Andromeda Rising

Andromeda Chronicles I

Jay Allan

ISBN: 978-1-946451-13-2

Books by Jay Allan

Flames of Rebellion Series
(Published by Harper Voyager)
Flames of Rebellion
Rebellion's Fury

The Crimson Worlds Series
Marines
The Cost of Victory
A Little Rebellion
The First Imperium
The Line Must Hold
To Hell's Heart
The Shadow Legions
Even Legends Die
The Fall

Crimson Worlds Refugees Series
Into the Darkness
Shadows of the Gods
Revenge of the Ancients
Winds of Vengeance
Storm of Vengeance

Crimson Worlds Successors Trilogy
MERCS
The Prisoner of Eldaron
The Black Flag

Crimson Worlds Prequels
Tombstone
Bitter Glory
The Gates of Hell
Red Team Alpha

Join my email list
at www.jayallanbooks.com

List members get publication announcements and special bonuses throughout the year (email addresses are never shared or used for any other purpose). Please feel free to email me with any questions at jayallanwrites@gmail.com. I answer all reader emails

For all things Sci-Fi,
join my interactive Reader Group here:

facebook.com/groups/JayAllanReaders

Follow me on Twitter @jayallanwrites

Follow my blog at www.jayallanwrites.com

www.jayallanbooks.com
www.crimsonworlds.com

Books by Jay Allan

Blood on the Stars Series
Duel in the Dark
Call to Arms
Ruins of Empire
Echoes of Glory
Cauldron of Fire
Dauntless
The White Fleet
Black Dawn
Invasion
Nightfall
The Grand Alliance

Andromeda Chronicles
(Blood on the Stars Adventure Series)
Andromeda Rising

The Far Stars Series
Shadow of Empire
Enemy in the Dark
Funeral Games

Far Stars Legends Series
Blackhawk
The Wolf's Claw

Portal Wars Trilogy
Gehenna Dawn
The Ten Thousand
Homefront

Also by Jay Allan
The Dragon's Banner

Cast of Characters

Andromeda "Andi" Lafarge – An orphan from "The Gut," the worst slum on the industrial hellworld of Parsephon, turned Badlands adventurer.

"The Marine" – An ex-Marine officer, discharged amid scandal, and living now in The Gut, addicted to the drug Blast. The Marine befriends a young Andi, teaching her to fight and survive.

Captain Walter Hiram – Owner-captain of Belstar, a small freighter. An acquaintance of the Marine, and Andi's commander for a time.

Captain James Lorillard – Owner-captain of Nightrunner, a free trader engaged in illegal old tech prospecting along the Badlands frontier. Andi's commander along the frontier, and her second mentor.

Tyl Jammar – A member of Nightrunner's crew. A native of the planet Physalia.

Tyrell Stone – A member of Nightrunner's crew. The ship's communication's specialist.

Gregor – A member of Nightrunner's crew. A native of a high-gravity world, a virtual giant towering well over two meters and massing more than one hundred fifty kilograms.

The Jackal – A member of Nightrunner's crew. The Jackal is an ex-thief, stealthy and light footed.

Anna Fasarus – A member of Nightrunner's crew. A good fighter, with an unknown and shadowy past.

Barret – A member of Nightrunner's crew. Barret is an Ex-Confederation navy gunnery specialist.

Yarra Tork – A member of Nightrunner's crew, and the ship's gifted engineer.

"Doc" Rand – A member of Nightrunner's crew. A former first aid technician, and now the ship's de facto doctor.

Sylene Merrick – A member of Nightrunner's crew. A gifted programmer and expert hacker, and Andi's best friend.

Pierre Gavereaux – An agent from the Union's Sector Nine intelligence agency, posing as a frontier information broker.

Darvin – An unscrupulous Badlands information broker and Spacer's District gangster.

Chapter One

"The Gut"
Vulcan City
Planet Parsephon, Obliesk II
Year 295 AC

The girl raced through the haunted, perpetual dusk of the back alleys, ducking under low-hanging beams and sidestepping jagged holes in the cracked and broken pavement. Her desperate flight took her past strung out addicts, decomposing corpses, and putrid piles of rotting garbage alike.

Vulcan City was an industrial powerhouse and, from the outside at least, a shining gem of the Confederation, a megalopolis covering forty thousand square kilometers of Parsephon's scarred and polluted surface. The wares it produced were sold on every world of the Confederation, and beyond, even out on the Far Rim, on planets whose names were known only to the trading houses and cosmographers who had reason to possess such arcane knowledge.

Those compelled to live in its slums and work long shifts in its dirty and dangerous factories had another view of course. Vulcan City was only the largest of Parsephon's many industrial cities. The planet's surface was a checkboard of old, nearly exhausted, strip mines, intermixed with urban areas consisting mostly of vast stretches of factories and block after block of worker housing. The laborers and derelicts of Vulcan City were no different than those in Carpathia or Gruniswald, though outside the decrepit and overcrowded neighborhoods where they lived and worked, no one much cared. Not as long as the goods continued to flow from the factories to the waiting holds of the freighters in the spaceports and in orbit above.

The city *was* a wonder of sorts, however. Its vast industry had created almost limitless wealth, and claimed for it a place high in the ranks of the swath of worlds known as the Iron Belt. Those sixteen systems poured out such vast quantities of manufactured goods, almost alone, they powered both the war machine that had resisted constant Union aggression and the economy that made the Confederation the envy of every nation on the Rim.

It was a perverse wonder of a sort in its vast ghettos, as well, where human and inanimate debris existed in a strange unity, the morality that would have drawn a significant difference between the two almost entirely absent. Men and women who fell below the working class disappeared into the alleys and catacombs, where most of them died, clearing the way for the next group of lost souls. The bodies of the dead were collected, not unlike trash was, or they were simply left where they had fallen, to decompose once they were picked clean of clothing and anything else of value they possessed.

Parsephon's slums were infamous, and Vulcan City's the worst of all, but none anywhere, perhaps in the entire Confederation, was more notorious than the Gut. Barely ten square kilometers, in a long sliver running from the stench of the putrid riverfront to the heavy industry sector, it was home to six million officially, and an uncounted number of homeless and wanderers.

It was a living nightmare, a place reeking of human

waste, chemicals, and caustic smoke. Of all the worlds of the Confederation, it was by far the foulest, the most miserable, and the one most dominated by a corrupt and brutal ruling class that made the rest of the Confederation's politicians seem almost just and dedicated by comparison.

It was also the girl's home, the only one she had ever known.

Her hand was clasped tightly around a small gold chain. It was but a trinket to the enormously wealthy owner she'd stolen it from, a bit of ornamentation easily replaced, but to her it was two or three month's food, at least. A true haul, even at the miserable valuation Argus the fence would offer her. Assuming she got away, of course, which at that moment was still an open question.

She'd shaken the regular police. That had been easy enough, as it usually was. The police were scared to go into the Gut, unless they went in significant force, and the two cops that had been on her tail gave up almost as soon as she'd crossed back into the grim and familiar zone. The police weren't the problem, not this time. They were never much of a problem.

Chasing after petty thieves, and even ones that rated a designation somewhat north of 'petty,' wasn't something that really got the cops' blood running, not when there were several hundred fresh murders every day in Vulcan City to occupy their time. Their first priority, in reality if not official process, was to operate the patrols that maintained order, that kept the millions of workers moving peacefully to and from their shifts at the factories. Industrial production was the planet's lifeblood, and certainly it was the top priority of the great industrial families that controlled Parsephon's industry. The police departments themselves were entirely in the pockets of the industrialists, and all of the officers wearing the familiar brown uniforms knew they were a favored class, at least somewhat of one, at least when compared to the miserable factory workers or, worse, the dregs that slipped down into shitholes like the Gut.

No, the problem wasn't the cops, it was the private security agents on her tail. That was a charitable designation, she knew. The men chasing her were thugs, pure and simple, and she had a good idea what they would do to her if they caught her. The details were highly variable, of course, but none of the possibilities were pleasant, and they all made getting arrested look like a picnic.

She reached down, feeling around to reassure herself the blade was still stuck in the ragged piece of cloth she called a belt. She'd found the knife a few years ago in a pile of garbage, the same way she'd come upon just about everything else she possessed, except, of course, for the things she'd stolen. The blade had been in pretty bad shape, but she'd managed to tighten the handle and refasten the grip with some old synth leather. She'd sharpened the weapon to a keen edge on the hard masonry of an old warehouse. It had come in handy more than once. She'd used it to scare off those who had threatened her—almost an everyday occurrence in the Gut—and she'd wielded it in an actual fight or two, but this was by far the most desperate situation she'd faced with it.

She'd been sneaking into 'The Heights' and stealing what she needed to survive for almost a year now. The exclusive neighborhood was home to many of Vulcan City's wealthiest oligarchs, or at least it was the location of the manor houses they maintained near the factories and foundries they owned. They all had sophisticated security systems, of course, but she'd found her ways around them. She'd managed to score some success in her endeavors, mostly because she went there looking for scraps and not trying to pull of grand heists. Staying below the radar, keeping a low profile, had been crucial to her success, and it had also allowed her to sidestep the risk of the higher security and heavier police presence in the Heights. The leavings of the rich and powerful were meaningful treasures to her, and she'd become adept at crawling through the transport tunnels and underground infrastructure to get where she was going unseen.

This time, she realized, she'd simply picked the wrong house. Parsephon's industrialists were hard men and women, arrogant, and far from tolerant of thieves or disobedient members of the working class. Still, they rarely wasted much time chasing after the small scraps she stole. Until this time.

The two men behind her were familiar. She'd seen far too many of their sort preying on the denizens of the Gut. They were mobsters, and the house she'd chosen to rob apparently belonged to one of Vulcan City's crime bosses, or at least to an industrialist with significant underworld connections.

It had just been an accident, a mistake, and very likely to be her last. She had always given the mob crews a wide berth. She didn't want the wares they peddled, drugs to fight off the daily misery or numbers games offering false hope of escape for the dregs of humanity. And, she definitely didn't want any trouble.

Trouble like the kind she had now.

She had managed to stay ahead of them, but she was getting tired, and she could feel her legs slowing. She knew her pursuers had to be fatigued as well, but they had pursued her a good part of the way in a vehicle, and they'd only resorted to a chase on foot when she'd gotten back to the narrow alleys of the Gut.

Also, they were grown men, and she was a fourteen-year-old girl. In places less harsh than the Gut, she would still be considered a child.

She was losing hope of outrunning her pursuers, of getting away. She was going to have to fight. It was a battle she knew she couldn't win. She was tough, scrappy, and she had some experience fighting off other denizens of the Gut, but this fight would be another thing entirely.

She figured the thugs had guns, and that made stopping in the open and waiting to fight something akin to suicide. She had to pick a spot, somewhere she could hide and wait, and jump them once they were close. Her chances in a knife fight against two of them were beyond poor, but it was a better plan than getting shot down in the street.

There was a turn coming up, she remembered, almost ninety degrees, an even smaller, filthier, more ragged alley than the one she was on. It was too far ahead to see yet, in the gray monochrome of the dismal alley, but she knew where she was. Dirty, reeking, dangerous, the Gut was her home, and she was willing to bet she knew it better than the two gangsters chasing her down.

You're betting on it, alright. You're betting your life.

She tried to breathe deeply, regularly, struggled to get ahold of her fear. She had to be ready. She'd surprise her pursuers, at least if she did everything correctly. If she could take one down before they knew what was happening, just maybe…

She could see the turnoff, just ahead. She knew where it was, by heart, but now she was nervous, worried that she'd run past and give her pursuers the chance to catch her before she had another chance to ambush them.

She was soaked in sweat, from the running, of course, and now even more from the fear gripping her body like a vise. She'd lived her entire life on the streets, the last four years completely alone. She was tough, able to take care of herself, but this time she knew she'd gotten herself in deep. If she could escape from—or kill—the two thugs pursuing her, maybe, just maybe, she could slip away, become a mystery for whoever had sent two goons to kill her. There had been surveillance assets all around the house, of course, but she'd gone in with her hood over her head, looking like one of millions of vagabonds prowling around Vulcan City's lost neighborhoods. She'd left DNA evidence behind, almost certainly, but she was a street rat, born on the floor of an abandoned building. That had never seemed like an advantage before, but the fact that she had no profile in the planet's databases was certainly helpful.

She lurched to the side, just as she got to the turn, pulling her blade out as she did. She stepped back, perhaps a meter from the main alley, and she tried to breathe as softly as she could. She knew her life depended on what she did in the next few seconds, and she tried to ignore the cold realization that she had little chance of taking out both of her pursuers.

She'd been ready for death, in one way or another, since the day she'd knelt down beside her mother, providing what miserable comfort she could as the woman who'd protected her, and done God only knew what to feed them and keep them reasonably safe on the streets, died, choking up fountains of blood and bits of her diseased lungs as she did.

But now that death she'd thought herself ready to face seemed at hand, she was terrified…and determined to survive. Somehow.

She gripped her knife, her fingers tight around the weapon. Her eyes were focused on the alley, and her ears were attuned, listening for the sounds of her attackers approaching. The light was dim, as it always was in the Gut's maze of alleys, but her eyes were accustomed to it. With any luck, the two thugs weren't. And she needed every advantage she could get.

She heard the sounds of their boots on the loose gravel, and another sound, one of them kicking some bit of garbage or debris. She didn't doubt the two men could handily beat her in combat and kill her, but they didn't seem likely to sneak up on anyone soon.

Her heart was pounding, and she rubbed her arm on the frayed old material of her tunic, wiping away at least some of the sweat. She could hear them coming close, see vague shadows in the dusky light.

Then the first man moved into view. She'd been

planning, thinking, trying to stay focused, but suddenly, instinct took over. She lunged forward, her hand hitting the man's shoulder, pushing him with all the force her limited strength could muster…while she brought the knife down, plunging it into his back.

The thug, screamed in surprise and pain, and he lunged around, his fist swinging for his still unseen attacker as he stumbled down to his knees. The girl had tried to pull back, to duck the response she knew would come, but she wasn't fast enough. She dodged the main force of the blow, but the back of the man's fist caught her on the side of her face.

She staggered back under the impact, and her legs went limp, her strength draining away. She stumbled, struggling to stay on her feet, and even as she did, she saw the second man, his arm moving up, bringing his pistol to bear. She tried to move to the side, to evade the shot she knew was coming, but her legs were too wobbly, too weak. She'd yanked the blade back, out of her victim's back, and she held it in her hand. But her would be killer was too far away.

She didn't want to die, but if she had to, she damned well was going to face it with defiance. She owed herself that much, and she pushed down with all she had against the wild panic rising up from within. She brought her arm around, her eyes focused on the man with the gun. She'd never thrown a knife before, and what little she knew about such things told her the blade she had was ill-suited for such use.

But it was all she had.

It didn't matter anyway. The man was going to get off at least one shot before the knife could reach him, and probably two or three. And he could hardly miss at such short range.

Her arm was halfway through its motion when she heard the loud crack, followed by another. She winced, and she braced herself for the pain.

But there was nothing. She stood, frozen, the blade still

in her hand.

And then the man lunged forward, and she could see blood pouring from his mouth. He fell to the ground with a loud thud.

There was shock, and a strange mix of fear and relief. Then she saw the shadowy figure standing on the other side of the main alley. He was rumpled, clad in old and torn rags. But his eyes were clear and focused, and he held a pistol in his hand.

Her mind raced, trying to understand what was going on, and even as she stood there, she saw the first man, the one she had stabbed, getting up, his hand reaching toward his own weapon, dropped weapon.

She tried to remember afterward what had gone through her mind, but the best she could ever discern was that she'd acted on pure instinct. She leapt forward, with such force, a hard pain lanced up both her legs as her feet left the ground. She slammed into the thug, her blade held out in front of her, both of her hands wrapped around the hilt, gripping as tightly as she could, as she jammed it into her enemy's body. She felt the feeling of the knife driving through flesh, striking bone and then sliding off. Hot blood welled out of the wound, quickly covering her hands, and still, she pushed, with all the strength she could muster, driving it deeper.

She slid down as she lost her balance, her hands slipping from the knife, and she dropped to her knees, even as her victim fell to the ground with a deep thud. She gasped for air, and fought back a wave of nausea that tried to take her. Even before she forced herself to look down at what she had done, she knew, without the slightest doubt.

She had killed a man.

A criminal, a murderer, a man who would have killed her if he'd been able. But, still…she was a killer now.

"It's difficult, I know." The voice was hoarse, scratchy. She jerked her head up, and her hands moved to the side, an abortive move to grab her knife. But it was too far away, still protruding from her victim's body, and the man speaking to her still had a pistol in his hand.

Besides, he'd just helped her. Saved her. That didn't mean she trusted him, of course, or that he wasn't a threat. But a lightning fast assessment of her options told her to wait.

"What?" She tried to keep her voice as deep as she could, but the word ended up sounding more like a squawk than the ominous tone of a dangerous Gut-dweller.

"Killing. It's difficult, at least the first time." Something in the man's tone told her this had not been *his* first time, nor anything close to it. "It gets easier, though I'm not sure that's a good thing."

"He had it coming. He'd have killed me if I hadn't killed him." She managed to get a grip on her voice. At least she was doing a decent job of hiding the fact that she was still on the verge of expelling everything inside her stomach.

"Yes, it certainly looked that way. And that's a good reason to kill, one of the best. If your guts aren't doing flops right now, you're tougher than I was, I can tell you that." The man moved forward, very slowly, and as he did, he let his arm bring the pistol down to his side. "Anyway, you should be safe now. At least as safe as it gets around here."

"Thank you." The words came out almost on their own. She was still suspicious of the mysterious stranger, but there was no question, he *had* saved her life. Andi had lived an almost feral existence, but she still understood gratitude.

The man looked down at the bodies, his eyes focusing on the one he'd shot. "Two on one didn't seem quite fair, especially when they had guns, and you only a little knife." He gestured toward the man with the blade still protruding from his chest. "Go, take it back. Always retrieve your weapon as soon as possible. You never know what, or who, else is lurking somewhere."

She nodded, and she stepped forward, her eyes darting

between the knife and the man. She was still trying to decide how much of a threat he was. He seemed friendly enough, to her at least, but the Gut was full of all sorts of unpleasant types. Maybe he *was* trying to help her…or maybe he was planning to imprison her or sell her to some underground brothel.

She pulled the knife out of the body, feeling another wave of queasiness at the sensation. Then, she stood up and stared right back at her—she hoped—benefactor. "So, who are you?" She was scared out of her mind, but she managed to keep most of that out of her words.

"Besides some unknown derelict, who wanders around looking for other peoples' fights to jump into, you mean?" He paused. "My name is not important. I've fallen from grace, shamed myself, and ended up someplace I could never have imagined. I've left my name behind. I don't deserve it, but I go by a designation that reminds me of the time in my life when I was something, when I mattered. You can call me the Marine."

The girl looked at him, a skeptical expression on her face. "You were a Marine? A Confederation Marine?" She didn't know much about the Confederation's elite soldiers, but she'd seen a few, mostly when she'd wandered out of the Gut and into the city's more desirable areas. They'd always been well-dressed and perfectly groomed, nothing like the filthy and ragged creature standing there looking back at her.

"I was, a lifetime ago, but I veered from my path, and ended up lower than I could have imagined. I will tell you all about it, in time. But for now, why don't you come with me? My hovel is likely no better than whatever slice of hell you've carved out for yourself, but I've got food there, and a heater with a full charge. And it is close. I don't know if these two…" He gestured toward the bodies. "…have any friends out there, but I think you'd be better off laying low for a while."

She looked at him, trying to decide what to do. It was exactly what someone would say to try and lure her somewhere, and part of her mind screamed at her to run. But there was something about him, a dignity, well worn and battered, but still somehow there. Perhaps he *had* been a Marine.

The cold truth was, she didn't have many options. He was right. There were probably more thugs out there looking for her, and after the two bodies were discovered, there almost certainly would be. And she didn't really have her own place, hovel or not. She doubted the tiny corner she'd staked out for herself in an abandoned warehouse a few days before was even still unoccupied. One needed a certain level of respect to enforce claims to such things, and a rail thin girl her age lacked the needed gravitas. Likely, she'd have to fight for the spot when she got back, and just then, she didn't have much left in her.

"I could have killed you easily enough by now, or forced you to do whatever I wanted. Not the best basis of trust, perhaps, but worth something, wouldn't you say? Maybe a start, at least?" He slipped the pistol back into the makeshift holster he wore at his side. "And, I'm betting you're hungry after all that."

She just looked at him, perhaps for twenty or thirty seconds. Then, she just nodded.

She *was* hungry. Starving.

He smiled thinly, more of a friendly look than an outright grin. "So, you've got something to call me. I'm thinking I should have something to call you, too. Seems only fair, don't you think?"

"My name is Andromeda. Andromeda Lafarge."

A quizzical look slipped onto his face, and he paused for a few seconds.

"Andromeda? That's a hell of a name, don't you think? Way too much of a mouthful for a wiry little thing like you." The man looked back at her, his eyes moving over her body, inspecting her closely, but not in the leering way so many others had. He was sizing her up. Somehow, she knew that, though she wasn't sure how much he'd managed to discern about her visually.

"From now on, your name is Andi."

Chapter Two

"The Gut"
Vulcan City
Planet Parsephon, Obliesk II
Year 297 AC – 2 Years Later

Andi was hanging from the rafter, drenched in sweat, grinding her teeth as she tried one more time to pull her body up. She'd managed thirty-eight times, her best so far, but dammit, she wanted forty!

She grunted loudly, putting all she had into the effort, but she fell short about a third of the way up. Her arms and back ached, and her eyes burned from the perspiration pouring into them like a torrent. Finally, she let go, dropping the quarter-meter to the ground and letting out a wave of self-directed invective between greedy gulps of air.

"That was good. A new best for you, no?" The voice was neutral, not cloyingly encouraging, but also unaffected by her blistering bout of foul-mouthed rage.

Andi hadn't noticed the Marine walk into the room while she was working out. She was usually very aware of her surroundings, but she'd been completely focused on pushing herself.

"Yes," she answered, sounding less than pleased. "But I wanted forty."

"You'll get there, Andi. You've come a long way from that skinny little kid I found in that alley. But you're *still* impatient. Everything takes its own time. Some things you can rush, others you can't."

She nodded, knowing he was right, but somehow still not really believing it. She was much older than her years in ways, matured by her hard life, but her youthful spirit was still there, too, providing her with energy, but also sometimes also battling the results of factual observation. Part of her was completely convinced that effort was *all* that mattered, that if she pushed herself hard enough, she could do anything.

And yet you both still live in part of a burnt out old warehouse in the most decrepit slum on a planet famous for them. Effort hasn't done a thing to change that for either of you.

"You look tired. I think you should rest. I'll go out and scavenge up some dinner for us." She looked at the Marine with genuine sympathy in her eyes. She'd never had a father, at least not one she'd ever known, and she'd come to think of the kindly old warrior in that way. As a mentor, at least, and something more, too. She had no real perspective on what a father was supposed to be, but she'd come to care about her benefactor, deeply, and to appreciate that he'd taken her in and protected her when she had needed it.

That part of their relationship had begun to change, too, she realized. The Marine had clearly been the dominant one in the beginning, the protector. Since then, she had grown stronger, more able to deal with threats…and her companion had become weaker, his health and strength drained by the addiction wracking his body.

"That would be nice, Andi. I *am* tired."

She nodded and smiled, but inside she felt a flush of anger. She knew fatigue wasn't the problem, though she had no doubt he *was* tired. The Blast was the real issue. She'd known about the Marine's addiction since shortly after the two had met. She'd badgered him to stop at first, but then she'd realized it just wasn't possible. Blast was the most addictive drug known, and prolonged usage actually altered the junkie's DNA, creating an addiction that was not only irresistible but also almost always irreversible. She'd heard about advanced gene therapies that could free addicts from the desperate need for the drug, but they cost a king's ransom. Such things were no better than fantasy to Gut dwellers.

"I'll be back soon." She grabbed a torn rag she used as a towel and wiped the sweat from her face. Then she bent down and pulled up the thin belt that held her small purse and her trusty blade. She wrapped it around her waist, and then she slipped through the hole in the concrete wall and out of the small residence the two of them shared.

She had a sense of confidence she'd lacked two years before. She'd always been tentative then, at least a little scared, but now she was confident, and she walked through the main section of the warehouse, and past the small encampments scattered all around, with grim purpose.

She'd changed in other ways, too. When she'd first encountered the Marine, she'd been fourteen, thin and bony. She'd matured considerably in the two years that had passed, filled out in ways that increased her strength and combat abilities, and in others that attracted attention that was rarely wanted in a place like the Gut.

She'd progressed in her reactions to such things, as well. The fourteen-year-old girl, street smart and still wary of the dangers all around, had mostly ignored and avoided situations that made her uncomfortable or afraid. And, she'd run when she had to. Now, Andi responded to such things more directly.

More violently.

She was a killer now, something that had made her uncomfortable at first, but a fact she'd later come to accept and even embrace. She hadn't murdered some innocent somewhere. She'd killed a man who was trying to kill her, a gangster with God only knew how much blood on his hands. It was an extermination, the removal of vermin from the universe, and now she looked back on the whole encounter with a grim sense of pride.

She'd been a killer, of course, for two years, but now she backed it up in ways the young girl she'd been never could have. She was muscular, strong, fast. And she'd been training for two years under the Marine's direction. The old man was past his prime, his body ravaged by his drug habit, but he remembered how to kill. And he had shared his knowledge with her.

She was a fighter now, and her confidence had grown with her skills. The Marine had taken care of her when they'd first met, but now, more and more, she took care of him.

There was one other difference between her and the Marine. He had given up. He was on the downslope of his life, his best days behind him, deeply mired in addiction and hopelessness. She, on the other hand, had no intention of living her entire life and dying in the Gut, or anywhere like it. She was going to get out of Vulcan City one day, and off Parsephon entirely. There was a whole universe out there, and somewhere in that great expanse, Andi Lafarge had promised herself she would make her fortune.

She didn't want a normal life, nor even a prosperous one. She wanted the kind of wealth she saw among the industrialists, the people from whom she stole and carved out her meager existence. She wanted vast treasure, and the power that came with it. Most of all, she wanted the seeming invulnerability the industrialists enjoyed. She wanted to feel safe, to come down on anyone who threatened her not only with her fists and blade, but with the awesome might the industrial princes could unleash on those who dared to offend them.

It was fantasy, part of her insisted, unattainable, but deep down, she believed she could do it. That, one day, she *would* do it. Somehow.

She walked down the street, more or less ignoring the familiar misery. There were the usual types, the lost, the addicts, those who had fallen down through society's drain. The toughs were out, too, intimidating the weaker denizens of the desperate slum, and stripping them of what little they possessed. But none of them even looked in her direction. They knew better, at least the ones who frequented the area around her tiny hovel. Andi had dealt with more than one would be bully—or worse—and the word had spread, some bruises and a few broken bones serving to add to the stories that had long passed back and forth in the streets of the Marine's exploits, and now, of those his sidekick. Andi had developed a considerable rep, and a rough form of respect from the street predators, and most of them gave her a wide berth.

Tracking down something for dinner often involved some sort of sleight of hand or petty theft, but she was flush just then, her purse was filled with coin from her latest score.

Well, perhaps *filled* was an exaggeration, but dinner for two was something she could readily afford. She'd even decided she would bypass the street vendors in the Gut, and slip out into one of the better sectors in search of food from less questionable sources.

She headed down the main street, toward the Fairmont. The adjoining neighborhood was nothing special, but it was a solid step up from the nightmare that was the Gut, a fact that was obvious enough in the far fresher air as she crossed through the broken down old gates that separated the two neighborhoods.

There were two cops standing around as usual, mostly keeping an eye on the gateway to ensure that those who clearly belonged in the Gut stayed there. There were no laws against moving between neighborhoods, of course, but she suspected the business owners in the Fairmont greased the local law enforcement to keep the worst specimens out. A Gut resident like her, with coin to spend and fitting in well enough, was more than welcome, at least as long as her purse held out. But the Gut was full of dangerous sorts with nothing to offer save theft and violence.

She never had any problems moving back and forth between the neighborhoods. She was cold-blooded and deadly, in many ways just what the Fairmonters wanted confined to the Gut. But it was far from obvious, and to uninformed eyes, she was just a teenaged girl. Anyone looking was more likely to wonder what the hell she'd been doing in the Gut in the first place, rather than trying to keep her there. Still, she'd pulled her tunic low, over the small sheath that held her knife. It wasn't exactly heavy ordnance, but she wasn't in the mood to answer any questions either, and the anti-weapons laws in Vulcan City were deliberately vague, constructed so the cops could charge just about anyone with a crime if they desired.

She headed down to Portlandt Street. There was an open-air market there, again, nothing special, but decently clean and with a good selection. A few of the stalls even had fresh meat sometimes, and not just cheap synth-protein. She would enjoy a good meal, but it was mostly her companion she was thinking about as she browsed the tables of the various vendors. The Marine had very little in his life to look forward to, and while she knew he disapproved of her various thefts and larcenies, he was always pleased to see some decent food or another power cell for the heater.

She knew something terrible had happened to the Marine years before, something horribly unfair. He'd been forced to resign from the Corps, she'd gleaned that much. He'd come close to telling her the specifics on a couple occasions—always in the middle of a Blast stupor—but he'd never been able to talk about it, not beyond disordered snippets that didn't make any real sense to her.

She had discerned his weakness, at least to her way of

thinking, the thing that had broken him, consigned him to a life of poverty and drug abuse as a desperate attempt to manage the pain. He believed in the Corps, he'd believed in the Confederation. He still did, in his own fashion, even then. But Andi saw only that his devotion had not been returned. He'd been cast aside, left to die in grim obscurity. His faith had been his undoing, his blind loyalty.

Andi didn't believe in anything, and her cynicism and dark outlook protected her like a shield. The universe was harsh and cold, and above all, it was corrupt. Her father had died because he'd clashed with someone more powerful. He'd never even lived to see his daughter born. Her mother had died after years of pain and misery and giving all she had to give to protect her child.

Now, she saw the Marine, a good man, even to her jaded perspective, lost and thrown away, killing himself slowly as he tried to dull the ache inside him. No, Andi had promised herself, she might believe in people—very occasionally— ones she knew well, ones who truly revealed themselves to her, proven themselves, but systems and governments? No way. Not ever. They were all foul and twisted, jammed full of the worst of humanity, driven by lust for personal power and for privilege out of reach of most of those they purported to represent. They were dangerous monstrosities, and most of humanity's worst nightmares had been brought on by its ruling bodies, by the actions of its leaders. The failings of such institutions had led to the Cataclysm, to uncounted deaths and unimaginable suffering.

The closer, more focused viewpoint was no less discouraging. She'd watched what loyalty and devotion to such ideals had done to the Marine, to one good man, and she'd sworn then and there.

Never. Not me.

The powers out there might defeat her, they might kill her. But she would never kneel before them, never trust in them or give them that part of herself that made her unique.

She would not obey, not become a slave to those who would rule her life, her actions…her very thought.

She wandered around the market, carefully choosing her items, and taking care not to let on how much coin she had in her purse. The Fairmont wasn't the Gut, but it wasn't a place where it was wise to advertise anything worth stealing.

Is there anyplace where that is wise?

Her last stop was at a small baker's stall. She looked around at the assortment of items, and she bought two large pastries. The Marine had a wicked sweet tooth, and she smiled as she reached out and took the bag. It would be a nice surprise, one that would make him happy.

For a fleeting moment, at least.

She made her way back to the Gut, back to the tiny corner of hell she called home. She went the longer way, as usual. The section of the Strand that cut through the Gut was more direct, knocking maybe a quarter of a kilometer from the route, but it also passed by Bannon Street, where her mother had died. Andi always avoided the place. She'd run that terrible day, half in panic and half because she couldn't bear to see her mother lying there, dead and bloodied. She'd left the body where she'd found it—an action that had always troubled her—and she hadn't been back since.

She made her way back, and she walked into the warehouse, past the same lineup of empty, vacant stares, and through the hole in the back wall, the entryway to what passed for home.

"I'm back," she said, setting her sack down on the old crate they used for a table. "I got us a true feast!" That was an exaggeration, of course, but she had gone a bit crazy, at least by the standards of thrift that usually governed their meager existence.

She looked across the room, toward the half-collapsed box they used as a shelf. Among his handful of weapons and meager personal possessions, the Marine had something else Andi had never seen before she'd met him. A stack of books.

Not data chips, not electronic tablets, but actual paper books, about a dozen of them. They were old technology, ancient really, rarely used anywhere save as curiosity pieces, but they didn't require power to use, and that made them ideal for squatters in the Gut. At least the few of them who were literate and had any real desire to read.

The Marine had taught her to fight, to survive...and he'd taught her to read as well. Sometimes she wondered what that was worth in a place like the Gut, but then she sat and read one of the books—working her way fitfully through at first—and she escaped from the cold dreariness of her existence. At least for a short time.

"Maybe we can read together after dinner," she said. She walked across the room, reaching down and scooping up her favorite of the books. It was *old*, how old she couldn't even guess. It was in pretty rough shape, nothing but the title legible on its worn cover. But most of the inside pages were still readable, and she'd loved the fantastic stories in it from the moment she'd first read them with the Marine, him teaching her with every word, pulling her from illiteracy and ignorance.

She didn't know where it had come from, nor of course, did the Marine, save that he'd found it years before, paying a few centicredits for it. Even its title was a mystery. Favorite Myths. She had no idea what a myth was, but she'd reasoned it had to be some kind of fiction. The stories told of fantastic settings, with gods of all sorts and superhuman heroes engaging in wild adventures.

She'd read it a dozen times, savoring each of the stories, and, in her favorite of them all, there was something truly fantastic, at least to her imagination. A white horse, with wings. A horse named Pegasus.

Chapter Three

"The Gut"
Vulcan City
Planet Parsephon, Obliesk II
Year 298 AC

Andi jumped up, hurling herself over the fence and landing with practiced grace. She was tall, her legs long, well-suited to leaping over obstacles. She'd grown more than five centimeters in the last twelve months, and three years of constant training under the Marine's instruction and watchful eye had turned her into a razor…fast, strong, alert. Deadly in a fight. Far more dangerous than many people expected a seventeen-year-old girl trailing a long ponytail behind her to be. Which was good. Surprise, also, could be a deadly weapon.

She was pleased with herself, with what she'd become over the past three years, but there was a dark side there as well, a grim comparison that troubled her greatly. As she had risen, as her abilities had grown and expanded, the Marine had fallen, his health and vigor fading with each passing day, it seemed. His Blast habit had gotten worse and worse, his binges more and more frequent, driven ever more by a growing physical addiction he was powerless to resist. She'd long since learned to look the other way, but it tore at her guts to see him weakening, failing, deriving pleasure from fewer and fewer pursuits, save only the drug that enslaved him, the one he was taking almost every day.

He was in trouble for money, too, she was almost sure of that. He'd never had much, mostly because what retirement pay he'd gotten from the Corps, whatever pension he'd managed to cling to after the shadowy conditions surrounding his discharge, had gone almost entirely to support his habit. He'd been edgier than usual of late, even scared, so much so that she'd offered him her own money to pay for his drugs, something she'd sworn she would never do.

She would help him anyway she could, with food, clothing, medicine—but the idea of supporting the habit that was killing him was anathema to her. Still, she would have done it. Anything to help him, to pull him back from the precipice she could see up ahead, and not too far down the road.

He'd refused, though, as she knew he would, insisting he was fine. Still, she was sure he was in trouble. She just didn't know what to do about it.

She climbed up a rusted old ladder leading to the roof of a large warehouse. It was a shortcut of sorts, one she'd been using for about six months, a way to avoid the crowds, and the unsavory types hanging around the main road. She'd been afraid of many of them once, but now it was more a desire to avoid problems. The fear was gone, for the most part, but killing someone in broad daylight in the middle of the street could lead to entanglements she didn't want. Even in the Gut, killings were best kept in dark alleys and crumbling buildings.

The warehouse she used as a cut through was actually an active storage facility, unlike so many of the abandoned buildings in the Gut. Still, she'd only been given a hard time once. A foreman or some kind of supervisor tried to chase her away one day, but she'd looked him right in the eye and told him if she ever so much as heard his voice again, she would cut his throat for the sheer pleasure of watching him bleed to death. She didn't mean it, not really, at least not if he didn't try to harm her first—she wasn't a sadist—but she thought it sounded right, almost poetic. If scaring the fool could keep him away from her, it would also keep him safe.

And, so it had. The man's face had turned white as a sheet, and he'd spun around and rushed back to the ladder. She'd never seen him—nor heard his voice—again.

She climbed back down the other side of the building and raced through the depressingly familiar streets. They were the same as always, but she barely noticed the usual misery and squalor. She'd been out for hours, since before dawn, and she was nervous. She didn't like leaving the Marine alone, not for so long. Not in the state he'd been in. It was well past time to check on him.

She patted her hand down at the small purse hanging from her belt as she turned the corner, doublechecking that her score was still there. She'd snatched it with practiced, almost ludicrous, ease, pulling it right from her victim's bag. It had been a personal indulgence or a present or something of the sort, she guessed, and no doubt, it's former owner would pull her hair out wondering where it went.

And then she'll just buy another one with money she won't miss, and this will feed us for half the year...

Andi had become quite adept at snatching things from unsuspecting marks, a far safer and simpler pursuit than her old tactic of robbing well-protected homes. She could escape pursuit if necessary—she'd done it dozens of times—but it was far easier to avoid it entirely.

The bracelet was valuable, she was sure of that. She'd developed quite a good eye for picking out her marks, especially since she'd found that the depreciation was a bit less severe when she fenced items of true quality. One bit of precious jewelry was worth far more than a sack full of lesser items.

Of course, she was pretty sure Argus had been giving her better deals the last year or two, anyway. She wondered how much had to do with the quality of the goods she'd brought in, and how much with the increased chance that she might slit his guts open if he tried to cheat her.

There was a lesson in that, too, one she would be sure not to forget. She was developing an understanding of how things worked, how the universe functioned, one far more accurate than the lies most people willingly believed.

She turned the corner onto the street that led to the dismal abode she shared with her companion…and she saw three men walking toward her.

For an instant, she tensed up. There was something about them, something sinister. More so than the typical Gut inhabitant. It took her a few seconds, but then she realized. They reminded her of the thugs who'd almost run her down three years before, the day the Marine had saved her. They were laughing, a foul, guttural sound, and one of them held a rag. He was wiping blood from his hands.

Andi got a cold feeling in the pit of her stomach. Her hand went to her side, hovering just over the knife. She wasn't that fourteen-year-old waif anymore, vulnerable, uncertain. She figured she had a chance, even against all three, at least with surprise on her side.

But she didn't know why they were there. She had fears, concerns, a bad feeling…but was that enough reason to kill three men?

They deserve it, you know they do, whatever they're doing here. Just look at them.

The thoughts were there, swirling around, urging her to strike, but there was one thing that overruled them all. She had to get back. She had to check on the Marine.

She raced down the street, abruptly breaking into a dead run, and she burst through the main entrance of the warehouse, shoving aside anyone who got in her way.

Her heart was racing, and the fear was choking her,

making each gasp of air painful and difficult. There were millions in the Gut, thousands even in her tiny section of it, and no small percentage of them were in some kind of trouble with the rackets. Those men could have come for anyone.

But, somehow, she knew they'd been there for the Marine.

She slipped through the small opening in the wall, her eyes darting back and forth as she did. Then, she saw him. Lying on the floor, blood all around. Her worst fears had been realized.

For an instant she thought he was dead. Then she heard a forced, raspy breath.

She ran over, dropping to her knees next to him. She reached out, put her palm against his face. "Can you hear me?" She was sobbing even before the words left her lips.

Her eyes moved over him, evaluating his condition, his wounds, and with each passing instant, what little hope she'd had slipped away. His clothes were soaked in blood, and she could see half a dozen knife wounds, at least. A cold realization sunk in as she knelt next to her only friend in the all the vast universe.

He hadn't just been attacked, she realized with growing anger. He had been tortured.

She leaned down, bringing her face closer to his. "Can you hear me?" She spoke softly, trying to sound as soothing as possible. She wanted to cry, to sob uncontrollably, but somehow, she held it back.

"Andi…" His voice was weak, and she could hear a fluid sound. *Blood in his lungs…*

"Just lay back. I'm going to get help. You'll…" She was going to say he would be okay, but she didn't want her last words to him to be lies. And there was no help to get. There were no hospitals in the Gut, and no ambulances would come into the lost ghetto.

"Andi…I'm sorry…fell behind…owed too much…"

Andi's fury hardened as the Marine's words confirmed her suspicions. She'd seen his Blast habit worsen, and she'd wondered how he was paying for the drug. Now, she knew. He was going into debt to his suppliers, and finally, they'd lost patience with him.

She looked down at her friend...the only one she'd ever had.

And now you're going to watch him die.

She pulled out her knife and cut a slice from her tunic. She set it down over a gash on his chest. She pressed hard, trying to stop the bleeding, but even as she did, she knew there was no point.

"Andi...we both...know I'm...done."

"No," she said, the sobs she'd held back starting to escape. "No...you can't..."

"Listen...you have...to get out...not sure...safe here." He gasped hard, his struggled breathing a sickly rattle.

"Don't worry about me. We have to do something about these wounds. I can't let you..." Her words trailed off to silence.

"Andi..." His voice was softer, fading even as he spoke to her. "...you have to...let me...go..." He sucked in another breath, clearly with great difficulty. "Go...leave here...now. Go to...spaceport. Freighter...*Belstar*. Find..."

"Please...you have to rest..." She kept her hand on his face, doing all she could to sooth him.

"No...listen! Important. Find Captain...Hiram...owes me favor...show him..." He held out his hand. His arm was shaking, and it was clearly taking all his strength. "Take..." He sucked in another breath. "Take," he said again, and he opened his hand.

There was a small steel chain, and a set of ID tags. Marine ID tags. She'd seen them around his neck a thousand times. This was the first time she'd seen them off.

"Show...to Hiram...tell him...want him...take you off...Parsephon..."

Andi reached out, took the tags, pausing for a few seconds, holding the Marine's hand. The tears were streaming down her cheeks by then, all pretense at control gone.

Her mind raced, things she wanted to say to him, words she knew should be—*had* to be—spoken between them. He had saved her life, taught her, protected her when she needed it. He was the only father she'd ever had.

But she just knelt there, his hand in hers, silent as she watched him draw one last breath, and then she felt the last strength fade from his arm.

A fresh torrent of tears poured from her eyes, and she set his arm down gently. She knelt where she was, for how long she could never remember, but finally, it was his words echoing in her mind that drove her to move. She had to leave, he'd been right about that. There was nothing she could do for him, nothing anyone could do. Still, the thought of leaving him lying on the cold cement floor, alone and untended, was almost too much for her. In the end, it took everything she had to drag herself away, to gather her meager possessions, and her favorite book—the thing she knew she would always remember him by—and to take one last look at her friend, her mentor, before slipping out into the main warehouse, and onto the street beyond.

She was morbidly sad, overcome by a grief that stabbed at her like a jagged blade, but there was something else there, too, even stronger, building up inside, pressure growing, pushing to blast out like a violent eruption.

Rage.

Andi was wildly, uncontrollably, desperately angry.

She was finished with Vulcan City, with all of Parsephon and its putrid cities and corrupt government. She would go to the spaceport, and find this freighter…*Belstar*, the Marine had said. She would leave the foul world upon which she was born, and where she'd lost everyone who'd ever meant anything to her. And, when she escaped, she was never coming back.

She didn't know what lay ahead, where fate would take her, but just then, anyplace but Parsephon was okay with her.

But she couldn't leave. Not yet.

No, first, she had one last task, one thing to do before she could move on. One achievement she needed if she was going to live with herself, find a way forward. One last goal to fulfill before she started her new life.

Revenge.

Chapter Four

"The Gut"
Vulcan City
Planet Parsephon, Obliesk II
Year 298 AC

Andi crouched down on the roof, watching the street below. It was a good spot, a great vantage point, with reasonable cover to hide behind. The crumbling masonry at the edge of the roof wasn't something she'd count on to protect her from heavy gunfire, but it served well enough as a hiding place.

She'd been scouting the area for days. She wasn't more than a quarter of a kilometer from her home of the past three years, but she knew she would never see that place again. It was about fifty-fifty whether some kind of authorities would ever discover the Marine's body and dispose of it in some fashion or whether it would be left to rot where it lay. Andi had seen death often enough—everyone in the Gut had—but the thought of staring down at the lifeless body of her friend—or even the place he had died—was too much for her. She'd added it to the list of places to avoid, right next to the street where her mother had died so many years before.

It would be easy enough to stay away from both spots,

since she never intended to see anyplace on the whole miserable rock that called itself Parsephon. Not once she'd finished what she had to do.

The Marine had trained her physically, put her through grueling exercises, and he had taught her how to fight. But scouting and surveillance had been subjects for brief discussions, only. She wondered, if they'd had more time, if he would have taken her out into the streets of the Gut, taught her how to track targets, how to seek out and find cover and vantage points for ambushes.

She'd listened to the talks intently, soaking up all he would teach her, and her own experiences as an accomplished thief combined with the Marine's advice, to make the whole thing feel natural, like some kind of carefully planned orchestration.

It all made tracking down people she intended to kill feel like a normal thing.

The Marine had once been a capable man, devoted to a cause, trained to the highest level, part of an organization shrouded in pride and commitment. She'd never known that version of him, of course. The man she'd come to know, and love almost as a father, had been broken, discarded, wallowing in misery, both self-inflicted and caused by unfairness from outside. Her companionship had brought him some happiness in his last years, or at least the closest he was still able to come to true contentment. She was sure of that. But the more she thought of how he had died, how whatever miserable amount of time he might have had left before his own addiction killed him had been stripped away, the angrier she got.

She had images in her mind, moments they might have shared that she knew he would have enjoyed, reading the books in his meager and worn library, splurging on some real food and not the nasty Synth that most of the Gut subsisted on. Such miserable little pleasures, and even that modest bit of joy had been stolen away.

Andi's rage had been fiery hot right after she'd found the Marine dying, but it had cooled since, though not in the normal sense, not in any way that reduced its intensity. It had morphed into a frozen hatred, as cold as space itself. She was going to leave Parsephon, just as the Marine had begged her to do—and good riddance to the miserable place. But first, she was going to find the men who had killed her only friend, and whoever had sent them as well.

She was going to find them, and she was going to kill them. All of them.

Tracking down the actual killers hadn't been difficult at all. Their faces were branded into her mind, and her continued analysis shook loose old familiarity. She didn't know them, nor really recognize them, not exactly. But she was sure she'd seen them around the area.

Blast addicts weren't exactly uncommon creatures in the Gut. She hadn't been sure if the men she was seeking were low level bagmen or street dealers, or if they were one step above, enforcers sent in when problems arose, but either way, she'd bet it wouldn't be long before she spotted them again.

She'd been right about that. It had taken less than a week, four days in fact. She'd raced along the rooftops once she'd spotted them, keeping tabs as they went about their routes. Her assessment seemed to be correct. They weren't regular mules dropping off drug shipments and collecting money. Their jobs were to lean on delinquents, and to make sure regular business went on uninterrupted. Of course, when just leaning on a deadbeat didn't work, they took things to the next step, which generally included sending a message for others to see.

As they had done with the Marine.

It took all she had not to drop down behind them and kill them all then and there. She wanted them dead so badly, she could taste it. She'd imagined tormenting them, killing them slowly, as they had done to the Marine. But she knew that goal was likely beyond her reach. She was looking at a three to one matchup to begin with, and even if she caught them in an alley or a side street, she doubted she'd get them anywhere private enough for the slow carving job she'd fantasized about.

However she eventually did it, however, she couldn't move yet. She wanted the men who'd actually killed the Marine, and she would have them, see their terrified expressions as they died. But she also wanted whoever had sent them, whatever wealthy druglord had dispatched his minions to kill her friend, sitting back, dripping arrogance as he'd uttered the words that ended a life.

She would see him die, too, before she left. And the three killers were her guides to that end result, her only lead to find whoever had decided the Marine would die. She'd watched them for several days now, forced herself to stay hidden and uninvolved, even as they beat their terrified victims in the street. Even as they had killed another addict.

Andi sympathized with the victims, on some level, but she had her job to do, and she was focused. Life on the streets of the Gut was hard, and there was little room for such things as charity and sympathy.

She was a killer herself, and vengeance was her master. If she tipped the thugs off, even to help one of their helpless victims, she'd never find their master. Her deadly justice would go unfinished.

That was unthinkable.

She crept along the edge of the roof, following quietly as the men moved back toward the decrepit gateway that marked the entrance to the Gut. It had been a busy day for them, and they'd left a trail of bruised and battered victims in their wake. Andi had never been more than ten kilometers from where she'd been born, but she was worldly enough to understand that drug dealers weren't patient with slow payers. They might advance a hit or two on a primitive form of credit, but the collateral was always the same. A borrower's health, his bones and his tolerance for pain.

And, ultimately, his life.

She'd seethed as she had watched, at the injustice of it all. To a point. But what really fueled her rage was the arrogance. Those bastards knew they were untouchable. Everyone in the Gut knew who they were, and no one had the courage to stand up to them.

That was about to change.

She moved along the roof until she got to the far edge. There was another building just across a narrow alley, and her mind raced, doing quick and informal calculations. Yes, she could make it across.

She thought.

She picked up the pace, breaking into a run over the last couple meters, and she hurled herself over the three meters or so of the alley. She landed hard on the other roof, rolling forward a bit more clumsily than she'd intended, and with a little more pain, but more or less unhurt.

She continued following the men walking down the street, until she reached the end of the road, at least the end of the roofs. She climbed quickly down a rusted old ladder and landed on the cracked pavement of a tiny side street. She stepped quickly but cautiously out to the main avenue. She didn't want to draw attention to herself by moving too quickly, but she wasn't about to lose sight of her prey, either.

She turned the corner, her eyes darting back and forth, seeking out those she was following. They were about ten meters ahead, just walking through the wrecked old gateway. She stepped out into the street, trying to keep a few others between her and the three men. She didn't know if they'd recognize her—to them, she was probably just be some kid passing by—but if there was one thing the Marine had pounded into her head, it was never to be careless, not in life and death situations.

She followed the men as they continued walking,

through the Fairmont now, then stopping for a few minutes at a tavern that looked, from the outside at least, just a cut above any of the gritty establishments in the Gut. That was about all she could say, at least everything positive. In a less relative sense, it was clearly a shithole, filthy and no doubt peddling the worst cheap liquor available, not to mention a number of other things, of a quality also pretty close to the bottom of the barrel.

She thought about going inside. Technically, sixteen-year olds weren't allowed in bars in Vulcan City, but the idea that anyone really cared almost made her laugh. No, it wasn't that. But the Marine had taught her more than simply fighting. He'd pounded the idea of tactical analysis into her head, of gathering intel and going into a possible fight as prepared to win as possible. She didn't know how big the place was or how many people were inside, what the layout was, or if her prey had friends in there.

And she suspected slicing up some uninvolved asshole who tried to proposition her would draw more attention than she wanted.

It was safer to wait. She did a quick scout around the building, making sure there was no back exit the men could use to escape from her. Then she sat down on the crumbling remains of an old half wall, far enough away not to draw attention to herself, but near enough to keep a close watch on the door.

Her hand moved down to her side, checking the knife. It was something she did frequently, almost without conscious thought, and she'd gotten quite good as disguising it, making it look like she was scratching an itch or something of the sort.

Another lesson from the Marine, one she suspected he'd learned in the Gut and not at the Academy. It was always wise to keep people from knowing just how ready you were to fight. Surprise was an ally you wanted, and not an enemy you wanted to face.

The men stayed inside for over an hour. She might have gotten impatient, but she was hunting, and it felt strangely natural to her. She was focused, and she would stay where she was as long as it took. She didn't know if the fools inside were downing drink after drink, or if they were spending their ill-gotten swag in the rooms that no doubt existed above the bar. It didn't matter. Either way, they'd be buzzed, distracted, tired…more vulnerable when the time came. When they'd led her where she wanted to go and, in the process, outlived their usefulness, any distraction would just make her work that much easier.

She watched them walking out, and while they weren't falling down drunk, she sensed they were a little impaired. That was perfect. The difference between victory and defeat, between life and death, often came down to slight differences in reaction time.

That was another thing she had learned from the Marine.

She waited a few seconds, allowing a few small groups to move by. She'd been following the men for a while, and even one of those fools might suspect if they noticed her. It was a little more stressful, following from farther back. She had to keep her eyes open, pay attention. She wasn't going to lose them, not if she could help it. She'd spent days following them around the Gut, but today was the day. The day she would avenge her friend, the day she would make those responsible pay.

And then she would leave Parsephon forever.

The men turned left on the Strasse, one of Vulcan City's main thoroughfares, and then they headed uphill, to the south.

Toward the Heights.

Andi knew the exclusive neighborhood well from her days of robbing houses, but it surprised her to see her quarry moving that way. The residents of the Heights were industrialists, executives, highly placed politicians. It had never seemed like a place some drug dealing gangster would live.

It also made her pursuit more difficult. It was gated, not with rusting old hunks of unattended metal, like those heralding the entrance to the Gut, but closed, high tech portals, guarded day and night. She'd found ways to sneak in, of course, but now she worried she might lose track of her prey in the process.

There was a way in, reasonably hidden, and not far from the gate the thugs were heading toward. It required some physical prowess to get over the wall there, but she'd managed it three years earlier, when she was smaller, weaker, and untrained. It wouldn't be a problem for her now.

What would be dangerous, however, was making her way through the streets. When she'd come before, she'd tried to look like someone's domestic staff or servant, but now, she looked like what she was. A street rat from the Gut. She'd stand out in the streets of the Heights like she had a flashing light floating over her head.

Damn...

She knew what the Marine would have said. He would have told her to know when to pull back, to give up the chase. To acknowledge the effort had become too dangerous and regroup, try another day.

Hell, he'd have told her to forget the whole thing, that vengeance wouldn't bring him back, that is wasn't worth the risk. He'd have wanted her to just get herself to safety, somewhere far from Parsephon. Someplace she had a chance at a life. A real life.

But that wasn't possible. Not for her. No, she *had* to avenge the Marine. That was the only way she could live with herself, the only road that offered even the chance of a future, at least one free from madness.

She would stay off the road as much as possible, do what she could to keep tabs on the men she was following. She had to avoid security systems, guards, even some resident shouting out after seeing her climbing a fence or something. But it was the only way. All she could do was stay focused, and hope for the best.

Chapter Five

"The Gut"
Vulcan City
Planet Parsephon, Obliesk II
Year 298 AC

She stared up at the house, her shock growing as her eyes moved over the massive structure, and familiarity hit her like a train.

She'd been there before. Three years before. The day she'd met the Marine.

The day she'd been fleeing from the very house looming up above her now.

Drug dealing was a profitable business, certainly, but the vast mansion was beyond anything she'd expected to find at the end of her search. She'd imagined some kind of wealthy gangster, probably a residence of ostentatious luxury, but situated in a less…prestigious…location. The homes surrounding the one in front of her were owned by the richest industrial families on the planet, and if few of their members spent much time in Vulcan City, they all maintained residences there.

The more she thought about it, though, the more it made sense. She'd wondered a few times, why the industrialists, so all powerful on Parsephon, had put up with the mobsters and the dealers. The criminals were dangerous, of course, and powerful, but they were nothing on a planet owned lock, stock, and barrel by a dozen or more great mercantile families. Those clans, whose power stretched all the way to Megara, could have shut down the rackets any time they'd wanted to. They could have had fifty thousand Confederation Marines dispatched to root the gangs out of every slum on the planet, if they'd wished, to destroy every hidden stronghold of the criminal cartels.

Now, however, she understood, and she scolded herself for never realizing it before, for allowing even her own dark view of things stray from being dark enough. The industrial families didn't do anything about organized crime, because the gangsters worked for them, even as everyone else on the planet did, from factory laborers to police and prosecutors.

It was a stark realization. The wealth of Parsephon's ruling families came not just from the mass production at thousands of factories, but from control of the black markets, from illegal loansharking operations, and likely, she thought, from wholesale government corruption as well.

She'd thought she couldn't have been more disgusted, more disillusioned with the foul and miserable planet of her birth. But she'd been wrong.

She hesitated, for a minute or two, trying to get control of her thoughts, to steel her nerve. She'd been ready for action as she'd patiently followed her targets, prepared to do what had to be done. She'd managed to track the three men, to remain hidden as she shadowed their steps. It was no small achievement, and she knew just how great the danger was, how easily one tiny slip up could cost her everything.

But the sight of the familiar house, and the cascade of revelations it triggered, stunned her, all the more because after that day years before, when she'd barely made good her flight from it, she'd checked around, and determined just who it was she had robbed, who had been so aggressive as to send killers after a thief who'd stolen one insignificant item.

Niles O'Bannon.

The O'Bannons weren't just a wealthy industrial family. They were enormously rich, obscenely so, the most powerful clan in Vulcan City, arguably on the whole planet. And Niles was the head of the family. His sons ran most of the family's businesses now, at least from what she'd been told. There were four O'Bannon children, all boys, and all but one occupied lofty executive positions and directed tens of thousands of workers, and billions of credits. The fourth son, Ian, represented Parsephon in the Confederation Senate on Megara.

Niles O'Bannon was one of the most powerful men on the planet, and despite the veneer of legitimacy and respectability, she understood now just how deadly dangerous he was.

He controls the Vulcan City drug trades, too. Maybe the ones in the other cities, as well.

Drug dealing was a profit center, of course, a big one, but now as she thought about it, she realized there was much more to the whole sordid system. Blast and other dangerous drugs offered more than just a massive flow of profit. They were a population control mechanism, for one thing, one that preyed most heavily on the disenfranchised and the down and out, precisely those of the least value to the industrialists…and the government. And, also the most likely to cause trouble. The drug trades created excuses for aggressive law enforcement activities and curtailments of individual liberties, especially useful when such things could be directed at crushing protests and dissent, instead of actually trying to meet the ostensible goal of reducing the flow of illicit drugs. The industrialists wanted people focusing on their work, and remaining obedient and pliable while they did it, and the government wanted that, too.

Andi felt sick to her stomach. She'd been cynical already,

or at least she'd thought she was. She hadn't thought she believed in anything. But just then, she realized how much faith had lingered in the back of her mind, how much desire to believe…in something. Anything. That understanding was particularly clear at that moment, because she could feel every bit of it falling away.

Her face hardened, and her hands curled up into tight fists. She didn't care *who* was involved, or how powerful or wealthy they were. If Niles O'Bannon was responsible for the Marine's death, then Niles O'Bannon had to die. If the president of the Confederation Senate had killed her friend, then she would have found a way to get to Megara…and put that bastard down, too.

Niles O'Bannon had to die. He had to die now.

She'd come over the fence right where she had years before, exploiting the same weakness in the security system. She was appalled at the carelessness that allowed such gaps not only to exist, but to remain for so long unaddressed. She imagined how much the O'Bannon's paid annually on their security operations, and she drew a hint of satisfaction from the idea that someone was robbing them in that way, taking their money and doing a shoddy job.

Your tech people are lazy, Niles. They let you down on this one…and not even you, I'm sure, every imagined what the consequences would be…

She moved cautiously, as quickly as she could, trying to minimize the time she had to spend in the open, while staying as quiet as she could. There were scanners everywhere, but she'd scoped them all out three years before, and she remembered the course she'd plotted then. It was rough—and she was far from sure her memory was perfect—but it was the best she could do.

She moved up, toward a large walled garden, and she hopped over the low masonry wall, ducking behind a large, flowering tree. She was close to the house now, and she could hear the sounds of boots on the ground up ahead. She peered through the branches, taking care not to move anything enough to draw attention. There was one guard for sure, close to where she was, and it looked like a second one, about fifty meters farther down, in the back of the house.

When she'd been there before, she'd waited, probed for a chance to rush toward the house when there was a blind spot between the guards. It had taken hours then, waiting for the sentries to get careless, but this time, she didn't have that much time to waste.

She moved slowly, carefully, through the garden, doing all she could to ensure any view from the guards was obscured. She watched them go through their rounds, three times, four. Five.

Then, there was an opening. Not enough to sneak all the way to the house, but a few seconds when the closest guard was around the edge of the building, out of visibility of the other. Maybe enough time. Just.

Enough time to kill the guard.

There were still scanners everywhere, and no doubt AI's watching and controlling them. She knew that once she moved, the clock would really start. She'd have minutes at best, and possibly a lot less.

She'd imagined pulling off the job, taking her revenge, and then fleeing, slipping back into the anonymity of the streets. But now, she began to realize how slim her chances of escape truly were. The likelihood of hitting her targets, of getting all those she'd come to kill, was poor enough. But getting out afterward, when every alarm was going off, every guard rushing to answer?

The fear she'd controlled with such discipline surged back against her defenses, and she thought seriously about turning and simply trying to get back out. That would be dangerous enough, but she figured she had a good enough chance. It's what the Marine would have wanted, too. She knew that, almost without a doubt. The last thing he would have wanted was her dying to avenge him.

But she couldn't do it. Whatever the chance of success, whatever the risks to herself, she just couldn't let the Marine's killers escape retribution. Not while she drew breath into her lungs. It just wasn't her, who she was. There was a coldness inside her, a dark and hard core that drove her…and right now, that part of Andi Lafarge demanded blood.

She watched the guards make their rounds twice more, counting off the seconds. They were a little sloppy, which was good in one sense, but it also made the amount of time she'd have more unpredictable. She waited, watching the guard move around the corner again, continuing his path along the side of the house.

Suddenly, she sprang forward, almost on instinct, not giving herself time to hesitate, time for fear to intervene. She raced across the short expanse of neatly trimmed ground cover, her hand whipping the knife out from her belt as she approached her target.

Her eyes focused on the guard's back. She was going to jam the knife into the man's heart. It had to be an immediate kill. The press of an alarm button, a shout, almost anything that alerted others would cost her the miniscule amount of time she was starting with.

Ribs…remember the ribs. Shove hard, but let the blade give, to slide off the bone and push through…

She remembered the Marine's words, the lessons he'd taught her on how to survive, which all too often meant how to kill.

She rushed toward her victim, and even as she closed the distance, she could see him starting to turn. He'd heard her, and he was reacting.

She'd gotten close, but she wasn't quite there yet, not in striking distance. She moved her hand over, tried to adjust to the aspect change of the target. And she pushed forward with all the strength and speed she could muster.

She slammed into the man, about a third of the way through his turn, and she jammed the blade into his back. She missed her intended spot, by a few centimeters, but she shifted, and even as she felt the blade strike something hard and then slide around, she knew she'd done what she had to.

The guard grunted, once, and then his body went limp, even as she was still pushing the blade in to the hilt. She tried to hold him up the best she could, to lower him slowly to the ground, and then she yanked hard, retrieving her blade and letting loose a torrent of blood.

The other guard had not reacted—yet—at least not that she could see, but she had no idea what the surveillance system had picked up. For all she knew, fifty guards were grabbing weapons even then, and heading out to find her.

To kill her.

She grabbed the guard's gun, and she jumped up, slipping around the corner, toward the window she'd forced her way into the first time she'd been there. Just like the fence, the defect in the lock had not been repaired. She was always amazed at the degree to which laziness and incompetence permeated so much human activity, not to mention arrogance. The house was like a fortress, guards everywhere, scanners, alarms…but no one paid attention to small imperfections.

The O'Bannon's think they're invincible, that no one would dare to strike at them…

If she survived the next moments, if she got away from Parsephon to live a new life somewhere, she promised herself, she would never overlook small details. She would trust nothing, rely on nothing. She would believe only her own eyes, and then no more than halfway. That was the way to stay alive.

She moved quickly, again, almost totally on instinct. She remembered the layout of the house, at least the parts she had seen. She'd passed a room that first time, one that had looked like an office or a study of some kind. It was a wild guess that such a place was where Niles O'Bannon would meet with his underworld associates, but she didn't have anything else, and she was taking the gamble.

It was a bet with large stakes, she knew. Revenge for the Marine.

And, on the other side of the table, her life.

She could hear a commotion, first shouts coming from outside, and then, a few seconds later, alarms going off.

Damn!

She'd hoped to have more time. But whatever chance she was going to have, it was now.

She broke into a run, down the hallway and out into a large gallery. There were open archways leading into several other rooms, all magnificently decorated. And all empty, at least at that moment.

She turned right and moved quickly across the room, retracing her recollection of the route toward the study. Halfway across the room, she heard voices…and then two men walked into the room from the far side.

Her eyes locked on them instantly, her mind racing, focusing on the details. Then confirmation. The man in front was definitely one of the ones she'd seen coming back from the warehouse, one of the ones she'd pursued all day.

One of the men who'd tortured and killed the Marine.

She had held back earlier, when she was tracking her targets, fought to restrain the almost irresistible urge to kill the bastards on sight. But she'd needed them then. She'd needed them to lead her back to their paymaster. Whoever was in charge.

She didn't need them now.

The man in her steely gaze had done all he could to serve her purpose. His value was exhausted.

He had reached his expiration date.

She whipped up the guard's gun she had taken, and she fired twice. The first shot hit her target along the top of his head. It was a nasty wound, and blood mixed with bits of bone and tiny chunks of brain in a grotesque spray. The second shot was cleaner, neater. Right between the eyes.

The man fell with a hard thud, but by the time he hit the ground, she was already firing at the second. He had been partially obscured, and she hadn't completely recognized him yet when she fired, delivering two more shots, again, both to the head. Her victim was dead by the time she got a decent look at what was left of his face, and confirmed that he too was one of the three men she'd followed there.

She felt satisfaction at the kills, at putting down the vermin who had murdered her friend, but there wasn't time for celebration. She had more people to kill, and then she had to figure some way—any way—to escape. That last goal was beginning to seem nearly out of reach.

There were guards everywhere now, running around outside on the grounds. But she could hear some in the house as well. They were getting closer. She was down to her last seconds.

She caught movement ahead, in the direction of the study. The third man? And Niles O'Bannon?

She moved forward, but she stopped after a few steps, her ears and instincts combining to dictate the action. To save her life. She spun around, just as a guard stepped into her line of sight in the gallery just outside the room where she stood. She had a clean shot, and before she had conscious thought of what to do, she realized she had already fired, and the man was crumpling where he stood, dropping to the floor with a loud thud.

The gun bounced across the wood floor, landing perhaps a meter from where she stood. It was a small automatic of some kind, one that looked pretty high-end. She raced back and scooped it up, another instinctive move. She wasn't sure if the impetus was training the Marine had given her, or her own instincts, acting on their own, surprising her again, even without the involvement of her conscious mind?

What did he turn me into?

She turned back and ran toward the study. The third man was standing there, weapon drawn, partially hidden by a bookcase. He fired once and missed.

Never let fear distract you. Not when you're fighting for your life.

Andi opened up with the automatic rifle, not entirely sure how to use the thing. She sprayed the entire area around the bookcase, and she could see that at least three of her shots had hit her target. He slumped back, and then he fell to his knees, dropping his weapon and hanging onto the edge of the bookcase to hold himself up. He was trying to hide as much of his body as he could, but he was still exposed.

Andi stared at the wounded man, whimpering, sobbing, begging for his life, and she felt no remorse. None. She wondered how the Marine had died. Had he done the same? Had he begged for his life?

She brought the rifle up to finish the job. *No mercy...not for you...*

But something was wrong. The weapon didn't move. Her arm didn't move.

And there was pain.

She glanced down, startled, biting back on the panic rising within her. Her shoulder covered in wet redness. She'd been hit. She hadn't even noticed the man getting off a second shot. She'd been so pumped up on adrenalin, so focused on killing her prey, she hadn't even felt the bullet slam into her.

Now, the pain radiated out like fire. The sixteen-year-old girl inside her wanted to turn and run, to find someplace to hide. To try somehow to stop the pain.

But only the smallest part of her was still that sixteen-year-old. Inside her, completely dominant, lived what the Marine had created. The fighter, the warrior. The angel of death. Determined, focused. That part of her—most of her now—would never yield. Not while she still drew breath.

She caught the movement in the corner of her eye. The fourth man in the room, the one who'd been hiding behind the desk. He had a pistol in his hand now.

She was uncertain what to do, but only for the slightest fraction of a second. Then the discipline slammed down. Her shoulder was a mess, and she knew she'd never manage to aim the rifle. But she pushed through the pain, jerking her ruined arm forward with every bit of force she could muster, throwing the gun at the man with the pistol.

The weapon hit the man's arm, pushing it aside, and two shots rang out, both far wide of Andi's position.

What had been Andi's position.

She was already in motion, leaping across the desk. There was something lurking in her mind, a faint realization of how much pain would explode in her shoulder when she hit the man she was lunging toward. But fear hadn't stopped her. It hadn't even delayed the instinctive action.

She got the first good look at the man as she came down on top of him. He was old, to her standards at least, a shock of thick gray hair covering his head. She'd heard the name Niles O'Bannon, of course. Everyone had. But she had no idea what the magnate looked like. Still, the age was right, and the location.

Was this the man who'd sent his minions to kill the Marine?

Yes, she decided. At least with enough certainty to decide he was going to pay for that crime.

Her shoulder slammed hard into the man, hard, and the two of them fell back behind the desk, slamming into the chair and flipping it over, as they dropped hard to the floor.

She'd been right about the pain. The initial impact had been sheer agony. She could feel her eyes watering, and a deep and guttural grunt escaping from her mouth. Then, more pain, even worse, as the two of them landed on the hardwood floor.

It was agonizing, like a raging fire running down one side

of her body, but she allowed none of it to interfere, to distract her from her deadly purpose. Her left arm was useless, immobile, but she already had her knife out in her right hand, ready to do what had to be done.

Her mind was a torrent of thoughts—lust for vengeance, fear, rage, recognition of sounds, realization of approaching guards.

She was out of time, certainly if she was going to escape, but likely in any event. If she was going to take her vengeance, if she was going to kill the rich and powerful man sprawled out on the floor next to her—the arrogant son of a bitch who had taken her only friend from her—it had to be now.

She plunged the blade into the man's side, reveling at his screams of pain. She knew a great deal about lethal spots, killing blows. She had discussed such things often with the Marine, just part of the training he'd given her in how to survive, how to kill her enemies.

She'd struck this time, however, where she'd been able, and she knew it wasn't a fatal blow. Not yet at least.

The guards would be there in seconds, and Niles O'Bannon would get the finest medical treatment available. He would be airlifted to the hospital, and a dozen surgeons would work on him. If she was going to succeed, she had to make sure the bastard was dead.

She twisted the knife, even as the man's screams increased in volume and intensity. She'd enjoyed his pain at first, but now all she wanted to do was finish and get the hell out. Only seconds had passed, but each one had felt like an age.

She jerked her hand back and forth, widening the wound, doing all she could to make sure her victim bled to death before anyone could help him. Then, her sense of self-preservation kicked in. The entire fight had been vastly shorter than it had seemed, but it had still been all the time she had.

Maybe more.

She pushed herself up, her teeth biting down from the pain, catching her lip, splitting it open. But she managed to get to her feet. He reached down, grabbed O'Bannon's discarded pistol. She glanced quickly at the stricken magnate, her eyes moving rapidly, looking for any signs of breathing or motion.

Nothing. He was dead.

She turned abruptly, her eyes moving to the third thug, lying in the far corner of the room, badly hurt, possibly dying, but still alive. She looked at the man, for perhaps half a second, and thoughts of mercy drifted through her mind.

Then she saw the Marine, a flashback from one of their times together, sitting, books open, and some sort of sugary confections in their hands. They were smiling, laughing, as he taught her to read. As he helped her become something more than a Gut street rat.

Her face hardened, and her eyes narrowed as she looked down at the helpless man.

"No," she said softly, grimly. "No way you live."

Her finger tightened on the trigger, and the gun fired. The bullet took the man in the side of the head, ripping through and exploding out the other side in a torrent of blood and brain.

Then, she turned, even as she heard guards moving into the next room. She looked around, frantically searching for an escape, and she threw herself at the large picture window behind the desk, bracing for the cuts and pain she knew would come.

Chapter Six

"Spacers District"
Vulcan City
Planet Parsephon, Obliesk II
Year 298 AC

Andi leaned back against the cold stone wall. She was
miserable, shivering, her entire body aching. The wound on
her shoulder throbbed, and despite her best efforts to clean
it out, it was badly infected. She'd done all she could, but
beyond squeezing out an astonishing amount of pus every
morning and engaging in yet another, extremely painful,
effort at cutting out the infected bits, there wasn't much she
could do. Antibiotics and antiseptic creams were as out of
her reach as the presidential suite on a five star liner to
Megara.

Her legs hurt, and her back, her arms. Her hands were
still cut up from the barbed wire fence she'd climbed in her
ongoing effort to escape pursuit. She was bruised and
battered, and for all her natural stubbornness and
determination, she was starting to lose hope. The depression
from the loss of her only friend weighed her down, even as
the grim reality of her situation slammed into her.

She'd done what she'd sworn to do, avenged the Marine,
and that provided *some* solace. Dying for something seemed

a damned sight better than dying for nothing.

Yet, as driven as she was to gain vengeance, she found it unsatisfying. She'd had to do it—she just couldn't have lived with herself if she'd let the killers live—but now she was just worse off than she'd been, and the only person on the entire Godforsaken planet she cared about was still dead.

Is he still lying where I left him?

She didn't know. In the Gut, it was possible, though more than likely, someone had at least hauled him out into the street and tossed him aside. Their spot, in the very back of the old warehouse, was too prime to stay long unclaimed.

Such thoughts upset her, though her rational mind didn't place much stock in the value of her friend's dead flesh, and she couldn't put it out of her mind. She'd even thought about going back herself, but that just wasn't in her. She couldn't bring herself to do it, just as she'd never gone back down the street where her mother had died. Andi had become cold, grim, unmerciful to her enemies and hardened to the images of suffering around her, but she had a weak spot for the very few people in her life she'd actually cared about.

Four people had died to atone for their involvement in the Marine's death, plus another three who'd carried no guilt save working as security guards and being in the wrong place at the wrong time. She regretted that she'd had to kill them, but she didn't dwell much on it. She'd escaped by the slimmest of margins as it was. If she'd delayed anywhere, hesitated to kill when she'd had to, she would already be captured. Or more likely, dead.

Kill or be killed. It was a fundamental choice one had to make, at least those born into circumstances like hers.

She wondered what would be worse, death or capture. She faced almost certain execution at the hands of Parsephon's authorities, there was little doubt about that. Murder was tolerated sometimes, in places like the Gut, for example, where no one expended too much effort trying to track down the killers of a derelict or addict long written off.

But killing *the* Niles O'Bannon was a capital offense on Parsephon, without question.

She wondered if a jury of O'Bannon factory workers would convict her. She dared to imagine perhaps they wouldn't, but then she realized the courage voting for acquittal would require. The O'Bannons could destroy the life of a normal Parsephonian worker in an instant, and she had no doubt, jurors who let Niles O'Bannon's killer go would rue that decision.

Not that it mattered. Confederation law entitled her to a jury trial, but she knew she'd never get one, and she had no doubt a panel of Parsephon's judges would return a guilty verdict, along with the maximum sentence, as quickly as they could get away with. Most of the judges were owned more or less, by the O'Bannons and by the rival industrial dynasties. The magnates didn't always get along—and she suspected more than a few had broken out cherished old vintages for toasts when they'd heard the news that Niles O'Bannon was dead—but as a group, on one front they agreed without exception, inseparable and totally united.

Rabble from the streets who dared to inflict violence on one of their number could *never* be tolerated.

The magnates owned the government and the judges, but the whole affair being in the public eye assured, at least, that execution by the judicial authorities would be quick and relatively painless.

She expected far, far worse if the O'Bannon security forces or their underworld allies found her first.

She'd been on the run for days. Hiding during the daylight, sneaking around at night. She had money, a little at least, but she didn't dare go anywhere she could spend it. She'd gotten into the O'Bannon compound, and back out again. That had been miracle enough, but she hadn't been able to prevent the security system from getting hundreds of images of her. She'd tried her best to disguised herself, but the hood covering her head had fallen off during the fighting.

Her picture was everywhere, on the nets, on posters hanging on the streets. It was a cliché, but one based in fact…there was no place to run to, no place to hide.

Almost no place.

She'd worked her way down to the Spacer's District, adjacent to the spaceport. Some lingering thought had driven her, some clinging recollection of her original plan, of the ship the Marine had told her to find, the captain who would help her.

That was then…

The Marine hadn't imagined she'd be on the run, though, fleeing from every cop, thug, even bounty hunter, on Parsephon. No freighter captain would help her now. None could. Even if he was willing to get involved.

There was only one way out. Besides surrender or death. She had to get them all off her tail, and the only way to do that was to convince them she was dead.

But how? She could get a body, she was sure enough of that. Sadly, there was no shortage of deaths in places like the Gut. Disease, violence, overdoses…there were a hundred contributors to the grim death toll every day. It would be harder, certainly, to find the corpse of a girl close to her age, though in the Gut and the other slums of Vulcan City, depressingly, it wouldn't be *that* much harder.

She'd left DNA samples behind at the scene of her crime, there was no question about that. The blood from her shoulder wound, if nothing else, and probably a lot more. But there was one advantage to being born on the streets in the Gut and living her whole life there. She wasn't in any of the planet's extensive databases on its people. That thought had always pleased her somehow, supported her sense of herself as something other than a mindless sheep doing as she was told. This was the first time it had produced a tangible advantage, though.

She had worked her way through her plan, pushing back her own thoughts when they cast doubt, or reminded her how many things had to go just right for it all to succeed. None of that mattered. She had no other choice, no other way out.

Either she convinced them all she was dead.

Or she waited until they came and found her. She was good, but she knew she couldn't stay ahead of the manhunt forever. There were too many resources deployed, too many people after her, too many rewards offered, sums of money that seemed like a king's ransom to the destitute and desperate people who inhabited the areas where she was hiding.

She was out of time, almost. Someone would see her, turn her in. She had to execute her plan as soon as possible, three days, four at most.

And that meant she had work to do.

*   *   *

Andi stood on the dank and quiet street. It was late, or more accurately, early, and the small side street was empty, save for her and the vehicle she had stolen and driven there. She'd been working feverishly, struggling to pull off the fraud she'd devised, the one intended to convince anyone interested in her that she was dead.

She'd been going at it nonstop for hours, but now she needed a rest, just a few minutes. That was all she could spare, if she could even spare that.

She focused on her breathing, inhaling deeply and exhaling, in a very controlled manner. She was trying to calm herself, at least to the extent that was even possible, considering what she was about to do. She managed some limited success. At least her heart wasn't pounding like a drum in her ears at the moment.

She'd even managed to relax her mind for an instant, and

her thoughts drifted from intense analysis of her plan to more philosophical subjects.

The Confederation Charter demanded that member worlds respect certain rights and privileges of its citizens. The Marine had told her that many times, espousing on his continued loyalties and insisting the Confederation was a beacon of freedom, despite the way it had treated him. She'd been skeptical, but she'd always listened, and wondered.

Now, she knew for sure. Unlike almost everything else he'd told her or taught her, that was pure bullshit. At least it was on Parsephon.

She'd killed Niles O'Bannon. To her, it had been simple, a deep need to avenge her friend. She hadn't been trying to make a political statement, nor strike a blow for the workers in the O'Bannon factories. And she certainly hadn't intended to bring every facet of law enforcement on the planet down on her head. But that's exactly what she'd done.

She *had* murdered O'Bannon. She realized that. It wasn't the prospect of being held accountable for vigilantism that angered her, nor a system which would not allow one to avenge a friend or loved one. She wasn't sure how she felt about that in a clinical sense, but she understood the advantages of retaining order. It was the difference in responses that infuriated her. People were killed in the Gut every day, and no one cared. Yet, the death of a magnate triggered a planetwide manhunt.

Why were two killings treated so differently? Especially when O'Bannon almost certainly had it coming more than some vagrant in the Gut, murdered for his coat.

She supposed there could be other worlds out there, ones that more closely followed the expressed ideals of the Confederation, but she was far from convinced. It seemed, at least, if a planet produced enough valuable exports, enough hulls for the navy, enough tax revenue for Megara, such lofty sentiments could be ignored easily enough.

Kill a Marine veteran, a decent man living in squalor and poverty, and no one cared. Kill a corrupt magnate, a power broker in local politics, and someone deeply involved in the planet's organized crime rackets to boot? Throw up barricades and send every cop and soldier available out into the street to hunt the villain down.

Well, not this villain. They'll chase me down, hunt me endlessly…but not if they think I'm dead.

She glanced down at the body lying on the ground next to her. The woman had been a bit older than she was, at least that was her best guess—her murderers had worked her over pretty savagely, not leaving much in the way of identifiable features. Still, the only other candidate she'd found was considerably younger, likely no more than twelve or thirteen. Andi had been that age on the streets, alone, and perhaps it was as much desire not to use the unfortunate young girl's body as it was anything else, but she'd opted for the older woman.

She was far from knowledgeable at just what forensic abilities the police could employ, but she'd done everything possible to ensure the body would be completely incinerated, just enough left to make it clear there had been a victim of the crash she was devising. She wasn't sure that would be enough to foil the DNA testing, but it was the best she could do.

She reached down to her side, her hand clasping on the grip of the blade she'd carried for more than five years, pulling it free and looking down at it. She'd found it, restored it, carried it with her everywhere, and used it to deadly effect. It had saved her life, and it was precious to her, as much as any inanimate object she possessed.

Now she had to leave it behind. She'd packed the stolen vehicle with every flammable substance she'd been able to steal, done all she could to ensure the remains of the body could pass for her. But that was a double-edged sword. The authorities *had* to believe it had been her in the car, without being able to prove it. She'd thought for days about how to achieve that result, and then she remembered the one thing that would have been captured on the surveillance vids, the only thing she'd had with her that could survive the blaze that would consume the body.

The grip would be burnt to cinders, of course, everything but the blade. But that would survive, and when the authorities investigated, when they watched the surveillance videos, they would match it to the one she'd carried then.

Her knife was going to save her one more time.

One last time.

She sighed softly, and she set the blade down on the top of the vehicle, bending over and grabbing the body, shoving her hands under the dead woman's arms. The corpse was stiff, and she had a difficult time moving it, forcing it into the driver's station of the small vehicle. The car was nothing special, just the kind of thing she might have tried to steal if she was on the run—which, of course, she was. She had it rigged perfectly, at least she hoped she did. The automated driving system would take the car out into the Fairmont, and then, if she'd changed the wiring correctly, it would accelerate to full speed and disengage.

Then the small charges would go off.

She'd gone well beyond her knowledge in rigging the whole thing, and she figured there was maybe a fifty-fifty chance it would work.

But one chance in two looked damned good just then, considering her circumstances.

If she pulled it off, if the vehicle crashed and ignited, if the inferno was hot enough to damage the corpse beyond the reach of DNA identification—and a hundred other 'ifs'—she just might convince her hunters she was dead.

Then, maybe, after a while, she would be able to find a way off Parsephon.

And out into a universe just waiting for Andi Lafarge to blaze her trail, and win her fortune.

Chapter Seven

"Spacers District"
Vulcan City
Planet Parsephon, Obliesk II
Year 298 AC

"So, Chuck told you to come see me?" The freighter captain was an almost perfect cliché, weathered, rough, with a clear and attentive stare, though looking a bit worn out by life. He held the ID tags she'd handed him, the ones the Marine had given her. They were old and battered, and they bore no name, only a number. But the captain had recognized them immediately.

Andi just looked back for a few seconds before she responded. She'd never had a name to call her friend, no labels at all, save for 'the Marine.' It seemed strange to suddenly assign a name to the face she remembered so well. *Chuck...his name was Chuck...*

"Yes. He and I were friends. He told me to leave Parsephon...after he was gone." She'd already told the captain the Marine was dead. He hadn't seemed surprised, and she got the impression that her mentor's friend had been aware of the drug habit that had led, indirectly at least, to his death.

"Well, that's just good sense. I make this run three times

a year, but I don't stay here any longer than I have to." He paused. "This place is a disgrace. Worst shithole in the Confederation. If Parsephon didn't pump so much tax revenue back to Megara, somebody would do something about what goes on here. But nobody wants to knock over the honeypot. And, this planet breeds a particularly skilled form of corrupt and immoral politician."

Andi lacked any knowledge of the rest of the Confederation, but she didn't have any trouble believing Parsephon was near the bottom of the barrel, or dead center in it. No quarrel, either, none at all, with the designation, 'shithole.'

She turned her head instinctively, looking quickly to the left and then the right. It was the third or fourth time she'd done it, despite her attempts to look natural and relaxed. Her ploy to fake her death seemed to have worked, at least for a while, but she was far from sure deeper investigation would fail to reveal that the body that had been found—and touted on multiple media outlets as that of Niles O'Bannon's killer—was not, in fact, that of the woman who'd invaded the family's compound and murdered the industrialist.

"So, tell me—what did you say your name was, Andi?—what kind of trouble are you in?"

She felt a rush of anger at herself. She'd laid low, despite the apparent respite from pursuit, coming out only to check on the arrival schedule for *Belstar*. It had been a few weeks, and she'd been on edge every passing hour, jumping at every sound, real or imagined. *If you screwed this up because you couldn't stay calm for a few minutes…*

"Trouble?" She was annoyed with herself even as the word came out of her mouth. *Couldn't you even try to sound convincing?*

The captain sighed softly. "Andi, Chuck was a good friend, and I definitely owe him, and I know damned well he wouldn't have given these…" He held up the ID tags. "…to anyone who wasn't close to him. So, I believe he told you to find me, and I'm willing to help. But you've got to be straight with me, girl, or it's no dice. Do we understand each other?"

She nodded slowly, still trying to decide what to do. She'd gone in thinking of the captain as a means to an end, a way to get off of Parsephon. But she found herself liking the man, feeling as though she could trust him.

Except she didn't trust anyone.

"Yes, I am in trouble…and, I think it would be better if you didn't know all the details. Let's just say, I was angry at the way the Marine…Chuck…died, and I wasn't willing to leave it be." It wasn't trust, not exactly, but she knew she wasn't getting on *Belstar* unless she gave the captain *something*. And she had a strong impression of his character. It made sense to her, at least, that he and the Marine had been friends.

The captain hesitated, and Andi could see his expression change slightly. Was it respect she was seeing, or at least something similar?

"You wouldn't leave it be?" A pause. "Maybe you're right. Maybe I *don't* want to know." He looked at her again, clearly trying to size her up. "Well, Andi, every bit of sense I've got inside is telling me to send you on your way…"

She felt her stomach tense. She *had* to get off Parsephon, and she had no idea how else she was going to manage it. If the captain sent her packing, she couldn't see any other way out. The authorities may have bought the burned body scam she'd pulled off, but there were still thousands of images of her floating around. If she stayed for too long, someone was bound to take a closer look.

Perhaps more importantly, even, she just *had* to get off of Parsephon. She detested the place. She'd have cast the whole miserable rock into its sun if she could have, and the idea of being stuck there, of missing her only chance at escape, was more than she could bear.

But her near-panic was needless. The captain managed something of a smile as he continued, "...but, if old Chuck saw something in you, well, he always did have a good sense of people. And I *do* owe him. Big." He hesitated again, staring at her intently. "Okay, go get your stuff and meet me back here in an hour. And, don't make me wait. I'm already sure enough this is a hassle I don't need...so don't prove me right, or at least, don't make it worse." He shook his head as he looked at her. "We'll be stuck here about a week waiting for our cargo, but my guess is, you're probably better off laying low on *Belstar* than prowling around the Spacer's District. Am I right?"

"Thank you. And, yes. Definitely." Her tone was emphatic, and sincere. Andi expected nothing from anyone, save perhaps grief, and whatever faults she had, ingratitude to someone who helped her wasn't one of them. "Truly, thank you. And, I don't need an hour. I'm ready now."

"What about your things?"

She held up the small bag that had been slung over her back. It was an answer, one that didn't need any words. The small sack held a change of clothes, a scrap of leather she'd taken from her old knife before she'd left it in the vehicle, and her favorite book. She'd wanted to take all the volumes in the Marine's tiny library, but they were heavy and bulky, and she'd spent weeks running from one place to another.

Those few things, save for the handful of coins left in the small bag on her waist, were all she cared about.

"Anyplace you need to go, anyone you need to see? Anyone you'd like to say goodbye to? It may be a while before you're back here."

Andi almost laughed. "No, nothing, no one."

"Are you sure? It may be quite some time before you see any of it again."

It's going to be a lot longer than you think...

She almost said what she was thinking, but then she held it back, concerned it would sound more obnoxious than she intended. She was never coming back to Parsephon, and if she remained on *Belstar* long enough for the ship to return, at least she had no intention of ever leaving the vessel and setting foot on the planet she'd learned to hate with almost unrestrained anger.

"There is nothing here for me." Everything good she'd had on Parsephon was gone, and all that remained, a few memories, would go with her wherever her travels took her.

Those memories were very few indeed for sixteen years. Her remembrances of her mother, and of the Marine, for a few pleasant moments she could recall with each. And, as for the rest of Parsephon, the less said the better.

"Okay, then come with me now. My guess is, the sooner we get you stashed out of sight, the better."

She didn't answer, she just nodded. She knew the captain was taking a risk harboring her, and she knew he knew it. She could offer appreciation, but she figured doing everything possible to avoid trouble was a more useful gesture, a more sincere way to express her gratitude.

Better for both of them.

The captain looked her over again. "We're going to have a few passengers on this run, a little extra income to cover expenses. What kind of cabin steward do you think we can make out of you?"

*   *   *

"Can I bring you anything else?" Andi stood just inside the cabin door, looking over at the man and the woman.

"No, this will be fine for now, but do try to come more quickly the next time we hit the call button." The woman's words grated on her, each of them clawing at her ears, as if trying to awaken her anger. She'd probably have given the woman—and her equally arrogant traveling companion—a good scare at the least, and quite possibly a few scars by which to remember their trip, but for all her rugged life and her upbringing among some of humanity's dregs, Andi Lafarge was not an ingrate. The captain had taken her in, gotten her off of Parsephon, and he'd treated her well enough in the six months she'd served aboard *Belstar*, even adding her to the crew roster and paying her what small amount he could afford from the bare sustenance revenues from his meager shipping contracts.

She would not repay that kindness by upsetting his passengers, and causing more problems for him. However much she wanted to carve her initials into their faces.

"I will make every effort possible." A pause, mostly so she could bite down on her temper. "I will leave you for now, but please ring if you need anything more."

She slipped back out of the door, as quickly as possible, staring at the hatch, trying somehow to will it to close faster. Then, she let out the frown she'd been holding back.

Frown? It was an outright scowl, and a nasty one at that.

She disliked the two passengers because they were arrogant and condescending, but even more because they were posers. Booking passage on a small freighter like *Belstar* was hardly the first choice of the spacefaring elite. There were liners that plied the star lanes in obscene luxury, with prices to match. The people in stateroom two were there because that was all they could afford, and however much they shit on the freighter's crew—and Andi, mostly, as their cabin steward—they were bargain travelers, plain and simple.

It took all Andi had not to remind them of that fact. *Hell, I killed a man who could have bought and sold both of you a million times over...*

She almost chuckled at the thought. She knew she shouldn't draw so much satisfaction from killing, but now that she was away from the scene and out of immediate danger, she realized just how pleased with herself she was. The bastard had deserved to die, and laws that protected someone like him were not fit to be obeyed.

In truth, Andi felt very little obligation to do what she was told, whether she was being bullied in some back alley or bludgeoned with laws passed in the middle of the night by corrupt politicians. She had a moral code, certainly, and she followed her own sense of fairness. But most politicians were so detached from morality and justice, she wondered why anyone heeded their diktats.

Save only out of fear. Laws were imposed, almost always at gunpoint, whether directly or indirectly, and she was well aware of the dangers of ending up on their wrong side. She'd come a hair's breadth from the scaffold already, and she was barely seventeen. She knew why people were subjugated by such laws, but she felt sorry for those who somehow believed in most of them.

Andi hated the fact that *Belstar* often carried passengers. She understood why the captain took the fares, and she knew there wasn't much choice, but she'd become accustomed to the crew, and she was as comfortable with them as she ever really was with anyone. If the four staterooms had been empty instead of occupied with difficult fools who were never happy with anything she did, she'd almost have enjoyed her time on *Belstar*. She had enough food, a climate-controlled environment, and freedom from most serious danger. That alone might have been paradise, but she had something else, too. A bed. A small cot, really, in the narrow back cabin that housed more than half of the crew. It was a top bunk, and she'd lain there many times now, listening to the rest of the crew complaining about the sparseness of *Belstar*'s comforts or the narrowness of its cots.

Andi always smiled when she listened. She thought she had found heaven. She'd never had a bed, not for one night in her sixteen years, and to her, the thin, hard cot seemed the ultimate luxury imaginable. It was so foreign, so alien, that she'd found, for the first few weeks, at least, she'd been unable to fall asleep. She'd almost wandered off to find some floorspace somewhere, something that more closely matched what she was used to…but she'd never been able to tear herself away from the decadent comfort. It was inconceivable to leave her cot behind, and she'd lain there night after night, fitfully slipping in and out of sleep, immovable, as though her body was almost part of the dingy metal bunk, welded there, immobile.

She'd quickly come to understand the realities of the freighter, and the ship's ragged and haphazard economy. *Belstar* was typical for a small, individually owned ship. She couldn't compete with the massive vessels of the large freight lines, nor with the luxurious liners that traveled back and forth across the Confederation's heavily-traveled commerce lanes. So, she carried small cargoes, specialized shipments—occasionally ones straddling the line of legality—and she supplemented that revenue by carrying a few passengers. The four staterooms were small, but they were considerably more luxurious than the crew quarters.

The captain owned *Belstar*, after a fashion, but the vessel carried a considerable mortgage, one that its freight runs barely covered after other expenses. Usually. Captain Hiram was wealthy, in a somewhat hazy and ephemeral way. The ship was worth more than he owed, usually. Assuming he sold in a good market, and that no massive repairs came up, and that he didn't lose the ship to the bank after a series of bad runs.

Hiram would retire comfortably, as long as he hung up his stars in the right port at the right time, when he could find a legitimate buyer for *Belstar*, one who could qualify to assume the ship's mortgage, as he had done himself years before. Otherwise, he'd have little or nothing to show for his years of work. Andi had gathered that the captain had little in the way of conventional savings. Constant repairs and upgrades made *Belstar* somewhat of an ongoing cash drain, and the bank accounts that might have held his thin profits had proven to be theoretical in the face of the realities of owning and maintaining a spacefaring vessel.

Belstar was his savings. Assuming he could sell out when he was ready.

Andi had always been aware of the difficulty of life in the slums, of the crushing pressure on the poverty-stricken denizens of places like the Gut. Now, she saw something else, a man she once would have considered rich, privileged.

But Captain Hiram was running every day, even as she always had, in his own way perhaps, and in somewhat more comfortable circumstances, but running, nevertheless. He struggled, with every trip, with every patched repair, and with every extra passenger he could book, to keep his head above water, and Andi respected him for it.

She genuinely liked Hiram, and *Belstar* was a far better place to be than the Gut. But she'd come to realize, it wasn't where she wanted to be. Where she *needed* to be. Grinding out credits, making one or two percent profit on a run—if nothing went wrong—that wasn't what she'd left Parsephon to find.

No, there was more out there, somewhere. She knew she'd find it one day, a new life, a place she could begin building her future. Her fortune.

Then, one day, Captain Hiram took a different job, a longer one, and riskier, too. One designed to help him get a few credits ahead for once.

One that would take *Belstar*—and Andi—someplace where fortunes were made.

And where people died trying to make them.

Chapter Eight

Spaceport, Port Royal City
Planet Dannith, Ventica III
Year 299 AC

"Are you sure, Andi?" Hiram didn't sound surprised, in fact his tone suggested he'd expected just what Andi had told him. But the sadness was still there. "I will really miss you on *Belstar*. I know you don't want to be a steward for the rest of your life, but maybe we could start training you in navigation." Even as he spoke the words, it was clear he knew Andi was going to leave no matter what.

"Captain, I can't express to you my appreciation for what you did for me. If I can ever repay you, all you have to do is ask. But I've got things I need to do, and I can't do them on *Belstar*."

And I've already figured out a lot more than you think about navigation, and piloting and engineering, too. I'll never be able to thank you enough for my time on Belstar.

Hiram looked like he was going to try again to convince her, but then she saw the resignation take hold. He'd come to know her, well enough she suspected, to realize she was ill-suited to spending years hauling routine cargoes.

"I'm sorry to see you go, Andi. I took you in because I owed Chuck, but you never gave me reason to regret it. It was a pleasure having you as part of the crew, and I know the others will miss you as much as I do."

"Will you say goodbye to them for me, Captain?" He voice was a little shaky, the strength that almost always drove her failing for a moment. She *had* become part of the crew, and she knew it was cowardly to just disappear, to let Hiram tell them all she was gone. But she was afraid if she delayed any longer, she'd allow herself to be persuaded to stay. Dannith was her real chance to strive for something bigger, and if she let it pass by, there was no way to know when another opportunity would come.

"I will, Andi…and good luck to you. Remember, go to the Shooting Star, and try to find Captain Lorillard of the *Nightrunner*. I used to run some of his contraband cargoes back in the day." He paused, and he smiled at her. "You see, I wasn't always as timid as I am now. Back when I was scraping up enough to payback the loan sharks who gave me the down payment for *Belstar*, I ran just about anything profitable." He hesitated again and then added, "Age can take something out of you if you're not careful, Andi. Keep your eye out for that…because even you'll get old someday."

Andi just nodded. She was seventeen, young by almost any standards, but a lifetime spent scavenging in the Gut did something to wear away youth.

"I haven't seen Jim Lorillard in years, but tell him I sent you, and maybe he'll take you on his crew." Hiram paused, clearly struggling to hold back his emotion. "And, be careful. Things are rough out here." The captain knew she'd been trained by the Marine, and before that, he understood she'd survived alone on the streets of the Gut. That she'd faced and defeated deadly adversaries. She was capable of taking care of herself, and Andi had no doubt her friend realized that. But there was still concern in his voice.

"I will find him, Captain." She stood and looked at him for a few seconds. Then, she leaned forward and hugged him. "And, thank you again, for all you have done for me. I will never forget it. Or you."

She turned, and even as she did, she felt pressure behind her eyes, tears welling up. She hurried her pace, determined to get farther away before the water escaped and ran down her face. She knew what she had to do, but that didn't make it easy to leave the safest environment she had ever known...and the third person in her life who'd been kind to her.

She just couldn't turn her back on the opportunities the Badlands offered.

Those opportunities hadn't registered entirely, not when Hiram had first told her *Belstar* was going to set course for an alternate destination, a change from the milkruns that constituted the freighter's normal route. Moving small loads of routine cargoes through the heart of the Confederation had become too unprofitable, at least to pay the bank and the crew, and have anything at all left over. Hiram was a risk averse captain, and the run to Dannith was a gamble of sorts, but one that offered the potential of two or three times normal delivery rates.

Ten times or more if *Belstar*'s captain was willing to stash some contraband old tech in his ship's hold.

Andi wasn't sure how much financial pressure was weighing down on Hiram, or whether the captain was prepared to step clearly over the line into outright illegality, or if he was just hoping to benefit from frontier rates on more standard freight.

But she knew the answer for herself.

She'd killed already, multiple times, and she'd fled from a world to escape from the law. She'd knelt beside her mother's body, looking down through a mask of tears, and again next to the Marine who'd taken her in and taught her almost everything she knew. She had nothing but resentment for those in positions of authority, people she'd only seen abuse their power. They could drop dead as far as she was concerned, and they could take their rules and their laws and shove them.

She didn't think of herself as evil, nor even criminal, and she followed her own code, with significantly more consistency than she'd seen laws enforced. She'd long ago promised herself she'd always be loyal to her friends, and she'd tried to do just that. But she had no respect for burdens she knew existed to keep people like her down.

Dannith was on the frontier, the planet closest to the region of space known as the Badlands. There were hundreds of systems, thousands, in that dead and haunted stretch of space, the ghostly remnants of imperial worlds, once prosperous and massively populated...before they were destroyed in the Cataclysm.

The people who'd lived on those planets were long dead, their cities reduced to ruins and dust. But in the debris, covered over by resurgent jungles and deserts, remained imperial technology. Bits and pieces of various instruments and machinery, creations of mankind that were now well beyond the understanding of humanity's survivors.

Scraps of ancient tech of incalculable value, to researchers working to reconstruct the knowledge that had been lost, and to the adventurers who'd gone out into the Badlands to find it, braving ancient security systems, the hazards of deep space and, not least of all, each other. Men killed other men for reasons far more trifling than scraps of technology worth millions of credits. Many crews went out into the unknown reaches, but not all of them returned.

There was danger, without question, waiting in the future along the course she'd chosen, and the pain of saying goodbye to friends in the present.

But for the first time in her life, Andi was somewhere she could put her skills to work, where her intellect and grit gave her a chance to really rise out of the pit, where she'd been consigned since birth. She would take the risks, work hard, struggle, fight...anything to achieve the goals that had long seemed impossible dreams.

Anything to make her fortune.

*   *   *

The place was dismal, a seedy pit, with old worn seats and tables that looked like they'd been patched back together after one too many bar fights. The patrons were a mixed bag, somehow a bit sleazy while also substantive in a way she couldn't quite wrap her head around. It was early, at least for a bar to be as full as this one was, but Andi had heard enough about Badlands prospectors to know they were different from any people she'd ever encountered.

She'd wandered around the Spacer's District for a few weeks, finding out what she could about Captain Lorillard and *Nightrunner*, but mostly waiting for the ship to return. She had money, enough to last her a while, at least, but as the days turned into weeks, she'd begun to get concerned. That worry escalated considerably when *Belstar* finished loading its cargo and launched. Until then, she'd known Captain Hiram would take her back. Now, she was truly stranded, wandering around a strange—and, in ways, dangerous—neighborhood, with perhaps enough money to last her six weeks.

She'd even started looking around for potential marks, people or places that seemed likely targets for a petty theft or two, if *Nightrunner* didn't show up soon. She'd told herself her days as a thief were behind her, but she realized such oaths wore away quickly when other options failed to appear. The Gut was a more violent place, without question, but the occupants of Port Royal City's Spacers District looked like tougher targets. Half the people walking around were hardened spacers and not one in ten of those even went to the bathroom without a pistol at their sides. There were easy marks, she was sure—there were everywhere— but they were harder to spot on Dannith.

Then, just as she'd almost become resigned to becoming a street rat on Dannith, as she had been on Parsephon, *Nightrunner* landed at the spaceport.

The ship and its crew had a pretty heavy rep in the District, and rumor had it, Captain Lorillard and his crew had hauled in some significant scores. Andi knew they couldn't have hit real paydirt—it hadn't taken her long to confirm that the crews that had tended to vanish into comfortable retirement. But of the active ships, *Nightrunner* was one of the more renowned and respected.

That was good. It meant the crew got the best leads, which increased the chances of hitting it big.

But it didn't take long for the word to spread that the ship's latest mission had been a bust. They'd come back with a few trinkets, enough to pay the expedition's expenses—maybe—perhaps even with enough extra to buy a few rounds of drinks to ease the pain.

Andi had gotten to the Shooting Star early, sure Captain Lorillard and his people would head there once they'd secured their ship's docking. She'd waited for hours now, drinking as little as she could and still avoid getting bounced out, and sticking as much as she could to non-alcoholic beverages. Andi wasn't much of a drinker. She'd watched the Marine whittle his life away with his Blast, and the images had stuck. She didn't like giving up the clarity of her mind, not for a second. Besides, back in the Gut, the last thing she was going to do was waste money on decent liquor…and the rot gut the street vendors sold seemed more useful for stripping paint than ingesting.

Still, she'd realized already, in just a few hours, that some level of drinking was going to ride hand in hand with a career as a frontier adventurer. She'd seen a couple other crews walk in and drink what she would have thought was enough to kill them all, without any more apparent effect than increasing the volume of their voices. Clearly, drinking was tightly woven into the frontier culture, and she was prepared to do whatever it took to fit in, at least long enough to get her start.

She was thinking about giving up for the night and leaving, when she saw a group walk through the door. The had swagger to their gait, but they were quieter, less pointlessly loud than many of the others. She had a pretty good idea they were the ones she was looking for, when the bartender more or less confirmed it.

"Jim…I heard you came up empty. Sorry to hear that, man…I figured you guys had it on that run." A short pause. "Still, I'd have been sorry to lose such good customers, and I'm guessing you'd have all been off to some pleasure world to whittle away the time and count your money."

It was clear the crew coming in were regulars, and Hiram had told her Lorillard's first name was 'James.'

"I wouldn't say 'empty,' Clevus, but damned sure not what we hoped for." Lorillard didn't elaborate, though from the bartender's expression, it was clear the man had expected him to.

She liked that. She, too, was thrifty with words. What you didn't tell people, they couldn't use against you.

"We'll take the usual, Cletus…" Lorillard paused for a moment, looking around. Then he jerked his hand toward a large table toward the back of the bar. "…we'll be back here. So, keep 'em coming."

Andi sat for a few minutes, waiting, and, if she was being honest with herself, building up her nerve. She could tell immediately that Lorillard was no joke, and he seemed a man unlikely to suffer fools. She had her introduction, for what it was, but nothing more, not even any real proof that she had served aboard *Belstar*. But if she didn't want to end up sweeping floors in some Spacers District dive, this was her best chance.

She sucked in a deep breath, and she slid off her barstool, and walked back toward the large round table, and the seven men and three women sitting there.

There are moments that alter the course of your life…it was something the Marine had told her.

And now is one of those moments…

Chapter Nine

The Shooting Star
Spacer's District, Port Royal City
Planet Dannith, Ventica III
Year 299 AC

"So, old Walt Hiram sent you, eh?" Andi couldn't tell from Lorillard's tone whether he believed her or not.

"Yes, sir. I served just over a year on *Belstar*."

"And you got off on Dannith?" The captain laughed, along with the rest of the crew. "Who the hell would pick Dannith of all places? What really happened? Did they put you off for stealing?"

"I don't steal from my friends."

Lorillard laughed again. "But you *do* steal from others?"

Andi didn't answer. She just stood, stone still, her face devoid of emotion.

"Well, it doesn't matter. Old Walt is a top-notch freighter captain. The poor bastard could have been rich by now if he had the nerve to keep running old tech instead of hauling bullshit loads of machine parts and grain seeds." He looked at Andi, clearly trying to size her up. "Anyway, if he really sent you, that carries some weight..." He hesitated again. "...but you're just a little pup, kid. I don't take babies on my ship, not for the runs we make. You'll piss yourself at the

79

first sign of trouble, and you'll run, probably just when the rest of us need you the most. Go, do yourself a favor, get a real job, even if it's shoveling shit somewhere. I know you think prospecting on the frontier is romantic, and you've heard all kinds of stories about big strikes and giant piles of money, but there's more hard work and death out here than prime old tech. Come back if you still want it when you're twenty-five, and I'll give you a go for old Walt's sake."

Andi stood where she was, not backing down, and despite the emotions threatening to burst out, not letting anyone on to her disappointment. Her mind was racing, trying to think of something to say, some way to change Lorillard's mind. He seemed a hard man, a tough man, not someone likely to be swayed by pleading. She couldn't show weakness.

But how could she push her case when the very act of begging someone who didn't want you to take you was weakness defined?

"Don't waste your time." Lorillard seemed almost to have read her mind. "You look like a scrappy kid. Maybe you'll make it out here, after all, but I don't do rookie training. If you've got a place here now, it's not on *Nightrunner*, not yet at least. Now, my crew and I have some serious drinking to do, so if you don't mind…"

Andi wanted to burst into tears, and inside she hated herself for that. She was a fighter—a killer, she reminded herself—yet she was woefully inexperienced in dealing with people, at least beyond chasing them away with a knife in her hand.

She turned and walked away, inhaling deeply as she tried to maintain her cold outward appearance. She wanted to go right for the door, to run back to the tiny, filthy room she'd rented, and yell or scream, or whatever else might give her an outlet for the anger and frustration she felt.

But she wasn't going to give Lorillard and his people the satisfaction. Whatever it took, whatever it cost her, she wasn't going to show weakness. She wasn't going to let them think they had gotten the best of her.

She went back to her stool and sat down, waving toward the bartender, ordering another drink. She'd started with coffee when she'd first come in, but the bartender's snickering told her that wasn't going to help her credibility with the spacers in the place. So, she'd switched to some kind of local beer. She'd been concerned at first about drinking too much, but the swill was so watered down, she figured a few mugs weren't going to affect her at all.

She reached down and grabbed the battered old mug, and raised it to her lips. She wanted to leave, and she had to go and think about her next move, what she was going to do. But her pride flared up as well, and she wasn't going to leave, not before Lorillard and his people did.

She drank slowly, gauging the glares from the bartender to judge just how gradually she could go through her drinks without drawing unwanted attention. She stewed and analyzed and tried to think of her next move, without any real success.

Then it happened.

She heard voices first, caustic and loud, coming from the back of the bar.

"Lorillard, you useless piece of shit…that was a good lead I gave you. And you threw it away and came back with nothing. Almost nothing, at least. I'm here for my cut of the miserable scraps you and your pack of mongrels managed to find. I should take it all, for compensation for your screwups."

"Get the hell out of here, Darvin, before I forget I'm here to blow off steam with my people, and I show you just what I think of that miserable info you sold me. You almost got half of my people killed, and the few items we managed to salvage will barely refuel and refit my ship. You aren't getting a thing from me, parasite, so why don't you get out of here while you still can?"

Andi felt a rush of excitement. She didn't know what was happening or, more accurately, what was about to happen, but just maybe there would be some kind of opportunity. Her hand moved down to her side. The old knife, familiar friend that it had been, wasn't there of course. But the new one was.

Serving as a steward on *Belstar* didn't pay anything anyone would call a good wage, nor even a moderately decent one, but with her room and board essentially free, what little she'd gotten had fallen right into her pocket. The crew wasted their wages in spaceport bars, and in the brothels and casinos that inevitably surrounded the landing areas. Andi had no desire to waste what little money she possessed, but she had splurged on something she knew would be truly useful.

A new knife.

Not a scavenged, hand-repaired, half-rusted old thing like she'd had before. This time she went to a proper store, and bought a large survival knife. It was properly weighted and razor sharp, and in every way, save the soft spot she retained for her old—and first—weapon, it was a superior blade. She'd bought a pair of proper sheaths as well, one for her belt, and one that fit under her arm, for when stealth was an issue.

Her fingers moved slowly over the soft leather of the hilt, but otherwise, she sat calmly, staring straight ahead, still nursing the beer in front of her. And listening intently.

"You're lucky I don't cut your throat, Lorillard. You think you're a tough guy, but you don't know shit." Even as the man was speaking, another half dozen walked into the bar. Andi flashed a quick glance their way, her eyes settling on a large, muscular man with a nasty scar running at an angle down his face. She didn't know *exactly* what was happening, but her years in the Gut left no doubt at all.

Those guys are here for a fight.

She slid slowly off the stool, trying to look as nonchalant

as possible. But no one was paying any attention to her. By that time, every set of eyes in the place was locked on the back table.

"Darvin, I'm only going to say this one more time." Lorillard stood up as he spoke, shoving the chair hard behind him as he did. The old wooden seat slid back half a meter before it tipped over and fell on its side. The crew lurched up immediately after their leader, and they stood there with scowls on their faces, arms down at their sides, not doubt hovering near weapons of one sort or another. "Get your miserable ass out of here now, Darvin, or by the Spacer's gods, I will make you pay for my people went through chasing down your shitty leads."

Andi could feel her heart racing, the invigoration of a pending fight. She was no stranger to violence, nor to the constant presence of death hovering on the edge of almost everything. Usually, she'd tried to avoid conflicts, and certainly fights that weren't hers. But this time, she sensed the opportunity she'd hoped for. Lorillard had called her a kid, sent her away.

I'll show him who is a kid…

The situation was deteriorating rapidly. The new arrivals outnumbered Lorillard and his people now, but the crew of the *Nightrunner* stood their ground. For a few seconds, it looked like Darvin and his thugs were going to back down.

And then, all hell broke loose.

Andi was watching, and she saw it before anyone else did.

One of the men, near the back of Darvin's group, reached for a pistol. Lorillard didn't see it, not quickly enough.

Andi's mind raced. This wasn't a random confrontation, nor a real argument. It was a hit. Darvin hadn't come to demand money from Lorillard, not really.

He'd come to kill *Nightrunner*'s captain.

Andi was still thinking about what to do when she acted,

her body lunging forward on instinct, before her conscious mind had even decided to intervene. She was halfway to the man with the gun when he noticed her, and then she crashed into him, knife in hand, even as he was turning the weapon toward her.

She was much smaller than her adversary, not much more than half his mass. But she had momentum, and he stumbled back as her body slammed into his.

It was a painful hit, likely for him as well as her, at least from the sound of his deep grunt. They both tumbled to the ground, even as the rest of the two groups leapt into action.

Andi was struggling with her opponent, her eyes locked on the man's pistol, which was still in his hand, despite the hard fall. He was bringing it around, trying to point it toward her. She almost reached out to grab his hand, but she knew she wasn't close to strong enough to stop him that way.

Her other hand tightened around the new knife, the successor to her trusty old weapon. She had intended to avoid trouble on Dannith, at least at first. Her narrow escape from Vulcan City had left its mark, and the last thing she wanted was to become a hunted criminal on Dannith as well. But the time for such considerations was over. She was in a fight to the death, and that being the case, she knew damned well whose death she intended it be.

She swung her arm with every bit of strength she could muster, her hand clenched hard on the hilt, determined to hold on, even as the blade's point hit its target. A jarring feeling raced up her arm as the knife hit the man's wide, thick leather belt. There was a pause, no more than a quarter second, she later guessed, but it seemed like an eternity. Then the blade slid off the hard leather…and plunged into the man's midsection.

Andi felt the knife strike the soft flesh, and the killer instinct in her took control. Her opponent was massive, and strong…and he still had the pistol in his hand. She had no doubt he could kill her, even wounded.

She jerked her arm hard, pulling the blade up, practically gutting her victim as she did. The two were rolling around in their desperate struggle, and the man's body ended up on top of her. She could feel the warmth, as what felt like liters of blood poured out, even as she continued to drag the knife up through flesh and guts, until it struck the bottom rib.

The howls of pain had stopped a few seconds before, and now she felt the full weight of the man bearing down. The pistol was on the floor now, laying in the middle of a large pool of blood.

She slid to the side, shoving with all her strength as she did, half pushing the man off her and half crawling out from under. She looked down as she scrambled away, over toward the side of the room, but she didn't really need to. She knew already.

She had killed again.

She paused for a few seconds, a failure of discipline for which she scolded herself, and then she jumped up, knife in hand, her head moving back and forth, eyes searching for any threats. There had been a number of gunshots, but she hadn't been able to get a fix on exactly who had fired…or who might have been hit. But there was no one right near her, nor anyone who seemed about to fire in her direction, so she lunged forward, sliding through the widening pool of blood as she did, and grabbed the pistol her defeated opponent had dropped.

Given a choice, Andi wasn't about to bring a knife to a gunfight.

She snapped back up to her feet, wincing at the pain in her legs as she did. But even as she was ready to jump back into the fight, she could see Darvin and his people moving back toward the exit. They left two of their own behind, the man she'd killed and another who was badly wounded, and probably dying. She glanced quickly over at Lorillard and his crew. Two of them had been shot, and two others had knife wounds. None of it looked life threatening, but they didn't seem to have any appetite to chase their retreating enemies either.

She stood where she was for a few seconds, not sure what to do. Should she run? She'd intervened to save Captain Lorillard, but who was going to believe some vagrant with no identification, no one to vouch for her? Had she escaped a murder conviction on Parsephon only to exchange it for one on Dannith?

She could hear Lorillard snapping out commands. "Get Jammar, bandaged up. Doc will have to get the bullet out later. And, Tyrell, you help Jackal. We'd better be careful on the way back to the ship. I think those fools had enough, but you never know."

"Yes, Cap…we're on it."

Andi turned slowly, thinking she'd better get the hell out, too. She took one step, and then she heard the voice behind her.

"You *are* a scrappy little thing, aren't you?"

She stopped, and her heart rate surged again. The voice was Lorillard's.

She turned around. "I try." She was struggling to stay calm, which was far from easy under the circumstances.

"You're a cool customer, too. I'm impressed. It can't be easy to pull that off, not after a fight like we just had. I'd have been shitting my pants when I was your age."

"I'm from Vulcan City, on Parsephon. Neighborhood called the Gut. They stack the bodies like cordwood there." She stared back at Lorillard, her eyes cold, focused. She was flipping out inside, but she kept it there, hidden from view.

"I've heard of the Gut. Might be the worst dump in the Confederation, at least some say."

"Not if they've been there. Wouldn't be any 'might' in that if they had."

"Well, you're sure handy with a knife, so maybe I could

make an exception to my usual requirements. Don't make me regret it, though. Don't turn into some kind of snotnosed kid on me. *Nightrunner*'s a tight ship, and we all do our jobs.

"I'm no kid. I told you that." Her heart was racing now. She was trying not to jump to conclusions or get ahead of things.

"So, where's your stuff?"

She reached behind her, realizing her bag was gone. She looked around her, spying it on the floor about a meter away. She reached down and grabbed it, holding it up. "Here."

"You travel light. I like that." A pause. "Well, we better get the hell out of here. Clevus over there will smooth things out with the authorities…" He turned and looked over at the bartender, nodding to one of his people as he did. The spacer threw a small sack of coins onto the bar.

"Yeah, I'll do what I can, Jim." Clevus scooped up the small purse as he spoke. "But we got one body, and from the looks of things, we're gonna have two in a minute. I'll do my best, but they're gonna want to *talk* to you at least."

"Good enough. I'll go down and straighten things out in the morning, okay?" He nodded to Clevus, and then he turned back to Andi.

"Well, you ready to go?"

"You mean…" She was trying to contain her excitement.

"Spacer's gods, kid…you saved my life. What kind of shit would I be if I left you behind now?" A pause, short, no more than two or three seconds. "Now let's get the hell out of here. And welcome to *Nightrunner*."

Chapter Ten

Free Trader Nightrunner
Approaching Dannith
Ventica III
Year 301 AC

"Andi stared across the table, her eyes fixed on the man opposite her. Everyone else had thrown in their cards, but Gregor had just raised her. Poker games on *Nightrunner* were cutthroat affairs, just about the only time the tightly-knit crew pitted themselves against each other and not as a team facing off against the rest of the universe. Andi missed the Marine every day, and she remembered her days on *Belstar* with wistful sadness.

But she'd come to realize *Nightrunner* was the only true home she'd ever had.

She caught a blink, no more than that. It was a nervous tick. Without another thought, she reached out and shoved her chips into the middle of the table. "I'm all in."

Gregor was her friend, almost like a brother, but he could expect no mercy, not at this table. Nor, she knew, would he show her any.

She waited, watching for a few seconds as her shipmate maintained the bluff. Then, she felt a wave of satisfaction as he threw his cards into the middle of the table. "Take it down," he said, morosely, as if she had just dealt him a fatal wound.

She smiled, and she reached out to pull the chips in. Poker was no joke on *Nightrunner*, and a 'take no prisoners' mentality was always in play. Andi had sat in for a few hands on *Belstar*, but the crew of the freighter used the AI to deal and to monitor the game. Her first day on *Nightrunner* was the first time she'd seen the game played with actual cards, and real, physical chips. She'd watched a couple sessions before she'd sat down at her first game, and she'd lost twice, badly, before she got the hang of it. But now, she was *Nightrunner*'s resident card shark, a sort of local hero, especially now, when the crew had informal plans to hit Port Royal City's best card games, and fleece the gamblers there.

The games in the ship were feral affairs, but once they went outside, they were one, as they were in all other things.

She stacked her chips, her fingers moving quickly, with practiced excellence. She counted them swiftly, coming up with about two hundred credits in winnings. That brought her total for the trip to just over a thousand. It was the most she'd ever won, but that was no real surprise. The stakes in *Nightrunner*'s games had increased with the successful conclusion of the mission. It hadn't been the big score—the retirement score—not by a longshot, but there were circuit boards and half a dozen highly advanced processor chips in a secure box in the hold. It was a haul, a good one, worth enough for the crew to go on one wild bender in Port Royal City, and even for them all to take suites in the Regency or Starlight, or one of the other high-end hotels far away from the Spacer's district, and its tawdry establishments.

There would be money left, a good amount, to add to their stash. The crew kept their funds together, mostly so the total was high enough to maintain an elite level numbered Aurelian account. Aurelius was the banking center of the Confederation, at least for those desiring privacy and discretion, and the *Nightrunner* account had become sizable. Andi's share was small, of course. After two years on the ship she was still the rookie. But it was more money than she'd ever had, and if it wasn't enough for a nineteen—soon to be twenty—year old to retire on, it was enough, at least, to make her feel strange. For the first time in her life, she didn't feel like she was standing on the brink, at least not financially. There was danger, of course, and she'd taken a pretty bad laser hit about nine months earlier. It had been painful, and it had left a large scar on her thigh, but beyond that, it had heeled completely, leaving her only with an increased appreciation for imperial defense systems well-constructed enough to remain operative more than three centuries after the Cataclysm.

She was still the newest member of the crew, but she was one of them now, utterly and completely. She'd gained her way onto the ship by saving Captain Lorillard's life, and she'd since saved Anna's as well, and possibly Jackal's, too. And, Yarra had saved hers, and taken a bullet for it. It was of such things that a Badlands prospecting crew—a team—was made.

Through all the danger, the last two years had been good ones. They'd been profitable, at least reasonably so and, more importantly, no one had been killed or injured seriously enough to be put out of the game. If they hadn't won their fortunes in one killer score, at least they'd moved steadily toward it. And they were all still there, still at it.

Andi sometimes felt a touch of guilt at how content she'd become on *Nightrunner*. She remembered her mother fondly, and the Marine, Captain Hiram…the people she now realized had helped her to survive, and ultimately to prosper. Some of them had paid a price for that, her mother certainly. She'd been ten when her mother died, too young to be of much help. She tried not to think of the things her mother had been forced to do to keep them alive, the constant fatigue and fear and sadness she had felt every day.

She didn't speak to anyone about her mother. She'd hardly even told the Marine about her, but she still missed her terribly, and some mornings she woke up sad, tears on her face.

She ached for the Marine, too, and she still seethed at the way he had died, but she'd come to understand she hadn't been responsible for his death. He had brought that on himself, and if anyone else had been to blame, it was those who had pushed undeserved misfortune on him, sending him on a downward spiral that ended in a pool of blood in the Gut. Thoughts of that angered her, and it only increased her hatred of authority and her grim certainty that all who tried to impose their will on her were her enemies. Appointments by political allies and corrupt elections didn't add any ethical validity to unjust laws, not in her view. The government, and the naval forces that patrolled the frontier and, periodically, went on a run of chasing down exploratory ships and searching them for contraband, were just like any other danger. To be watched and avoided—or defeated, if necessary—but never to be respected as some sort of moral authority.

She scooped up the chips, and walked over to the small bowl that held the coin the crew members had put up as their stakes. *Nightrunner*'s poker games were always played for hard currency, and never for electronic credits. The ship's AI could link to any normal bank on Dannith, of course, but the ship's crew kept their money in the numbered account…or in their pockets. Andi wasn't the only one aboard with little or no trust for the system.

"Alright, you gambling degenerates back there, pack it up and get yourselves all strapped in. We'll be moving into orbit in ten minutes, and commencing landing ops as soon as planetary control gives us the go ahead."

Andi took a deep breath. This had been her fifth run on *Nightrunner*, and the whole process had become familiar. She was somewhat excited about some time in port, though not as much as the others, if she was being honest with herself. Still, she knew they had to come back, if only to pick up some intel or leads for the next mission. A ship with *Nightrunner*'s reputation wasn't forced to simply wander around the Badlands hoping to find something. There were information brokers all through the Spacer's District, gathering data from scientific missions and other sources— even naval ships, Andi had been told—paying the sources in immediate cash and then leveraging their intel by partnering with experienced captains and crews. Captain Lorillard would put the word out that *Nightrunner* was looking for a mission. Then, he would comb through the offers, weeding out the ones that didn't smell right. There were enough scams and plenty of useless leads making their way around the District, and no small number of traps and deadly dangerous expeditions. A captain like Lorillard had considerable experience in sifting through such things looking for the best. It was far from a guarantee, of course, but Andi had come to trust the captain's judgment.

The rest of the crew would enjoy varying degrees of debauchery, but Andi mostly stayed behind when they did. She'd participate in the planned poker onslaught—the more money they could lift from District rubes, the closer she was to building her fortune—but the drinking and the rest of it had no allure for her. She'd grown up surrounded by the human debris of life, people living in misery, people who had ended up there, as often as not, because of their drinking or drugs or wild behavior. She didn't think anybody from *Nightrunner* was going to slide all the way down to the equivalent of Gut street trash, but her memories guided her own behavior, nevertheless.

She walked back to her chair, the last one in the row along the back of the ship's main wardroom, and she sat down, strapping herself in. Despite her lack of drive to hit the hotspots, she was anxious to get to Port Royal City, more so this time than most. Testing her poker skills against the Spacer's District hustlers would be an amusing diversion, especially knowing she had her shipmates at her back in case of trouble.

But even more exciting, she thought Captain Lorillard was going to take her with him when he scouted out the next mission. She wanted to learn from him, to understand as much as she could about how the game worked on the frontier. And, if she was right, she was about to take a big step forward.

* * *

"I trust you understand why I am here, Rolf." The man still stood at the doorway, looking inside, despite two invitations to come in and sit. He wasn't doing anything threatening, and his voice was calm and moderate in volume. Still, he was entirely menacing, and Rolf Gavereaux could feel the sweat beginning to bead on his forehead and along the back of his neck. He'd never before met the man standing before him, but he'd known about him for years. Sector Nine agent, confidante to the head of the agency, virtuoso killer. Ricard Lille was a living nightmare, one who struck terror into the hearts of enemies and allies alike. Gavereaux suppressed a shiver. Gaston Villieneuve would only have sent his top henchman for two reasons.

He'd have killed me already if that's what he'd come to do.

There was logic to the thought, but it was far from convincing enough to drive away the fear that had taken hold inside.

The other reason was nearly as foreboding. If Lille had come only to pass on orders, or to express disappointment at the results of the last mission, his presence as a messenger sent a message that couldn't be misinterpreted. Gavereaux knew whatever orders Lille had brought would have to be carried out successfully.

The 'or else' hung in the air like a thick fog.

"Certainly, Mr. Lille." A nervous pause. "I sent a complete report back to headquarters. I did everything possible to ensure…"

"I am not here to discuss the past. Let us simply state that Minister Villieneuve understands that there were certain…difficulties…at play that somewhat mitigate your failure. I imagine I might be here with other instructions myself if that were not the case."

Gavereaux sat where he was and suppressed a shudder, mostly at least. Then he just nodded. He'd almost gotten up—he felt intensely uncomfortable sitting while Lille stood—but he'd decided that might make things worse.

"With Minister Villieneuve's recent appointment to a seat on the Presidium, he is now tasked with wearing two hats. It is a considerable drain on his time, and he will be relying on his key aides, and on sector chiefs like yourself, to carry more of the burden." Lille paused. "Just to clarify, Rolf…your orders are to mount another mission to penetrate the imperial installation and retrieve the artifacts that are almost certainly there." Lille's didn't raise his voice, but the tone became deeper, colder. "And, you are not to fail this time. Is that understood? I do not want to be forced to come back to this miserable planet." Lille narrowed his eyes, and he stared right at Gavereaux. "And, I can assure you, Rolf, that you do not want that either. Do we understand each other?"

Gavereaux understood, all too well. It was taking everything he had to hold back the shivers trying to break loose in his body.

"Yes, Mr. Lille. I understand perfectly."

"Good." Lille took a few steps forward, and finally, to Gavereaux's relief, he sat down. "Then let us discuss specifics. Minister Lille has sent you more than orders. I have five million Confederation credits in untraceable coin for your use, as well as updated intel and scouting data on the subject system. And there is a small gunship that will be positioned in the Heckmere system, en route to the target. On it are two squads of Foudre Rouge soldiers, which are available for your use in penetrating the target and retrieving the artifacts."

Gavereaux felt tension and relief at the same time. The resources would be extremely helpful, no doubt, but he still remembered the results of the last mission he'd sent. No one had returned from the landing parties. The ship he'd sent returned with two crew remaining, both so profoundly terrified by what they'd seen, even his interrogations of them—harsh ones ending in eventual executions—had done nothing to increase his knowledge of what had happened. Something there, most likely some ancient imperial defense system, had killed the crew he'd hired, and he had no idea how to proceed, how to ensure that another mission didn't end with the same result.

"I will see it done, Mr. Lille. You may assure Minister Villieneuve that no resource, no effort will be spared."

"The minister is concerned only with results, Rolf." The assassin managed to make his use of Gavereaux's first name sound deeply sinister. "I will leave the details to you. With the added funding and increased intelligence, not to mention twenty elite soldiers of the Union, I have no doubt you will succeed…and redeem your reputation."

Gavereaux nodded silently for a few seconds, before he managed to force a verbal response through the tension and fear. "Your confidence is appreciated, Mr. Lille. I will see it done…whatever it takes."

It was all he could think to say, though he questioned how much faith Lille had that he would, in fact, succeed.

There was one thing he didn't doubt, however, not in the slightest.

The content of the assassin's next orders if he failed.

Chapter Eleven

The Shooting Star
Spacer's District, Port Royal City
Planet Dannith, Ventica III
Year 301 AC

"We could clean these fools out, Andi. There's nobody there that's a match for you, or for any of us, for that matter." Gregor was standing right next to Andi. She was tall, and a wiry kind of muscular, despite her overall slim build, but the blond, almost albino, giant soared a good quarter meter over her, and his bulk made her look almost skinny and waiflike.

"We had a saying in the Gut back on Parsephon, Gregor. Don't shit where you eat." She *had* heard the term back in Vulcan City, but she'd never quite understood its usage then. In her experience, people in the Gut would shit anywhere...both literally and figuratively. But she'd since decided it was good advice, and completely on point at that moment. The Shooting Star was no palace, but it was the crew's informal headquarters in Port Royal City and, save for the fight two years before—the disturbance which had given Andi her chance to push her way into the crew to begin with—Captain Lorillard always tried to keep things calm there. He'd always told the crew to avoid fights, or at least not to be the ones starting trouble in the ragged old bar.

The bar had very little difficulty finding trouble without their help.

The Star was a rough place, and not much to look at, but a quick glance at the crowds and the bar business left little doubt it was profitable enough. Perhaps more importantly, it hadn't taken Andi long to realize that Lorillard was friends of a sort with the owner, and not much longer for her to pick up on the fact that *Nightrunner*'s captain owned a stake in the place himself.

Definitely not the right place to cause trouble. And, fleecing drunk gamblers, however legitimately the game was played, had a pretty significant track record of leading to trouble.

Don't shit where you eat.

She reached out—and up—and slapped her hand on Gregor's massive shoulder. "Don't worry…we'll hit some of the other places later tonight. There are plenty of games out there." She had enough sense to step away from the Star when she was looking for marks, but she *was* anxious to put her newly honed skills up against some of the District hustlers. She'd been pretty good the last time *Nightrunner* had been docked at Port Royal City, but she was better now. The trip back from the last mission had been a long one, lengthened further by a detour to avoid a pack of naval escorts patrolling just beyond the frontier. That left a lot of time to hone her poker skills against her shipmates.

She had other advantages in a game, besides pure skill. She had a perfect poker face, utterly devoid of emotion. And, she hardly looked the part of a skilled and capable gambler.

Her body was tight, muscular, and she was an experienced killer, but she looked like anything but at first glance, especially when she wanted to. She could pass for somewhat of a lost young woman ripe for exploitation when it suited her, and with her hair pulled back and tied behind her head, she looked even younger than she was, especially if she dressed the part, too.

"You bet we will. I got taken last time, I'm sure of it. I think they used some kind of marked deck on me." Her shipmate's voice had a bit of edge to it.

Andi just nodded. Gregor *always* thought he'd been cheated when he lost. She found it amusing, and it certainly wasn't worth arguing with her shipmate. She always felt better crawling through some imperial ruin with the giant at her side, and humoring his ego defense for gambling losses didn't seem a large price to pay.

I wonder who would have the guts to actually cheat Gregor…

There were safer marks out there than a towering goliath who looked most of the time like he was on the verge of boiling rage. Andi knew Gregor, of course, and she was aware that he was actually more of a gentle giant most of the time, despite appearances. Some hustler in a card game lacked that knowledge, of course.

"Andi…you got a minute?" Captain Lorillard had walked out from the back room. Andi hadn't even known he was there.

"Sure, Cap. What can I do for you?"

"I'm putting out feelers now for our next mission. As soon as I find something that looks worthwhile, I'll let you know. Go ahead and hit the card games tonight, but stay in touch tomorrow, okay?"

"You got it, Captain." Andi was excited. She had been looking forward to sitting in as Lorillard negotiated their next deal, but she'd thought he was bringing her to humor her, because he was tired of her working him to do it. Now, she realized, he actually wanted her there. She was still the rookie on *Nightrunner*, technically at least, but the captain had come to rely on her more and more with each passing mission. The ship's crew were all experienced, but they were specialists, too. Gregor was handy in a fight, Yarra was a great engineer, Sylene could code and crack computer systems like no one she'd ever seen.

Andi was the most like Lorillard. She'd seen that, and she'd let herself begin to believe it, but now she suddenly realized the captain had also noticed. Andi had always been determined and stubborn, but she'd never considered herself especially smart. The Gut wasn't the kind of place that recognized intelligence, nor for the most part, rewarded it, save perhaps for a raw kind of street smarts. But two years on *Nightrunner* had exposed Andi to all kinds of new experiences—poker was just one of them—and she'd excelled at them all. She'd dared to think she could handle more, that her lofty goals, her determined effort to achieve great wealth one day, wasn't necessarily a fantasy, after all.

And the fact that Lorillard seemed to agree only bolstered her confidence. Poker games or not, she would damned sure be ready when the captain called.

Damned sure.

* * *

"Darvin, I have a job that needs to be done." Gavereaux sat in the corner, looking across the table at the Spacer's District hustler. Darvin had a reputation for turning up useful intel at times, and an equally-deserved one for a lack of discrimination for whom he dealt with. Gavereaux didn't know if the information broker suspected he was Sector Nine, but he didn't think the rogue would care. Not if the purse was large enough.

"What do you need, Rolf?" Darvin had worked for Gavereaux before. The Union spy had found the data Darvin peddled to be spotty at best, sometimes useful, other times looking more like some concocted scheme to create something to sell. But Gavereaux wasn't buying leads this time. He was looking to sell one in particular.

"I have a lead, Darvin, and considerable data to back it

up. It's a big score, possibly a *really* big one."

"You have your own crews, Rolf. What do you need from me?"

Gavereaux pulled a sack from the seat next to him and tossed it on the table. He knew nothing would capture Darvin's attention like a bag of platinum hectocredit coins.

"I need you to find me a crew. What I don't need are questions."

Darvin pulled his eyes from the sack, with some apparent difficulty. "What kind of crew?"

"A very good one. One that can penetrate an operational imperial defense system and retrieve the artifacts beyond." Gavereaux paused. "Or at least one that can overcome most of the defense net, and leave the door more open than they found it."

Gavereaux didn't care if the hired crew completed the mission and retrieved the artifacts, or if they only managed to blunt the defense network before they were killed. His Foudre Rouge could finish the job no matter what. They could go in, get past the damaged and disarmed imperial defenses, and find the artifacts themselves.

Or they could simply follow the crew in and kill any survivors, relieving them of whatever treasures they may have found.

The important thing was, to gain the skills of a veteran crew, a team that had more expertise with imperial systems than any of his people.

"You want a crew that will go in and get killed. You want to set them up, to send them into a trap." It was the kind of thing one might have said with disapproval and condemnation in their tone. But those emotions were absent from Darvin's voice.

"Yes, Darvin, that is exactly what I want. Though it is of little account if any survive, as long as they penetrate the main defenses." A pause. "And, when I say a good crew, I mean a *good* crew." There was no point in sending a bunch of fools in who would only get cut to ribbons before they'd achieved anything. Gavereaux glared across the table. "Do we understand each other?"

Darvin smiled broadly, an expression that should have been less creepy and disturbing than it was. "Yes, Rolf. I understand you perfectly." His grin widened even more. "And I have just the crew for the job. They're a little...annoyed with me right now. I'm afraid we had a misunderstanding a couple years ago. But they're one of the best teams on the frontier, and I think they just got back and are looking for a new job." He was silent for a few seconds. "I'll have to get someone else to front for me— and that's going to cost you extra—but I think we can pull it off." He sat silently again for a bit, looking extremely self-satisfied. Then, he added, "So, you are saying that, whatever happens, none of them will be coming back?"

Gavereaux returned the stare, and his eyes were cold. "I can promise you that, Darvin. This mission is a most definitely a one-way trip." He stood up. "Go, get your people lined up. I want this done as soon as possible." He reached out and dropped a small pile of data chips on the table. "This is the intel on the system and the site. It should be enough to get any ship's crew salivating. But it's sensitive data, Darvin." He paused. "Listen to me very clearly. That is very delicate information. If you lose it, or if you share it with *anyone* besides the crew you hire, I can promise you, they won't find enough scraps of you to get a decent DNA sample."

Darvin's smile shrunk a bit, and a look of unease slipped onto his face. But then he looked back at the money, and he just nodded.

Gavereaux reached out and slapped his hand against the sack on the table, jingling the coins inside. "This is only a down payment, Darvin. Get me a crew ready to go, and there's another sack just like this one." He paused. "And when the mission's done, there's two more. How's that for a bonus?" Gavereaux had always been convinced of the utility of greed as motivation.

He could see the avarice in the hustler's eyes. The money Gavereaux had just offered was a king's ransom, but it was nothing compared to the artifacts his people would retrieve if the crew Darvin chose managed to get past the defenses.

"I will get this done immediately, Rolf. You have my word."

Gavereaux struggled to control the snort that almost escaped his lips. Darvin's word might be worth something, but he wasn't sure what. But he was quite confident the scoundrel's greed would get the job done.

"See to it, and contact me the instant you have someone in place. I want this expedition launched in three or four days, a week at most. Understood?"

"Yes, I understand. I know just who I can get to approach them. Give me two days, and I'll get back to you."

Gavereaux nodded. He didn't like relying on the likes of Darvin, but there were few of his type on Dannith that were more dependable…and willing to set up a crew to send into a trap. And there were none as reliably greedy. The funds Lille had brought had proven quite useful, and he'd doubled the amount he'd initially intended to offer.

Just a bit of insurance, a bet on greed as motivation.

It was a bet he felt good about, especially when it was supported with just a bit of fear.

Chapter Twelve

Free Trader Nightrunner
Approaching Ventica Transit Point 3
Ventica System
Year 301 AC

"Prepare for jump in forty seconds."

Andi sat quietly as Lorillard spoke into the small comm unit. She was sitting at the number two station, and her hands were on the piloting controls. Lorillard had always helmed *Nightrunner*, but Andi had been working on him for a while to teach her how to fly the ship. She'd had some success, and he'd allowed her to watch as he flew the vessel, and even to pilot herself a number of times.

Still, she was shocked he was letting her take *Nightrunner* through the point.

She was a bit nervous about it, too. Flying the ship in the open was one thing. Navigating the strange alternate space that made interstellar travel possible was quite another.

It was a reminder of just how much confidence Lorillard had developed for her. It made her feel good, and reinforced her belief that she had found a family, at least one of sorts.

It also made her stomach feel like it was about to heave.

"AI systems engaged." The AI would take the ship right

into the point, but Andi herself would have to navigate through the tube and out into the destination system. The space inside the point had various effects on man and machine, but scrambling most electronics was one of the most difficult to handle. "Entering the tube in fifteen."

Her hands moved over the controls, switching the power flow, adjusting the thrust coordinators. She knew what to do, at least intellectually, but it was quite another thing to remember it all for the first time.

"Ten seconds." A thought flashed through her mind, and she wondered what the others thought of hearing her voice on the comm instead of the captain's. They'd all come to put their faith in her abilities...but she was far from sure piloting the ship could yet be categorized as an outright *ability*.

Five seconds." She reached out, cut the power flow to the engines. An instant later, *Nightrunner* was in freefall, slipping right into the center of the transit point's maw. She took a couple of deep breaths, trying to center herself. She'd come to realize that alternate space tended to make her a little nauseous. It wasn't serious, usually at least, but just then it combined with the effects of her nerves. She was at the controls, responsible for getting everyone through, and throwing up all over her workstation was not going to be helpful.

She'd heard about spacers who struggled with terrible problems inside points, severe vomiting, mind-splitting headaches, even near-psychotic episodes. A little queasiness was certainly nothing she was going to allow to interfere with her work.

She felt the—sensation was the only way she could label it—of moving through alien space. It was unsettling, but perhaps the strangest thing about it was the seeming inability to describe it after the fact. She'd tried several times, and she'd seen others, including lifelong spacers, fail as miserably as she had. It was just one more inexplicable aspect of the ancient imperial network of transit points.

Nightrunner moved steadily forward through the tube, though there was no sensation of motion at all, and with the instruments mostly down, no way to confirm that the ship was making its way through the tube. Except she knew it was.

They all knew it was.

She imagined the strange feelings of alternate space would wear her—anyone—down given enough time, but fortunately, most trips between systems took only seconds, and almost always less than a minute. Andi was looking straight forward when she felt it, the sudden return to normal sensations. The scanners and monitors were still down, and it would take them thirty seconds to two minutes to recover and reboot, but there wasn't a doubt in Andi's mind.

Nightrunner had emerged.

They were back out in the Badlands.

*   *   *

"Get your asses moving! Our takeoff slot is in six hours." Gavereaux was frustrated at the pace of loading the ship. *Clipper* was a freighter, designed and built in the Confederation, and bought second hand by Tristar Trading Company, a Confed-based entity with a home office on Dannith. The firm, like the ship, looked to all casual inspections like any of a hundred similar enterprises, small freight haulers supplementing commodity transit rates with some speculation in the purchase and resale of certain...controversial...cargoes.

Tristar was different from the others in one significant way, however. It was funded—and owned, through a bewilderingly complex web of dummy companies—by Sector Nine, the Union's premier espionage agency. Tristar and its ships were tools the Union used to spy on

Confederation activities, interfere in certain operations, and, most importantly, to operate within the Badlands, and the crucial efforts to find abandoned imperial technology that went on there.

"Yes, Chief. We'll be finished in an hour."

Gavereaux scowled, not believing what he was told for an instant. "What, a Patrovian hour?"

Patrovia was a world in the Union, one famous for its very long days, each of its hours lasting almost a conventional week.

"Nevermind…" He didn't want an answer, and even less a bullshit excuse. "…just be sure you're done in *two* hours, and not a second more." That would leave enough time to begin the launch sequence as scheduled, and anything that reduced tension on the ship, and its crew and cargo, the better.

The Union and the Confederation were enemies, bitter rivals who had fought no less than three wars in the previous seventy years. Those conflicts, and the underlying struggle that continued almost as fiercely in technical times of peace, were also fought in the Badlands, a vast stretch of space full of dead imperial worlds. That struggle was less conventional, and generally not fought by warships, but it was no less vital than any other front.

The Union had a route to the Badlands, but it was long, out of the way, and it snaked through an expanse of unsettled and barely explored systems on the Far Fringe. The Union sent expeditions through that long and torturous route, of course, unwilling to be left behind in the race to reclaim ancient knowledge. But they had achieved most of their successes through Sector Nine's clandestine activities on the Confederation's far more strategically-placed frontier worlds.

The Confederation's focus on freedom, one that existed more, perhaps, in rhetoric than reality, and the disorderly state of its politics, created a perfect atmosphere for the

Union spies to operate. The fact that the Confederation paid, at the very least, lip service to the international treaty compelling all nations to share any old technology finds helped the Union keep up in the tech race. That document, the butt of raucous laughs in some circles, was utterly ignored by every other signatory, save of course, those with no direct access to the Badlands and no practical way to violate its constraints.

Sector Nine didn't pull as much old tech out of the Badlands as the Confeds did, but since most of the Confederation finds were made by illegal prospectors who sold their booty on the black market, the Union was able to throw some cash at the problem, buying what they couldn't find themselves, and actually gaining a slight edge in the tonnage of ancient equipment acquired.

Most of the frontier adventurers refused to deal openly with Sector Nine, of course. The Union was the enemy, and even though most of the hardened prospectors considered the Confed navy that hunted them just another adversary, most of them retained a strange kind of patriotism. That was easily circumvented, of course, and Sector Nine maintained dozens of agents in Port Royal City, many of them in deep cover, able to withstand almost any level of investigation a prospecting crew was likely to conduct.

For the most part, however, values like patriotism were cheap, and in the end, many crews just went for the biggest payday, especially if there was no obvious Union involvement. Gavereaux sometimes wondered how many of them really cared where the money came from. Patriotism was an odd thing. Most of the frontier adventurers were far more persecuted by their own government than by Sector Nine or any Union forces, yet they maintained at least the façade of loyalty, if not the real thing.

Gavereaux stood and watched for another few minutes, and then he turned and walked back to his office. This time, he had more to think about than getting *Clipper* on its way.

He was going to lead the expedition himself. It was something he'd never done before, and he was scared. He would have far preferred to remain behind and direct operations from his comfortable office, as he usually did. But he knew his life was on the line this time—literally— and when he'd sat down and thought about who he trusted to pull his ass out of the fire, he came through the exercise with a small list. A *very* small list, with a single name on it.

His.

He knew what would happen if the mission failed, and that bolstered his courage against the dangers he knew waited in the Badlands. He'd actually considered running if things went bad, of disappearing and hiding somewhere far from the battlefields of the espionage wars. He had some funds stashed in secret, the result of a number of years of moderately successful embezzlement. His lifetime of espionage experience had even prepared him for such a flight. But he quickly discounted the idea. Against any normal agents, he'd have bet on himself to make good his escape.

But Ricard Lille would find him.

Gaston Villieneuve's top henchman had an uncanny ability to find his prey, and chasing down a fleeing agent with a signed kill order in hand would be dead center in Lille's area of expertise.

Hell, the psychopath would probably enjoy it more if I ran...

No, he had to see the mission through. He needed to make it work, to return with the promising old tech the scouting report suggested existed in the target system.

To restore his reputation and regain the favor of Gaston Villieneuve.

* * *

"All systems green-1, Captain. We're accelerating at 1.2g, heading toward the Ghosalon transit point." Andi sat bolt upright in her seat on the bridge, as she snapped out the crisp report. She could feel energy almost crackling through her body. She'd been nervous at first, but she'd quickly built up her confidence, and she fancied her ship and crewmates a match, ton for ton at least, for any ship in the Confed navy.

Not that she much liked the navy—the patrol ships stationed on the frontier spent most of their time half-heartedly harassing Badlands prospectors—but there was no arguing with the record of the Confederation's fleet. There might even be some things to emulate. A little polish of the sort common on military vessels could only help operations on *Nightrunner*.

Andi had been born a street rat in the darkest alleys of the Gut, scavenging for food, and now she could pilot an interstellar spacecraft. She'd nursed her lofty goals in those early years, but now she realized how ridiculous they had been, how wildly audacious. And yet, it seemed almost amazing how far she had come. She was still a long way from that vast fortune, but there was no question she was vastly closer than she had been.

"Very good, Andi. You fly *Nightrunner* as well as I do. Maybe better." Captain Lorillard looked over and met her gaze, giving her a smile she knew was genuine. She'd had two real mentors in her life, the Marine, of course, and now *Nightrunner*'s captain, the man who'd come so close to sending her on her way the day they'd first met two years before.

Both men had taught her many things and, almost uncontrollably aggressive in her desire to learn, she had soaked it all up, rapidly focusing and mastering the skills her instructors imparted to her. Flying *Nightrunner* through an empty system wasn't the same thing as handling the ship in a battle or other difficult situation, she knew, but she could also see Lorillard's surprise—bordering on shock—at just how quickly she'd become adept at the pilot's position.

She'd never taken *Nightrunner* into battle, of course, but she was beginning to fancy that she could pull it off if she had to.

"On a straight run through a clear system, I'm okay, Cap. But I've got a long way to go." It was appropriate modesty, but it wasn't completely honest. She was beginning to believe she could handle the controls in any situation.

"You're smart, too. Controlled. You never bite the hand that feeds you. You protect your teacher's feelings, understate your abilities, just that little bit. You'll go far out here, Andi. Unless this mission turns out to be what it looks like it might. Then, you'll just be gifted and skilled, sitting among the idle rich on some pleasure world while those hard-earned abilities atrophy." Lorillard clearly had high hopes for the expedition. Andi knew that much from his tone, and also from the edginess that had taken hold of him from the moment they'd left Dannith. He was anxious, hopeful…but also nervous. Even scared.

That gave Andi a bit of a chill every time she caught the concerned look on his face.

Andi had been on a number of missions, but they'd all been relatively normal, which is to say, dangerous, but not hopelessly so. She'd seen the scouting reports on this one herself, participated in the negotiations. She hadn't much cared for the broker who'd sold them the lead. Actually, she would have passed on the whole thing if it had been her call. She didn't think Lorillard had been overly comfortable with the details either. But *Nightrunner*'s crew had dealt with the man before, and everything he'd sold them in the past had proven to be at least reasonably legitimate.

And the payoff was potentially monstrous.

The target was an old space station, one that appeared to be in at least reasonable condition, even partially operational. That made it dangerous, no question, but even Andi's controlled mind raced at the thoughts of possible artifacts they might find.

Andi was still young, but even at her tender age, she was hesitant to allow greed to overrule good sense and caution. She was often surprised at how few people did the same.

Her eyes darted to the small screen on her workstation. There had been something there, for an instant, at least. She was sure of it.

She turned and looked over at Lorillard. "Cap, I think I saw something on the scanner, just a flash. Maybe we should change course and check it out before we move on."

Lorillard looked down at his own display for a few seconds before answering. "I don't see anything, Andi. AI shows a transient contact on the record, zero point three seconds in duration, low power. It's probably some natural occurrence, maybe two small meteors collided, or even a gas cloud burst." He paused a few seconds, clearly thinking. "I don't think it's a problem, not all the way out here."

Andi knew they were far out, and they were going farther. This mission was taking *Nightrunner*, and her with it, vastly deeper into the Badlands than she'd been before. Deeper than anyone on the ship had been, its captain included. That had her nervous. She tried to tell herself she was being foolish, that mere distance from the Confederation border meant nothing. But she couldn't push it from her mind. She looked again, intently, changing the readings on the scanners. But there was still nothing. Only the one brief contact.

"Cap, there are some pretty heavy dust clouds over there, and a small asteroid belt. Someone could be hiding in there, couldn't they?"

Lorillard looked down at his screen again, a demonstration of just how seriously he took his youngest crew member. But he shook his head and repeated the essence of his earlier response. "You're right, technically, at least. I suppose someone *could* be hiding somewhere on the edge of the system. But who would be all the way out here, engines shut down, laying low? It's always possible we could run into another prospecting ship, of course, but who would be running silent, waiting for…for what?"

Andi understood what Lorillard was saying, and she tried to push aside the concern. But it was still there.

"I'd run over there, Andi, just to take a look for caution's sake. Hell, it could be some kind of artifact as well as a threat of some kind…but it's probably nothing, almost certainly nothing in fact, and this trip is long as hell. We're going to be tight for fuel anyway, and we'd need to blast the engines hard to go over there, and then again to get back on course. I think cutting our fuel supply that close puts us at a lot more risk than whatever chance there's some danger sitting out there."

"Yes, Cap. Of course." Everything Lorillard said made perfect sense. But, if she'd been in charge, she still would have gone over and investigated.

But she wasn't in charge, and she wasn't about to dispute the captain's decision. So, she put it out of her mind.

At least as well as she could.

Chapter Thirteen

Sector Nine Freighter Clipper
Heckmere System
Year 301 AC

Gavereaux stood in *Clipper*'s small landing bay, watching as the robots pulled the shuttle into place and clamped it down. *Clipper* had a small crew, and most of those were specialists of one sort or another, in areas ranging from hand-to-hand combat to codebreaking, but there was no room for flight operations crew and the like. The robots were sophisticated units, and very expensive, something a vessel like *Clipper* would not normally possess, at least if the ship hadn't been an undercover Sector Nine asset.

The freighter wasn't anything special in most other ways. Improving the old vessel too much would only have only drawn suspicion, and since its primary purpose had been shuttling Sector Nine spies around the Confederation, the less attention it gained, the better. The two small laser turrets were an exception, very high tech and far superior to anything a normal freighter might carry. Still, the limitations of the reactor capped the ship's offensive capability. It could take on another freighter or similar craft and win, but it was nowhere close to strong enough to fight off even the smallest warships.

The doors on the shuttle opened, and a man stepped out.

Though Gavereaux wasn't entirely sure he would designate the new arrival in quite that way, and a *man*.

He was tall, and even through the light body armor he wore, Gavereaux could see he was lean and muscular. He had short-cropped brown hair, and he stared forward with a withering intensity. Gavereaux had seen Foudre Rouge before, but he'd never gotten comfortable around the clone-soldiers.

"Agent Gavereaux, Lieutenant Emile-2756 reporting as ordered. My soldiers are under your command." There was no detectable emotion in the officer's voice, though Gavereaux knew Foudre Rouge soldiers *did* have emotions, like any other human. The Union's elite troops had always seemed cold and robotic to him. He couldn't imagine being created in a lab and raised in a crèche before beginning a relentless regimen at age seven, one that continued into adulthood, and led only to a life of more training and war. He couldn't speak to what that kind of life did to the Foudre Rouge, but he subscribed to the generally accepted theory that it messed with their heads.

"Very well, Lieutenant. Thank you for shuttling over to discuss the mission. The scans of the system are clear, but I think it is best to maintain communications silence for as long as possible."

"No explanations are required, Agent Gavereaux. My soldiers and I have been placed under your command. Ours is to obey."

Gavereaux wanted to appreciate the lieutenant's pure obedience, but the man made the hair on his neck stand up. "Okay, Lieutenant, if you have no argument, perhaps we can do this right here. *Clipper* is a rather small ship, and there are no conference facilities to speak of."

"Ours is to obey."

The cold, robotic demeanor of the Foudre Rouge—the result, in no small part, of the relentless conditioning they'd received—was off-putting, though perhaps it was perfect for soldiers intended for war. One glance at the lieutenant suggested he considered himself a member of an almost invincible fighting force. But, Gavereaux had his own doubts. The Foudre Rouge were good, but they had never quite managed to outclass their primary enemies, the Confederation Marines.

"Very well. Your troops are ready for action, I presume."

"They are always prepared for combat, Agent Gavereaux."

"Then, I will simply brief you on the mission parameters, and you can then return to your ship before we depart." *And that can't be soon enough for me.*

"Yes, Agent Gavereaux. I must also advise you that our vessel tracked a scanner contact approximately three point six four days ago. Mass in a range of four to eight thousand tons."

Gavereaux felt a twinge of excitement, and maybe a bit of fear as well. The contact the officer was reporting had to be *Nightrunner.* That meant Captain Lorillard and his people would be approaching the target any time, even as he stood in the bay speaking with the lieutenant.

With any luck, Lorillard's crew will fight their way through most of the defenses, and leave the door something close to open for us. And, whatever is left of them, well, that's what these Foudre Rouge are for...

"Okay, Lieutenant. Let's go through the plan for when we arrive, and then you can return to your ship, and we can set a course for the final destination."

Gavereaux was going to see just how quickly he could cover everything, and relieve himself of the officer's disconcerting presence.

* * *

"Feeding additional power to the scanners, Captain. We've got the station, in orbit just where it's supposed to be..."

Andi paused, looking closely at her screen as a small dot moved around the planet and into view. "…and there's something else, too."

"A second contact?" Lorillard's voice showed concern, but he'd been uncharacteristically serious and glum the entire trip. Andi knew he was concerned about the mission, more so than usual. It was a perfect match. She was just as edgy.

She figured the blip was just another bit of imperial debris, perhaps an ancient ship flying around the planet, dead in a sustainable orbit. Until the second batch of readings came in.

She frowned as she stared at the screen. She'd learned a lot in her two years in *Nightrunner*, but she also understood what she didn't know. And, she was no expert in reading scanner reports and about the specific profiles of ships. But the new contact looked more to her like a half-rusted bucket of bolts than some sophisticated ancient imperial technology. The closer she looked, the more convinced she became.

And the more concerned.

"Cap, that thing's no imperial tech. I'm no scanning master, but I can tell you that much." Andi had never seen an actual imperial spaceship, nor even a decent-sized piece of one, but she'd looked at visual accounts and other images. The empire's ships were sleek, usually close to symmetrical, and they were built from high-tech materials that rarely showed wear, even when they were centuries old. An imperial ship could be blasted apart, of course, and the wreckage of more than one such vessel had been found, but short of that, they boasted incredible durability.

"Bring us in closer, Andi…and slow, one-tenth thrust." Andi heard the captain's voice, and she knew he was concerned too. The ship was the unexpected find, looking a lot more like a battered version of *Nightrunner* than a vessel of the old empire. The station was different…old imperial tech, certainly.

"Power to engines now…just a touch…" Her hands moved over the newly familiar navigational controls, and the ship lurched slightly along its new vector. She felt relief from the freefall, if only the one-tenth normal grav equivalent the engines were providing.

She didn't remove her eyes from the screen. There was more information scrolling down, both new data coming in and previous readings the AI was gradually cleaning up and enhancing. There were no energy readings, at least none that appeared to be from an active reactor, or even significant battery power to systems. There were some trace indications of radiation, and the ship's interior temperature was roughly three degrees warmer than the surrounding space. That wasn't much, and it was easily accounted for by the decay of radioactives inside the vessel.

"It looks dead, Captain…but it's definitely a ship, and not an imperial one, at least not like any we've seen before."

"No…I don't think it's imperial either." Lorillard was definitely concerned now and, either he was either making no effort to hide it, or he was failing completely. "Honestly, the mass, the hull material readings, even the general shape…it could almost be *Nightrunner.*"

Andi felt a quick shiver move through her body. The whole thing was an all too clear reminder of the risks they took on every mission. Andi was coming to the same conclusion she believed Lorillard was. That was another prospecting ship out there. Someone had been there before *Nightrunner*…and it was looking very much like they'd never made it out.

Andi worked her hands over the controls, as much to find a focus for her nervous energy as to actually accomplish anything. The scanner data was still coming in, and the image on the screen was becoming sharper, clearer.

It *was* a ship not too unlike *Nightrunner*, and the possibility that a crew just like theirs had been there recently—and the residual radiation levels indicated it hadn't been all *that* long—cast a pall over the bridge. Andi looked back at Lorillard, and he simply returned her gaze, wordlessly.

The image in front of her was becoming crisper and clearer, and now she could see a recreation of the ship's hull. And a series of holes all along its center.

She had hoped that whatever disaster had befallen the vessel, it was a mechanical problem, a systemic malfunction of some sort. But now there was no doubt.

The ship had been attacked.

"Activate subroutine sixty-three, Andi." Lorillard's voice was deep, serious in a grim way she'd never heard before. Andi reached down to her keyboard, her hands typing in the numbers the captain had given her. Her screen lit up, and as her eyes focused, she knew immediately what subroutine sixty-three was.

Nightrunner's weapons system.

The small ship had two laser turrets, nothing by the standards of naval warships perhaps but, from what little she knew of such things, pretty hard-hitting compared to most of the weapons carried by freighters and other prospecting craft.

"Activating weapons systems, Captain." The discovery of the dead ship hardly made it certain that *Nightrunner* would be attacked…but she found herself entirely in agreement with the captain's caution.

"Barret…get up here right now." Lorillard was hunched over the comm. As far as Andi knew, *Nightrunner* had never gotten into a serious ship versus ship battle, but Barret had served a term in the navy, the only member of the crew with that sometimes questionable honor.

And as Andi thought about it, the one time she'd heard him talk about him time in the service, he'd mentioned being a gunner, or a gunner's mate, or something.

Something that made him the likeliest candidate to man

Nightrunner's weapons.

A few seconds later, the door slid open and Barret walked through, grabbing the handholds on the wall to steady himself in the one-tenth normal gravity. "What's up, Cap?"

"We may have some trouble, Barret. There's a ship out there, another prospector's vessel from the looks of it, and somebody shot the hell out of her. She looks dead." Lorillard's words seemed to bring down a wave of cold across the bridge. "Get set up at the third station. We're charging up the guns…just in case."

"Got it, Cap." Barret's tone was far more serious than it had been. He turned and moved toward the third chair on *Nightrunner*'s small bridge. Andi had never seen all three stations occupied before, but then she'd never seen the ship as close to going into battle as it seemed just then.

"Andi, I want those young eyes of yours on the scanners. You see any kind of energy reading out there, I don't care if it's some guy lighting a cigar, you shout it out right away. Understand?"

The seriousness of Lorillard's tone slammed into Andi's gut like a fist. She'd been in fights before, even deadly ones…on the ground. But this was something new, and she suddenly felt very out of her element. She could watch the scanners well enough, but she felt the closest damned thing to useless if it came to a fight. And, Andi Lafarge wasn't the type who liked to sit and wait while others decided her fate.

"I'm on the scanners, Cap. Nothing new yet. The trace readings around the contact are almost certainly residual radioactive decay. AI calls it a 98.6% chance."

"Just keep your eyes focused." A pause, then Lorillard again, speaking to Barret this time. "How are we doing on charging the lasers?"

"Thirty-five seconds, Cap. The things haven't been fired in a while, and I had to run a quick check on the system before I could feed in the full power flow."

Andi had no real idea exactly what was happening, but it made enough sense to her. Firing the lasers and burning them out, or worse, seemed like a really bad idea.

She leaned forward, bringing her eyes closer to the screen. She was looking all around, searching for any signs of activity. The station itself read as nothing but pure mass. She knew that had more to do with the resistance of the imperial hull materials to scanners than it did to any certainty that the entire station was non-functional. For all she knew, there were batteries on that monster—ones far larger than those *Nightrunner* carried—even then tracking their approach, waiting for some old, but still functioning AI to give a command to fire.

"Everybody…get strapped in back there. Just in case we have some trouble." Lorillard hadn't filled the rest of the crew in, most likely because he didn't really *know* anything. But even what they'd heard, coupled with the call to Barret to come to the bridge, had to have everyone on edge.

Andi was feeling the pressure. She forced herself to remain still, rigid, focused like a laser on the job Lorillard had given her. But still, her mind wandered. She was no timid child, no frightened orphan slipping nervously around in the Gut, trying to avoid trouble. She was an experience prospector, and a fighter with training from a Confederation Marine and the blood of her enemies on her hands. But now she was sitting in a tin can, a hundred lightyears or more from Dannith, waiting to see if some ancient defensive grid was going to incinerate her along with the entire ship.

She took a deep breath, and then she exhaled, repeating the exercise with controlled breaths. It was something the Marine had taught her, a way to help center herself before battle. She'd always used it before when facing danger on the ground, but she imagined it would work just as well in space.

"Both turrets are charged, Captain, and ready to fire."

Andi sat quietly, focused on the scanner, but glancing quickly toward the captain every ten or twenty seconds. He looked calm, though she suspected that was an acting job, one for her benefit, and for the other members of the crew.

She had thought many times about fighting, survival, endurance, but always in the context of individual action. She was a loyal friend and shipmate, but her mind had always directed her own actions. Now, for the first time, she really thought about leadership. Watching Lorillard hold back his fear, broadcast an aura of confidence she knew he couldn't really feel, she began to understand what it took to lead people, to generate real loyalty from a group of followers. To be what they needed, even as they moved forward into danger.

That is leadership...

Suddenly, she saw something. A small flash on the screen.

"New contact, coordinates 230.157.302!" She was instantly angry with herself for the shrillness of her voice, for the panic and worry she'd allowed into her tone. "Energy spike, Captain...there was nothing there a second ago." She was confused, and she had no idea what to do.

But Lorillard was already snapping out an order. "Barret, open fire. Blast that thing now!"

Andi grabbed onto the armrests of her chair, an instinctive move. The adrenalin was coursing through her veins, and she could feel sweat pooling all over her body. She was about to experience something new.

Nightrunner was going into battle.

Chapter Fourteen

Free Trader Nightrunner
Osiron System
Year 301 AC

Andi sat in her chair and watched, feeling like she was going to crawl out of her skin for the very reason that all she *could* do was watch. Barret had control of the ship from his station, to allow him to adjust the vessel's aspect, to bring the lasers to bear. The target she'd spotted was clear now on the screen, and even more so its purpose and intent. The energy blast she'd just picked up had seemed strange to her at first, like nothing she'd ever seen before. But the AI gave her the answer before she figured it out.

It had been a laser pulse. The scanner contact had fired at *Nightrunner*.

The shot had been a miss, though it had come pretty close. She wondered if it had been poor targeting, but then it all fell into place. Barret had altered the ship's vector slightly, and he'd done it at just the right time to pull *Nightrunner* away from the shot's trajectory. It hadn't been deliberate evasion. No, it was that other tactical factor, the one Andi already knew was sometimes paramount above every discipline of war.

Luck.

It was a dangerous ally to rely upon, however, and one looking even less promising as a second contact appeared on her screen, just like the first.

They were satellites of some sort, she realized, or at least floating weapons systems positioned around the station. But were they imperial tech? Or just something positioned there by a crew that beat them there?

That answer, too, was obvious on more thought. Laser buoys or satellites were hardly beyond the available tech in the Confederation—though something like the devices they were facing would be tough for any civilians to procure—but the devices had just appeared, as if from nowhere. Something had blocked *Nightrunner*'s scanners from picking up the contacts...and whatever was doing that, it was beyond any Confed science she knew about.

The lasers were part of the floating platform's defensive network, almost certainly, and *they* had destroyed the orbiting hulk. She was sure of it, all the details falling into place.

She felt a cold feeling go down her spine. She'd faced some old imperial defenses before, but nothing anywhere near the guns threatening *Nightrunner*. She watched, shouted out a warning about the second contact, and otherwise sat frozen, with no idea at all what she could do.

The bridge lights dimmed slightly, and she heard a high-pitched whine. Barret had fired *Nightrunner*'s lasers. She felt her stomach clench, fighting back the wretch that tried to expel what remained of her last meal. She watched the scanner, feeling her heart sink when there was no immediate sign of a hit.

But Andi was still getting used to the distances in space travel and combat, and perhaps half a second after she'd hoped to see something, the first contact vanished from the screen. For an instant, she was afraid it had slipped back into whatever stealth mode had hidden it before, but then she saw the energy readings, the radiation.

Barret had scored a hit. He had destroyed it.

"Andi, bring us about 009.211.291." Lorillard's voice, and the urgency of his command, almost reached inside her and grabbed her by the spine. She turned in an instant, and even before she had conscious thought of obeying, her hands were moving over the controls, entering the navigational instructions.

"Thrust up to fifty percent."

Again, she followed the order instantly, without thought of the intent or even the wisdom of the command.

"Nav plan seven, Andi…engage the AI." Again, she was impressed with the constancy in Lorillard's voice. It was odd. The captain had seemed edgy before, concerned. But now that they were fighting for their lives, he was like a block of cold steel.

Leadership again, she knew. She took note, just in case she got out of the current mess and had use for the data someday.

She entered the codes and hit the button to engage the nav AI. *Nightrunner*'s computer took over immediately, and the ship began jerking wildly, as the positioning jets moved all around, small blasts of normal thrust pushing the ship every which way.

She saw another flash on the screen. The second satellite had fired. The shot came close, closer even than the first, but it too, had missed. That, Andi realized, was entirely the result of the evasive maneuvers. There wasn't a question in her mind they'd all be dead otherwise, or at least struggling to patch the damage from a hit and restore hull integrity.

Barret fired again, a clean miss this time. Andi knew the general theory of evasive maneuvers, and that the AI should be adjusting the gunnery solutions to offset the changes from the wild and seemingly random moves.

She also knew it was a far from perfect system.

Nightrunner jerked hard again…and then the ship spun around wildly.

Andi felt herself thrown against her harness, so hard she thought she might have cracked a rib. Then the ship went end over end, making three complete revolutions before the AI regained control and righted the vessel.

Andi was confused, unsure what had happened. Then, she heard Lorillard.

"Damage control, Yarra. How bad?"

Nightrunner had been hit.

She felt a shiver, and a wave of almost uncontrollable fear that lasted perhaps two seconds. Then her intellect pushed its way back to the forefront of her mind.

We're alive...

Whatever she'd imagined might happen if the ship took a hit, in reality, this time at least, it hadn't been the worst. She knew that by the simple expedient that she was still there, strapped in, drawing breath.

The quality of the air told her that life support was still functioning, at least on some level. There was a slight tinge to the air, a minor burning sensation with each breath, but nothing that seemed critical.

The continued jerking motions told her the AI and the engines were still there, too, though she realized the frequency and intensity of the maneuvers seemed somewhat lower than they had been.

Engines still functional, but damaged...

She turned her head abruptly, eyes focusing on Barret. He was still at the controls, still clearly trying to line up a shot.

But would the lasers fire? Were they, too, damaged?

She didn't know...and she had an unsettling feeling that Barret didn't either. Lorillard was still on the comm with Yarra, but he'd pulled his headset on, and she couldn't hear what the engineer was saying.

Leadership again. He doesn't know what she's going to tell him, but he damned well knows we're all scared...

She turned back toward Barret. He was almost ready to

fire, the still-operational meter on the display showing five seconds to a full charge.

That meant next to nothing, she realized. It could be displaying incorrect data, or the recharge system could be fine, but the turrets or the lens could be damaged. The lasers could fire perfectly, but even an infinitesimal irregularity on the mounting, from the shock of the hit or a hundred other causes, would throw off even a perfect shot.

At a distance of over ten thousand kilometers, the slightest fraction of a degree in misalignment was enough to send an otherwise perfect shot far wide of its target.

She sat, silent, and she realized she was holding her breath. She stared across the tiny bridge, doing nothing as a bead of sweat pushed its way from her scalp and slid down her face.

Then, the lights dimmed. A quick glance at the screen confirmed the weapons had fired. And an instant later, the contact disappeared from the screen.

It took a long instant, maybe three or four seconds, for her to realize just what had happened. Barret had taken out the second enemy laser buoy.

She felt hope, and as she stared at the screen, seeing nothing new appearing, she took a deep breath and let the relief flood over her.

We're…no, not safe…not safe at all…but maybe out of imminent danger. She stared at the main station on the screen, the hulking, circular structure, made up of three concentric rings, and she began to see dread. Suddenly, she understood what they had come to do, the staggering reality of it all pushing her to her limits.

She looked at the hulking monstrosity they'd come to find, and now she saw something that hadn't seen there before, something sinister. She'd been nervous about the mission from the outset, and she knew the captain had been, too.

Now, she knew why.

Now, she had an idea of what real imperial defenses looked like. And the idea of somehow docking with that thing, going inside. It seemed impossible. Or, at least, it seemed foolhardy, almost like the specter of certain death.

That didn't matter, though, she was sure of that. It was what they had come find, come to do.

Andi Lafarge had never backed down from a threat...and she wasn't about to start now.

* * *

"I almost had to put the ship in hock to afford it, but I knew that adjustable docking ring would come in handy one day." Lorillard stood in *Nightrunner*'s narrow central corridor as Yarra and Gregor pulled on the large metal bars protruding from the airlock. The chunks of reinforced steel were resisting their efforts with considerable stubbornness. That much was obvious from the fact that Gregor was sweating so profusely, his shirt plastered to his back.

The loud grunts had also been a pretty unmistakable sign.

If *Nightrunner*'s resident giant was having a hard time jamming the thing into place, that said something. Andi had seen Gregor carry two giant chests, close to a hundred kilos each, one on each shoulder, and give a good belly laugh at a joke while doing it.

It wasn't clear if the docking ring was the problem, or just the fact that the ancient imperial airlock was too different from anything in the Confederation. Andi was just about to give up on them ever getting it in place, when Gregor stumbled backwards, almost falling to the deck, and the thing slid suddenly into place with a loud clang.

The giant sucked in a deep breath, one that sounded like it must have consumed half the breathable air on *Nightrunner*, and he stared at Lorillard. "Next time you buy something like this secondhand, Cap, make sure its not rusted and half twisted out of shape."

"There's nothing in the Confederation that would be an easy match for that dock. Imperial military, I'm guessing, this whole place." The corridor was silent for a few seconds. Imperial tech was one thing, daunting enough. But military hardware and facilities were another thing entirely.

A much riskier thing for all involved.

Lorillard flashed a crooked smile and tried to draw attention from thoughts of what might lay inside. "Besides, that's what we've got you for, Gregor." Lorillard's smile widened, and Andi could hear a wave of snickers move along the assembled crew. "You don't want to work your way into complete obsolescence, do you, big guy? If we didn't need some muscle once in a while, I'm wagering we could find someone cheaper to feed."

Another flutter of soft laughs.

Andi was amazed at the crew's spirits, notwithstanding the brief somber moment they'd shared. She knew they were scared, *had* to be scared. They'd had a close call coming in, and while they'd escaped—by the slimmest of margins— it was damned near certain they hadn't seen the last danger the mission had in store for them.

Though only Barret, the Cap, and I really saw how close we came to...

The others knew, of course. She was sure of that. There were different personalities on *Nightrunner*, some she felt closer to than others. But none of them were fools.

She looked around, grabbing a quick glance at each of her shipmates. They had smiles of a sort on their faces, and a few were still chuckling. But she saw the truth in their eyes. They *were* scared, every one of them. As scared as she was.

Morale was a tricky thing, she'd come to realize. The dynamics of a group facing danger were far different than those of an individual. Andi had a bag of tricks she'd long used to push herself forward when terror threatened to hold her back, but they were all internal, manipulations she could only use on herself.

The camaraderie she was seeing around her...it was the crew's way, their own trick. They'd pushed the narrow escape away from their thoughts, and now they were ready to go inside the ancient space station, to do what they had come to do. Obsessing over the risks, both past and in front of them, could only sap their spirit, and distract them. That would make them less ready, more exposed to whatever threats lay ahead.

She wasn't sure if some of them were thinking of huge scores, of stunningly valuable technology, of returning to Dannith in triumph. Probably. Others were probably more focused on the urge to get it done, to go inside, search the place, and get back to *Nightrunner* as soon as possible for the trip home. She was sure it was a combination of thoughts and mental tricks that fortified *Nightrunner*'s crew, steeled their nerves as they stepped onto the station. None of it meant they weren't scared to death.

They would all do what they'd come to do. And she would, too.

"Alright, Tyrell, Doc...you stay on *Nightrunner*, and do what you can to keep a scanning beam on us." The old imperial hull materials were proof against scans, at least any made with devices of Rim technology levels, but there was some chance, at least, that the soon to be open hatch would allow *Nightrunner*'s sensors to at least keep tabs its crew members as they moved deeper within.

"On it, Cap." Tyrell was standing close to the back of the group in the corridor, and he moved a few steps toward the bridge.

"The rest of you, let's go. Stay close, and whatever you do, nobody get lost. This thing's huge, and if you wander somewhere and can't find your way back, you're probably screwed." He paused. "With any luck, those laser buoys were all that was left of the defensive systems. If so, we might just have a cakewalk the rest of the way…head inside and scoop up a bunch of serious old tech." He hesitated again. "But we're not going to count on that, you hear me?"

He looked around, acknowledging a series of nods.

"Everybody packed?"

Another ripple worked down the small group, this time including a few grunts of acknowledgement. Andi ran her hand down to her waist. Her knife was there, and her pistol. And she could feel the rifle strapped across her back. She was ready.

She was packed.

She added her own semi-intelligible response to the mix, and then she stood still and silent for a moment, while Lorillard opened the airlock hatch and stepped inside.

Chapter Fifteen

Abandoned Imperial Station
Orbiting Zensoria, Osiron VI
Year 301 AC

Andi shivered, a sudden, uncontrollable shake that ripped its way through her body. There was just *something* about the corridor, about the space station itself, that cut through her defenses. She had braved the harsh and filthy streets of the Gut, crawled through tunnels and sewers, faced enemies and dangers of all kinds and survived to tell about it. But she'd never seen anyplace as completely...different...as the corridors she and her comrades were passing through.

The walls were white, almost impossibly so, as though they had defied dust and wear for more than three centuries. The material looked almost like a high-gloss plastic, but to the touch, it was cool, feeling like a metal of some kind. The hallway was lit from the ceiling, though there were no visible fixtures or lamps, just a constant glow that seemed dim when stared at, yet provided more than adequate illumination.

The lighting, of course, also testified to the continued at least partly operational status of the station, as did the functioning life support. That is, of course, assuming the deadly laser attack on *Nightrunner* hadn't already pushed aside all thoughts of the station as a cold, dead hulk.

The breathable atmosphere and tolerable temperature certainly made the mission more physically comfortable. The crew all wore their survival suits under their normal clothes, and their helmets hung from clasps at their waists. Just in case. There was no way of knowing if the habitable conditions would continue, or if they would need their own life support to get back to *Nightrunner*.

Andi had wondered if they should risk the environment at all, and she'd almost suggested they go in with full gear in place. She'd only held back when it was clear that no one else, the captain included, seemed to share her thoughts. She knew they had to be aware of the risks, but they seemed comfortable enough simply to be ready to switch over if necessary.

Andi didn't have too much trouble going along with the rest. She hated the damned survival outfit as much as the others did, and besides, this way they were saving their power and air in case the need arose. She'd rather have the full two hours of life support from the moment a crisis struck, and not have to face an unexpected problem with half a tank or less remaining.

She wasn't sure how much of the choice came down to all of them justifying their desire for greater comfort, but she convinced herself it made sense, at least enough to push the doubts away.

There was even a reasonable simulated gravity generated by the ring's slow revolution around the station's core. It was just a little heavier than Parsephon's, or for that matter, most artificial gravity systems in the Confederation. But whoever had designed the thing had likely come from far coreward, from a world in the heart of the old empire, and not in a fringe sector like the Rim.

A place where billions once lived, with technology beyond anything we've ever seen.

A place that is dead now, an empty graveyard, slowly wasting away under the onslaught of merciless time.

Andi wasn't sure it was more than an old spacer's myth, but she'd heard more than once that planets tended to get larger the closer they were to the galactic core.

She took a deep breath, trying again to settle her nerves, to keep the almost alien feel of the station from shaking her focus. She'd prospected for old imperial technology before, of course, but she usually looked at it all in a somewhat clinical way. As far as she was concerned, they could easily have been searching for platinum, or gemstones, or anything else of value. But this time, it was different.

This time, the reality took shape in her mind, and she realized they were seeking the creations of people who'd been dead for three centuries, the handiwork of scientists and engineers and technicians, all of whom had faced the Cataclysm.

Who'd been destroyed by it.

She looked ahead, steering her focus to the present, to the reality laying before her. The corridor was long, stretching out of sight into the distance, and so far, there hadn't been any turnoffs or intersections, nor even a hatch leading anywhere. That seemed strange to her. Andi was no expert in spacecraft architecture, but she was pretty sure they were heading straight through one of the rings, and that meant there was *something* to either side of them, whether there was an accessible entrance or not.

She stopped for a second, abruptly. She'd heard something. Again.

It was a distant sound, faint, almost like metal knocking on metal. She looked around, as she had the other two times she'd heard it, but no one else had seemed to notice. She was the youngest by at least ten years, and it wasn't the first time her hearing had proven more sensitive than the others'.

"Cap, I keep hearing something. It's faint, far away. But it's definitely there, maybe every two minutes or so." She wondered if he was going to brush her off or tell her she was hearing things, but he just stopped and turned to look back at her.

"Still hear it?"

She paused silently, listening. "No, Cap. It stopped. That's what it did the other times, too."

"It's probably some system deeper in the station...most likely nothing to worry about." He didn't sound like he felt all that relaxed about it, and Andi knew damned well that *she* didn't. "Still, Andi...tell me as soon as you hear it again, and the rest of you, stay focused and listen. See if any of you can catch anything."

They all stood where they were for perhaps twenty seconds, and then Lorillard waved for them to follow as he continued forward. Andi stated walking again, right behind Gregor—not a bad place to be, she'd thought when the marching order shook down that way. *At least not if the threat comes from the front.*

They moved about another hundred meters, when Andi heard the sound again. She reached out behind her, tapping Anna on the shoulder. Her shipmate spoke almost immediately, before Andi could say anything, and said, "I hear it, too, Andi."

"It seems pretty regular." Andi paused a few seconds, listening. "It feels like it's been on a consistent schedule. Maybe it *is* some kind of regular system, and we're just hearing it here."

Anna nodded. "It could be, and if it is, we should try to head toward it." Anna's tone was odd. The idea of heading in the direction of the sound made sense, but there were doubts there, too.

"You may be right, Anna, but first, we're going to have to find a way to go anywhere but straight ahead...or straight back." Lorillard had stopped and turned. "So, until we can find another choice, we might as well just continue." He swung back around and took a couple steps forward before stopping again. "And, Andi...see if you *can* confirm that it's on a regular schedule."

The group moved forward again, and the sound repeated twice more. Andi had confirmed the timing, using her chronometer to get an exact time on the last two. It was exactly two minutes sixteen seconds from the completion of one to the start of the next. She wasn't sure whether to feel relief or apprehension at the regularity, so she split the difference, and did both.

The group's movement slowed a moment later, and then it came to a stop. Lorillard was at the head of the line, and he was standing in front of a hatch, one that was familiar.

It was familiar because it was an airlock, just like the one they'd entered through. They'd walked from one side of the ring straight across to the other, and they hadn't found a single corridor or hatch leading anywhere. It didn't make any sense. Andi was tracing her thoughts back over the entire stretch, trying to figure out what they had missed.

"Alright, we're going to head back the way we came, but this time, we're going to stop every fifty meters and do some intensive scans. There's something behind these walls…we don't need more than geometry to tell us that. And, if there are compartments, there has to be some way in. I know these walls are scan-resistant, but all we need to find is a section that's…different. If there are no doors we can see, there must be doors we can't see. And, however well-camouflaged, there has to be some difference, some kind of concealed mechanism or lock, and, we're damned well going to find it."

The rest of the crew nodded, and a few acknowledged verbally. Andi had been thinking almost exactly what Lorillard had said, and she turned around, reaching behind her and pulling out the small, portable scanner from her sack. She and Jammar had the miniature units. Gregor had the larger, high-powered scanner, along with most of the other heavy gear. It was the curse of being the largest member of the crew by a good fifty kilos.

Andi flipped the unit on and held it facing the wall as she began walking back the way they had come. She slowed her pace considerably, to give the unit the time to penetrate the ancient material of the walls. She didn't know what to expect, whether the small scanner would be able to find anything but, in the end, it was only a few seconds before she saw it.

It wasn't much, just a small blip. But she stopped and moved back and forth twice, confirming the initial result. There was something…different…there. She wasn't sure if it was open space beyond, or some kind of mechanical or electronic device—no doubt, there were both—but she was sure it was *something*.

"I've got a definite reading here, Cap." She paused. "I have no idea what it is, but it's there."

"I've got one, too, Cap." Jammar's voice was deep, shrouded in his thick Physalian accent. That had given Andi one hell of a time understanding her shipmate when she'd first come aboard, but she'd long since gotten fairly use to understanding what he said.

Lorillard stood silently for a few seconds before he started barking out orders. "Okay, let's figure all this out. Barret, behind me. Keep an eye in that direction…just in case. Anna, get back to the other end and stand guard there." Andi didn't know what might come at them from either side of the empty corridor, but she still agreed completely with the captain's caution.

"Gregor, get that bigger unit set up. Maybe it can get a little deeper, give us something useful." He turned his head. "Sylene, help Gregor…and get your own gear set up. As high tech as this place is, I'm betting the locks, hatches—everything—are AI controlled. I know it's a lot on your plate to hack into imperial tech like this, but if we can't get anywhere but this corridor, we've come a damned long way for nothing."

Gregor nodded, and he reached around, sliding the

massive pack from his back and setting it down.

Sylene had been behind Andi, and she worked her way toward the big man and the scanner suite he was already beginning to assemble. Sylene was Andi's closest friend on *Nightrunner*, a connection most would have pegged as unlikely. The programmer—and accomplished hacker—had a skillset that was almost the counterpart of Andi's own.

Sylene was massively educated, a celebrated professor at one of the Confederation's most prestigious universities, until some kind of scandal—the details of which she had never shared with anyone but the captain—ended that celebrated career. She was a virtuoso at bending computer systems to her will, and disillusioned and bitter at how she'd been treated in her former, very mainstream position, she'd rejected the private sector jobs she'd been offered, and ended up in Dannith's Spacer's Guild, one of the very few specialists there with even a prayer of decoding imperial information systems.

Sylene was the least violent of *Nightrunner*'s crew, the worst fighter by a good margin. Andi, on the other hand, didn't look like a deadly danger to anyone—at least anyone who didn't look too closely into her cold eyes—but all of her comrades knew just how dangerous she was.

Andi watched her friend crouch down next to Gregor and help the giant get the scanner set up. The tension lay heavily over them all. The station was a technological marvel, no doubt, and it was in the best condition—by far—from any other facility the crew had investigated, but there was still a haunted feel to it. Its aura felt not only of crew members long dead, but a while civilization lost, the great empire that had ruled humanity for millennia.

Andi, was nervous, edgy, and she found her hand moving down, sliding lightly over her holstered pistol. There was no enemy anywhere she could see, no signs of any imminent danger, but that didn't stop her.

The danger was there. She knew it was, somehow. And

no matter how careful they were, how prepared, she knew
something with a rock-solid certainty she couldn't explain.

When it happened—whatever was going to happen—
they weren't going to be ready for it.

Chapter Sixteen

Abandoned Imperial Station
Orbiting Zensoria, Osiron VI
Year 301 AC

"Another one bites the dust!" Sylene had been hunched forward, staring intently at the large tablet she'd set up in front of her. She'd been working steadily for more than an hour, but then, suddenly, a section of the shiny white wall vibrated. An instant later, there were visible lines around the edges, the clear delineation of a door or hatch of some kind, one that had been completely invisible just seconds before.

The programmer turned hacker leaned back, sitting on the floor of the corridor, and Andi could see from her expression, the shout had been almost a reflex action. Sylene looked anything but confident or triumphant, and her persona had never been the cocky sort so prevalent in her profession.

"Nice, Sy." Lorillard had been sitting, looking deep in his own thoughts, but he reacted immediately to her exclamation. "That looks like a hatch of some kind…" A short pause. "Can you get it open?"

"Honestly, Cap, I'm not sure how I did that. This system is…incredible. It's so far ahead of anything we've got on the Rim. I spent most of the last hour just trying to get in. I think I managed to trigger an unlocking sequence, but I'm not even sure of that. I'm as likely to electrocute us all or make poison gas come out of the thing as get it open."

"My money is on you, Sy. Nobody knows these systems better than you do. I trust you…we all trust you." There were a few nods, not exactly half-hearted, but not rousing signs of confidence either. It wasn't doubts about Sylene, Andi knew, but everyone was very aware just how advanced the station's systems were, how far beyond anything they'd seen before.

At least anything still operational. It wasn't just Sylene hacking into a system…it was a live system that could decide to strike back, to counter a perceived threat with whatever defense systems it had available.

"I think everybody should get back, Cap. Just in case. I've got a line, I think, into the system. Enough to trigger the open routine, at least, but I have no idea what security there might be and, honestly, it'd probably take me a week to figure it out. The defensive routines are heavily protected, much harder to reach than the lock controls." She turned and looked back at the rest of the crew clustered around her. "I'm just going to trigger the routine and see if the door opens…and whatever else happens happens."

Lorillard stared back for a few seconds, and it was clear from the expression on his face he was less than thrilled about the amount of guesswork in the plan. But whatever went through his mind, he obviously didn't come up with any alternatives, and he finally nodded and said, "Alright, everybody, pull back about five meters each way down the hall." A pause. "And, Sy, you…"

"Don't worry, Cap. I'm setting up a five second delay on this. I'll get out of the way, too."

Lorillard frowned, and Andi felt her own face twisting into somewhat of a grimace. Five seconds didn't seem like very long.

"Do it." The captain didn't sound happy, but Andi knew

there weren't many alternatives, save for returning to the ship empty handed and crawling back to Dannith with their tails between their legs. She knew enough about her shipmates—and herself—to be sure that wasn't really an option.

It took more than a haunted old space station to rattle *Nightrunner*'s crew.

At least to rattle them enough to send them running.

"Okay, Cap…I'm all set." Sylene stood up and took a quick look in each direction. The crew had split into two groups, each of them standing a few meters down one side of the hall. Gregor had the massive weapon he carried in his hands, at the ready—some kind of autocannon, Andi knew, a gun intended to be mounted on a tripod when wielded by anyone less enormous than *Nightrunner*'s resident giant. The others simply looked edgy and ready for action, their hands hovering near weapons.

Andi's own hand lay on her pistol, half-wrapped around the grip, but leaving the gun in the holster for the moment. She was quick, and she knew it. She defied anything to come out of that hatch before she could pull out the gun and put half a dozen shots in it.

Andi believed in avoiding arrogance…but she wasn't immune from a bit of cockiness herself, at times.

"Everybody ready?" The question was almost rhetorical. *Nightrunner*'s crew were all veterans, and they knew where they were. They were ready.

Lorillard flashed a last glance at both groups, and then he said, "Okay, Sy…do it."

Nightrunner's computer wizard stared down at the tablet, and then she set it down on the floor. She eased herself up, crouching forward, and she tapped the screen one last time. She was up in an instant afterward, lunging—half run, half wild dive—down the hall and away from the hatch.

Andi stared straight ahead, watching, waiting. She imagined all sorts of threats coming out—security robots, sprays of automatic fire, even deadly beams from high-energy lasers.

Then, the door slid open, and every muscle in Andi's body tensed. She'd only half believed Sylene would manage to get the hatch open—and release whatever nightmare lay beyond—and the sight and sound of success filled her bloodstream with adrenalin, he body preparing itself to face whatever dire threat came out of the now opened portal.

But there was nothing.

The two groups of the crew stared down the corridor from opposite ends, their eyes moving from the hatch to each other and back again, silent for close to a minute. Finally, Lorillard's arms moved out, a gesture for all of them to stay where they were. He moved forward, slowly, his eyes locked on the open doorway. Andi hadn't noticed him pulling his rifle around, but it was there, in his hands, ready for whatever might still come out of the hatch.

He crept forward until he was entirely in front of the door, and he looked directly into it. All kinds of images flashed before Andi's eyes, watching the captain obliterated by a burst of hypervelocity projectiles or incinerated by a great gout of flame. That was all foolish, of course. Anything like the thoughts in her mind would damage the very station the defensive system was trying to protect. Death, if it came to any of them from the system's internal defenses, would be far more prosaic.

But that didn't mean she wasn't about to see the captain, her friend, die in the next few seconds, as he stood there, peering into the unknown. She held her breath, watching, her hand still resting on the pistol at her side.

Nothing happened.

Lorillard stood where he was, seeming perhaps as surprised as Andi that he was still there, unmolested. "It's another corridor," he said softly. "It's long. I can't see the end."

That made sense, to an extent. The crew had been

moving across the width of one of the station's rings, but the new corridor, if it was perpendicular to the one they were in now, would extend all around the ring.

Andi stepped forward, the first of the crew to do so, and Sylene was just a half second behind her. The two peered around the edge of the opening. Andi was still on edge—she suspected she would be until *Nightrunner* was well on its way back to Dannith—but the sense of immediate, impending doom had receded significantly. The corridor looked similar to the one they were in, but she could see from where she stood that there were doors and hatches clearly visible at various points. It was a bit narrower, but still wide enough for them to march down two abreast.

At least if Gregor wasn't one of the two.

"Alright, let's not waste anymore time. We came out here to find old tech—and while this entire place is a marvel, we can't exactly shove an entire space station into *Nightrunner*'s hull. This one's beyond us, at least most of it is, but it looks to me like these information systems in here are working vastly better than anything we've run into before. A hold full of the circuit boards and processors running this place will put us all on a beach somewhere, living in mansions and boring the locals with tales of our days as adventurers in the Badlands."

Andi suspected the upbeat tone of Lorillard's short speech was intended, at least in part, to bolster morale. But that didn't mean every word of it wasn't true. In her two years on *Nightrunner*, Andi had never seen old tech as well preserved and functional as the station. Digging through centuries of dust for broken scraps was more commonly the work of the Badlands prospector. She'd never even heard of anyone finding something like the space station. She'd moved forward, prowled down the corridor with her shipmates, but only as she stood there, letting Lorillard's words sink in, did she fully realize.

She was close to her dream, to her—so long seemingly

impossible—goal of achieving truly vast wealth, and the power to protect herself that came with it. She'd always believed it, in one sense, at least…and she'd always doubted it as well, even if she'd never faced that realization. It had seemed so unattainable, but now there were standing there, in a vast imperial construct, full of technology beyond anything on the Rim.

"Let's go, Cap. Let's push on and get what we came for." Jammar was near the back of the group on the ship side of the new corridor, but his response was the first verbal one to Lorillard's words.

"Yes, let's go."

"Push on…let's find that old tech."

Most of the crew chimed in with one version or another of the same sentiment. They'd been scared, and no doubt they still were, but Lorillard had rallied them, at least to an extent. Andi wasn't sure if anyone had really understood what had just happened but her. The Marine had told her about leading men and women into battle, about reaching them on a level that existed below their fear, and even their good sense that told them of danger. She'd always respected Lorillard as a leader, but now her admiration grew.

She had been silent, but she stepped out in front of the corridor and looked over at the captain. "What do you say, Cap? Time to press on?"

Lorillard looked back and nodded. "Absolutely. Let's go find some choice tech, and then get the hell out of here. A few billion credits will do well for us, we don't have to be pigs about it. Maybe we'll even tip the navy off after we're done. Anonymously, of course."

Andi felt a bitter reaction, for a few seconds, but it faded quickly. She had the same resentment the others did for the Confederation's naval forces. She was a sort of patriot, to an extent at least, but she still harbored her share of anger and resentment. Certainly, for the squalor of the Gut and the abuses of Parsephon's government and industrialists. She could believe her homeworld was one of the worst in the Confederation, perhaps even *the* worst, but she didn't believe for a second that there weren't similar places, planets where people died in misery without tasting the slightest morsel of the vaunted liberty and protection of the Confederation.

She was furious, as well, at the harassment *Nightrunner*'s crew had suffered, that all prospectors had. Confederation law forbade private missions into the Badlands, and save for properly licensed research expeditions, ships heading out to explore became criminal enterprises the instant they entered an imperial artifact or scooped up a handful of crushed old electronics.

Worse, perhaps, was the uneven way the law was applied. To a great extent, the prospectors were tolerated, and yet, at times they were chased down, boarded, even imprisoned. Andi could accept different points of view—to an extent—but uneven application of laws destroyed any justice that might have existed in them.

"The navy can go…" Sylene spoke, but she let her words trail off before she finished. She had begun to say what Andi was thinking. What they all were thinking.

"This isn't a discussion to have now." Lorillard, clearly sorry he'd added the last words to what he'd said. "But remember, you're Confederation citizens. I have my grievances, as all of you do, but be damned glad you weren't born in the Union…or that your ancestors didn't live out here, where so many billions died long ago."

There was a spark in Lorillard's speech Andi had never seen before. She didn't know much about the captain's past, and she'd certainly seen him furious at naval harassment. Lorillard knew some damned fine curse words, and he'd never been hesitant to fire a few out when the ship was hiding or running from patrols. Andi had thought she'd known just about every way to swear, a side benefit of growing up in the Gut, but she'd learned a few more since she'd signed on the *Nightrunner*.

Andi was focused on the task at hand, and not on thinking about justice in the Confederation, or lack thereof, but Lorillard's words stuck with her, hanging just behind her conscious thoughts, waiting to return to the forefront as soon as the danger had passed.

It was hard to consider herself lucky for being born in the Gut, but she'd managed to escape it as well. Would she have in the Union? Or were the Andi's born in that totalitarian nightmare trapped forever in their miserable serfdom?

"Andi, take the lead with me." Lorillard's words sliced through the distraction, grabbing her attention like an iron vice.

"Yes, Cap." She'd moved forward, and she focused her thoughts on the mission. She could philosophize another day, try to figure out the Confederation, the Union, even who she herself truly was…when she was somewhere other than in the guts of a dead imperial artifact.

First, she had a job to do. It was time to find old tech, to score riches beyond the imaginings of the masses, back in the Gut or on any of a hundred planets.

It was time to find some juicy old tech.

Chapter Seventeen

Abandoned Imperial Station
Orbiting Zensoria, Osiron VI
Year 301 AC

"Hold."

The single word rattled off the high ceiling of the vast room, stopping Andi in her tracks. Stopping all of her comrades.

Her hand went to her side again, to the pistol, ready to draw at any second. But she waited. She had no idea what was happening, but she knew the last thing any of them needed was some kind of fight they could avoid.

"Who are you?" It seemed Captain Lorillard agreed with her assessment. His voice was calm, controlled, even assertive. He'd challenged the command with a demand for information, and he'd delivered the words with a level of focused authority she doubted she could have matched.

"I am Intelligence Sigma-7684, first activated Imperial Year 8,525, uploaded to Station Zensoria Primus, Imperial Year 8,526."

Andi stood, frozen, stunned at what she was hearing. She'd caught vague references to the old imperial dating system and calendar before, but nothing so clear and specific.

Was the empire really over eight thousand years old when it fell?

It was an amount of time she could barely comprehend. The three centuries since the Cataclysm had always seemed an eternity to her.

Andi watched and listened, in fear, but also in hypnotic fascination. The artificial intelligence—and, she knew, of course, that's what it *had* to be—spoke naturally, a bit of formality in its speech patterns perhaps, but then it *was* a military installation. Even the Marine had spoken with a reasonably strict cadence in his voice, a brittleness to his manner of speech.

Not entirely unlike the machine speaking to them.

Or on the verge of threatening us…

Andi had dealt with many AIs, the first when she was sneaking into houses in the Heights to steal. She didn't really understand the systems back then, but she'd developed enough familiarity with them to sidestep their defensive reactions, and even disable them once or twice. Later, of course, she'd become much more experienced with *Nightrunner*'s AI, and Sylene had taken her behind the curtain, so to speak, showed her how the thing worked, how its programming functioned.

None of the AIs she'd seen anywhere had been as natural-sounding as this one. She'd almost have believed there was a human being at the other end of the comm line, someone watching them, talking to them.

But that was not possible. The worlds of the Badlands were lifeless, save for small animals and insects encroaching on the remains of past human habitation. The Cataclysm had spared the Rim, if not from mass death and suffering, at least from total extermination. But the worlds closer to the galactic core, the ones that had been more populated and advanced, had fallen the hardest. The chance that *Nightrunner*'s crew had stumbled onto some kind of human survivor, three centuries after the Cataclysm was nil.

They were talking to a machine, and it was one they'd

never seen the likes of before. Andi was at a loss as to how to proceed, and she was grateful she wasn't in command.

"What should we call you?" Lorillard took a step forward as he spoke, probably, Andi figured, to test the AI's 'hold' command. She caught herself holding her breath as she watched, and she forced herself to breathe more regularly. If the shit hit the fan, she wanted to be ready, not gasping for air.

"Hold where you are. My informal designation is 'Zensoria Control,' and I am prepared to download a compete report on all system activities and statuses since the last human intervention. However, before we proceed, I must confirm your identification."

Andi's spirits sank, and she felt her stomach tighten. It had seemed too easy, especially when Sylene had managed to pull up something of a directory leading them to a place that looked an awful lot like a control room.

No, Andi realized, it had only *seemed* too easy. The control room was beginning to seriously resemble a trap, and she wondered nervously how an imperial military AI would react when they couldn't present any credentials.

She watched tensely as Lorillard stood still, waiting for the captain's perfunctory effort to talk his way through. She knew he would try, but she didn't have much hope of success. Her muscles were tight, her reflexes ready. She figured there was a good bet they'd all see action in a few seconds.

The captain was clever and capable, but none of them had any real knowledge at all about three-hundred-year-old imperial protocols, much less any forms of ancient ID.

"I am Captain James Lorillard, of the...imperial...ship *Nightrunner*, and this is my crew. We were ordered here to survey the station and take inventory of all holds and storage facilities."

"I have no record of a Captain James Lorillard, on the imperial roster. Neither is there a vessel, *Nightrunner*, on the naval ship list." The AI's voice was unchanged, no anger, no edge to it, nor signs of suspicion or threats.

Somehow, that made the whole thing worse.

"It has been a long time since any imperial personnel have been here. The perimeter defense systems have engaged and destroyed several vessels making unauthorized approach attempts in the two hundred ninety-seven years, three hundred four days, seven point six two hours since I last interacted with a command officer. Your ability to access this station and its supporting information systems suggests that you are, in fact, duly authorized imperial personnel. Nevertheless, I must confirm this. Please provide your operating number, and step forward alone for DNA scan. Your officers and spacers may line up behind you for their scans."

"The information I provided was correct. You just acknowledged you have been cut off for almost three centuries. Your knowledge banks are out of date, three hundred years behind. Even if I provided you with addition identification, it would be of no more use to you than my name or that of my ship."

Andi was impressed. She hadn't expected the captain to come up with anything nearly as convincing as that. She still didn't believe it would work—it wasn't in her to be that optimistic—but perhaps uncertainty would at least delay the AI from taking any kind of action.

For long enough to get back to the ship, maybe. Andi's determination to gain great wealth was strong, but she wasn't sure it was powerful enough to send her into action against an imperial AI and whatever resources it still retained. Not if getting back to the ship and getting out of there was a viable option.

Of course, it wasn't her choice. At least not hers alone.

"You are correct about the status of my data banks, however, I must confirm your identity and authorization to enter this station. I may not have access to current information, but if you came here to reassert control over this station, you would at least have the last access codes entered into the core system. Move forward to the lighted workstation, and enter the primary sequence to confirm your clearance to be here."

It was a reasonable request by the AI, and it suggested the machine they were dealing with was highly sophisticated, able to make decisions beyond a narrow flowchart. Of course, one of those decisions could very easily be to decide they were invaders or spies, and to try to kill them all. Andi found herself looking around the room, her eyes scanning for possible cover.

There wasn't much.

"I have current access codes. I am able to enter those, but it is doubtful they will match your data banks."

"It is not logical that duly authorized imperial personnel would have entered this station without access codes or some other credentials. Remain where you are."

"I order you to permit us access and to provide the…"

"Remain where you are."

Andi could hear sounds in the distance, and a few seconds later, a hatch opened, and two small shapes came out. They were about a meter tall, and there was a small sphere mounted on a cylinder over the stout bottom section. There were two thin tubes protruding from the top of the middle section.

Andi knew what they were the instant she saw them. Autocannons.

"You will be taken to the holding area and confined until I am able to verify your identity." No mention of what would happen if the AI *couldn't* confirm their identity which, of course, Andi knew it couldn't.

That's more tactful than I'd expect from an AI. Makes sense, too. Why tell us we'll be killed, or that we'll die in a cell somewhere?

It would only encourage resistance.

You're going to get resistance anyway, you…

Her thought was stopped abruptly. Some kind of klaxon went off, fairly distant, sounding very much like an alarm system that was only partly functional.

"Alert. Unauthorized ships approaching."

That can't be good…

Andi almost knew what the AI's next words were going to be, and she was already on the move when they came.

"The approaching vessels have opened fire."

The words hit like a hammer. Who the hell was out there, and why would they come so far just to try to blast the thing?

And, what kind of ship could have weapons powerful enough to damage something this big…

Cold realization hit Andi.

"*Nightrunner*, Cap…they're firing at *Nightrunner*."

Her words preceded his own realization by perhaps a second. Andi was looking right at him when she saw it on his face.

"We need to get back to the ship…now!" He turned and took two steps toward the door they'd entered through.

"Hold!" The AI's voice had changed, the relentlessly calm tone replaced by a clearly threatening one.

"We have to return to our ship." Lorillard took another step, the only one he managed before the AI's voice boomed out like a thunderclap.

"This is your final warning. Remain in place. I have calculated an unacceptable probability that you are some kind advanced guard or infiltration unit connected to the attacking strike force. As per standard procedure, this station is on Priority One Alert. You will be neutralized so you cannot take action to aide the attacking ships. If you resist, you will be terminated at once, without further warning."

Andi stood where she was, as did all the others. The bots moved, taking position where they had a line of fire at the entire landing party. Everything on the station was old, Andi knew, and there was a good chance some of it was no longer fully functional.

But that wasn't a bet she wanted to take, at least not on those autocannons.

* * *

"Break radio silence…advise *Embuscade* to close with the station and dock." Gavereaux sat in the middle of *Clipper*'s small bridge, his eyes fixed on the scanner display's image of the station. He'd read the reports, and he knew more or less what to expect, but he realized none of that had truly prepared him for the reality. The thing was *huge*, and perhaps more importantly, it was in decent shape. There was damage, of course, and unrepaired wear—he could see that plainly enough. But it was by far the best-preserved artifact he had ever seen.

"*Embuscade* acknowledges."

"Bring us in along a course to *Nightrunner*'s docking point. Take position two thousand kilometers from their position. Lasers at full power." *Clipper* didn't have all that impressive of a weapons suite, not by the standards of warships, at least. But then, neither did Captain Lorillard's vessel. And, coming in against a docked ship, *Clipper* would have a huge advantage if it came to fighting.

When it came to fighting.

Gavereaux wasn't ready to destroy the prospecting ship, not yet. He had no idea what was going on in the station, how many of Lorillard's people were in their ship, and how many had moved out into the imperial artifact. Ideally, he'd get *Nightrunner* in his sights, and wait until the Foudre Rouge landed and gave him a report from inside the station.

But if Lorillard's people tried to pull something…

"I want the lasers manned and ready to fire at the first signs *Nightrunner* is powering up to break away from the station."

He would let Lorillard's people live, a little longer. They may yet serve a valid purpose, root out some internal defenses that would cost him some of his own people. But he wasn't about to let them turn the whole thing into something approaching a fair fight. If he had to, he'd kill them all immediately.

They were all as good as dead anyway. He might use them a bit longer, but there was no way he could let any of them escape. He hadn't decided if he'd take prisoners if any of them surrendered, but letting them get back to Dannith—or anywhere else—was out of the question.

Lorillard's people were probably running around, grabbing trinkets, electronics and even data dumps if they were able to get some. That would be enough to make them rich. Crazy rich. But the station offered far more than that. It offered the entire Rim.

Artificial intelligence systems. Vast reactors and power generation. Weapons. Even if, as it appeared, none of the station's guns were operative, they were still there, manna for the scientists and engineers the Presidium would send to study them. To copy them.

Possession of the station—and keeping its location secret—was no less than a chance to alter the fundamental balance of power on the Rim, to give the Union irresistible dominance. The Union had fought three wars with its neighbor, and there was little question another was coming. It might be five years off, even ten—the fleet wasn't ready yet—but it would come. If the ships that fought that war were equipped with imperial-grade weapons, it would be a massacre. The conflict wouldn't be fought to gain frontier systems. The heart of the Confederation would be vulnerable. Foudre Rouge could march on the Senate Compound itself.

Gavereaux knew, if he was the one who discovered the ancient tech that could win that war, the rewards would be immense. Power, wealth, privilege. Perhaps even advancement that put him on a road to a seat on the Presidium someday.

He wasn't going to let it slip through his fingers, and certainly not by allowing any of Lorillard's pack of pirates to elude his grasp. They all had to die in this system, or they had to go back to the Union and a Sector Nine cell somewhere.

Gavereaux didn't care which it was, though he suspected a quick death in the Osiron system would be the most merciful. He didn't know whether *Nightrunner*'s crew knew anything else of value, save whatever they'd learned about the station, but he was well aware of Sector Nine's methods of interrogation, and the thoroughness of its inquisitors.

Yes, perhaps I will do them a favor killing them here. I owe them that much for clearing away the defenses, and opening the door for me.

Opening the door to so much…

Chapter Eighteen

Free Trader Nightrunner
Docked at Imperial Station
Orbiting Zensoria, Osiron VI
Year 301 AC

"Doc, get up here...I need some help." Tyrell was sitting in the command chair on *Nightrunner*'s bridge—the *captain's* chair—feeling very out of his depth. He'd stayed behind because the captain had asked him to. He might have read something in that once, but he'd come to know the captain's ways long before. Someone had to stay, and it was Tyrell's turn, more or less.

Beyond that, while Tyrell could hold his own in a fight, his real skills were in communication and scanning devices. That made him, aside from the captain, the logical choice to mind the ship, and wait for the others to return...and do his best to keep an eye on things in the system. Not that he'd expected to find anything so far out in the Badlands.

At least until a few seconds before.

"On the way." "Doc" Rand wasn't a real doctor, he was just the closest thing *Nightrunner* had to one. He'd been a medical technician of some kind, and he'd completed some percentage of the course requirements for a medical certification. The specifics of that percentage had varied, depending on the details of the telling, and how much drinking was involved.

The hatch slid open, and Rand raced onto the bridge. "What's up?" He sounded a little edgy, but then he saw the display, and his visible stress level increased well beyond "a little."

"What the hell is that?"

"That's why you're here. They're coming in right at us, and I need some help with the controls."

"I don't know how to fly this thing? I patch up your wounds, I don't pilot *Nightrunner.*"

"I don't pilot *Nightrunner* either, but we're going to have to do something. I can't reach the landing party. Whatever this station is made of, it blocks scanning and comm beams cold. They weren't twenty meters in when he lost contact."

"So, what do we do? Who are they?"

"How the hell should I know?"

"Well, what kind of ship does it look like? Another prospector?"

Tyrell shook his head. "My God, you really don't know how to read any of this, do you? There are *two* ships, not one, and they're both heading for the station…or for us, it's hard to tell."

"Two ships? It could still be a prospecting run. If anyone else had data on this…thing…well, there's probably plenty here to go around."

That was a reassuring thought, the idea of a few more prospectors come to join them, and even help with the gathering of tech. The only problem was, Badlands salvage teams had a bad history of *not* working together. Sharing wasn't a big part of the culture, and no matter how much loot there was for the taking, crews tended to get territorial. Tyrell knew that for a number of reasons, not the least of which was his own angry thought that *Nightrunner* had gotten there first.

Whoever this was, it was two ships to one, and maybe

worse. Tyrell didn't see a way to prevent them from getting a bead on *Nightrunner*, or just blasting the ship, before he could get the engines ready to break away.

Assuming he could manage that at all.

That all ignored the fact that such an action meant leaving the others on the station. He wasn't sure if he could execute the breakaway, but he was even less confident he could manage to pull off a docking run. If he pulled *Nightrunner* from its mooring, he might never be able to get the others back aboard.

And if he didn't break away, they'd be sitting ducks.

"I need you over there." Tyrell gestured toward the number two station. *Andi's station*, he thought. The seat had never been designated as belonging to any of the crew, but they'd all become used to Andi flying the ship along with the captain in recent months.

Doc looked like he might say something, but after a couple seconds, he just turned and sat down in the chair.

"We need to bring the reactor level up high enough to give us some thrust potential. But it's pretty cold now, and we can't raise it too quickly."

"You're kidding, right? I have no idea what I'm doing over here."

"Well, if you don't want to get roasted while you're sitting over there, start figuring it out."

Tyrell was watching the scanner, and even as he was trying to get the nav systems online, he began to realize it was too late. He *might* break away, just in time, but *Nightrunner* would never get away—or get her own weapons charged up—in time.

"Slow down on that reactor powerup." Tyrell was shaking his head and exhaling as what little hope he'd had drained away. "We don't have time to break free, not before those bastards can fire at us." His mind was still racing, despite the cold realization, trying to come up with something—anything—to do.

The best thing he could think of was to stay where they were, for the moment, at least. Maybe the approaching ships would hold their fire, not wanting to damage the station or trigger some kind of defensive response. That would buy a little time, at least.

But what the hell are you going to do with more time, trapped under their guns, without the Cap and the others?

* * *

"Let us return to our vessel. We are an imperial crew, and our ship is armed. Your defense grid is down. We can intercept those…"

"Negative. The approaching vessels are too close. There is insufficient time, and you cannot be allowed to leave until your identification is confirmed." The AI was stubborn, and all of Lorillard's efforts to extricate them from the room had been rebuffed.

Andi stood where she was, her head moving around, scanning the room. It was a control center of some kind, almost certainly, but she was willing to bet it wasn't the main one for the entire station. The AI speaking to them, and holding them as prisoners, was very likely located elsewhere in the station.

She had no idea what condition the station's comm lines were in, but the fact that the defense network—which he she imagined had once been vast and powerful—had been reduced to a pair of laser buoys suggested that, as much of the construct that remained intact, there was, nevertheless, considerable breakdown and wear. Not to mention the fact that the AI seemed unaware that the two lasers that had remained had been destroyed by *Nightrunner*. Clearly, there were huge gaps in the various systems.

The AI was clearly incredibly sophisticated, and not likely to be outsmarted or convinced to let them go…but its ability to hold them where they were was dependent, at that moment, almost entirely on maintaining communications with the two bots.

At least part of that ability was wireless—the bots were freestanding, not connected in any physical way. Andi didn't like the idea of guessing on the capabilities of imperial systems, but enough interference just might cut off the AI's connection to the bots. If only for a short time.

Her eyes caught the scanner, the large one Gregor had been carrying. The giant had set it down about a meter from where he stood. Andi had a clear line of sight to it.

A clear line of fire.

She didn't know if she could get a shot off before the bots took her out. Even if she managed it, she didn't know if the thing would overload the way she hoped. If she was even able to hit it.

She had no idea at all what kind of internal programming the bots had. Would they stand where they were, if they lost contact with the main AI, seeking to reconnect for instructions?

Or would they open fire and kill everyone in the room?

Her head ached. She didn't know what to do. If she took action, if she made that desperate gamble, she might get herself killed...get all her friends killed. But if she didn't...

The AI would never release them, and eventually, it would realize they weren't imperials at all. What would it do then? And what ships were approaching? Who was out there, and what would they do? To *Nightrunner*? To her friends?

Even to the station.

She could feel her hand shaking, and she felt nauseous. She understood her body's own signals. She'd decided to act.

She tried to think of some way to let her comrades, or at least the captain, know what she was doing, but there was nothing. The AI could hear everything she said, and it was monitoring her from multiple angles, she was sure. At best, she'd cause confusion. At worst, she'd warn the AI, or trigger some kind of unpleasant response.

She hesitated a few seconds, feeling an almost irresistible urge to procrastinate, to wait and see if the captain had a plan, if any other opportunity was going to develop.

But she knew there was nothing. Her plan was their only chance.

Lorillard had tried to persuade the AI, and there had been no movement at all, no change in the computer's position.

Do it.

She took a deep breath, trying to steady herself, trying to push back the desire to leave saving them to one of the others, to shy away from the terrible responsibility. She'd have one chance. One. If she was lucky. She couldn't miss. She had to hit the thing dead center, and hope for the best.

Do it now.

She acted, startling herself with the suddenness of it all, as some part of her deep inside overruled the fear, the hesitation.

Her hand had been close to her pistol, and now it was on the weapon, fingers clasping as she pulled it from the holster. She was quick, the fastest gun on *Nightrunner*, but her adversary was a machine. She had surprise, perhaps, but she knew she didn't have time.

*Aim, aim, aim…*her mind pounded the thought into her. But she ignored it, and just fired.

There hadn't been time to obsess, to line up the weapon. She'd had to rely on her gut, on the instinct that had taken her from the streets of the Gut to where she was now. She was consciously terrified, but some part of her had held firm, and she felt the kick from the weapon as it fired a second time, and then a third.

Even if the bots blast me now, maybe the others will get out.
If I hit the thing. And if it overloads.

Those 'ifs' were massive, huge shadows darkening her

soul, even as she dropped low, doing what little she could to protect herself from the bots if they attacked.

Gregor turned toward her, even as the scanner unit sitting next to him erupted in a shower of sparks. He had a horrified, confused look on his face.

Don't worry…I wasn't shooting at you, my friend…

Andi swung around, her eyes darting toward the closest bot. She held the gun down, behind her back. She didn't know what the bot's programming allowed, even if her desperate action had succeeded and cut it off from the AI's direction, but she didn't think threatening the thing directly was a good idea.

"Brilliant, Andi!" The captain turned toward her, and as he did, he pulled out his own rifle, and he fired three times at the far wall, the bullets shattering the speaker mounted there.

The only one that seemed to be functional.

Way to go, Cap. She hadn't even considered that the AI could issue verbal orders to the bots.

"Let's get out of here, before that interference fades." She listened to the captain's command, but she was far from as certain as he sounded that the bots were cut off. "Walk slowly, everyone. Don't threaten those things, don't even look at them with a funny expression on your face."

Andi had conceived the plan, and she'd bet her life—and quite possibly her friends' lives—on it, but she found herself stunned it seemed to be working.

She didn't let doubts or shock slow her response, though. The captain was right. The interference wouldn't last long. She'd bought them an escape from the room—*maybe*—but it was a long way back to the ship.

She moved toward the hatch they'd used to enter, slipping into the rough single file column the others had formed. Her eyes darted back and forth, checking on the bots. They were still motionless, sitting still where they had been. That didn't ease her worries, though. Any instant, she knew, they might attack, and if they did, she and all her comrades would be dead in seconds.

She could feel the small of her back tighten, a series of shivers running down her spine as she could almost feel autocannon rounds tearing into her, ripping her body to shreds. Andi had faced death before, but somehow, walking slowly and calmly, knowing with each passing second that the next was far from assured, was harder than anything she'd ever done, and battle she'd ever fought.

Her heart was pounding as she looked toward the hatch. Anna had been the closest to the door, and she was at the head of the column. She'd moved slowly, steadily as she slipped through the still-open door.

Barret followed her, and Sylene was next. Then, the captain walked through, and after that, Andi took a deep breath and followed. One by one, the others came out, and when they had all left the room, they paused for a moment in the corridor.

"Sy, can you close that door?"

Andi heard the captain's words, and she liked the idea of closing off the control room, with the security bots inside. But without knowing what the AI could control through the station's aging and battered circuitry, she didn't know if it made more sense to try o close off the portal, or just to run like hell.

"I think so, Cap." Sylene already had her tablet in her hand. "I think I'm still connected, unless that...thing...found me and cut me off." A few seconds passed. "Yup, I'm still in." An instant later, the door slid shut.

"Nice job." Lorillard stepped into the middle of the corridor. "All of you, get back." Then, he turned to Sylene. "The locking mechanism is there, right?" He pointed toward a section of wall next to the hatch.

"I think so, Cap."

"Alright, everybody back ten meters." He waited while

everyone stepped down the corridor. Then he opened fire with his assault rifle.

The walls were *almost* invulnerable, whatever incredible material the imperials used to construct them proof against most damage. But Lorillard's assault rifle wasn't the normal kind the rest of the crew carried. It was a Marine issue, hypervelocity weapon, firing a depleted uranium projectile at speed in excess of three thousand meters per second.

And Lorillard opened fire on full auto from a range of less than a meter.

The spray of projectiles slammed into the smooth white surface, and for an instant, they were proof even against that awesome kinetic energy. But then, a split appeared, and a chunk of the wall material flew off, landing on the floor about a meter to the side.

A burst of sparks sprayed out from the internal mechanism, and Lorillard turned and nodded. Andi didn't know if the captain had managed to jam the door—she called it about 50/50, and she suspected he would have been right around the same figure—but she knew it was time to go.

Time to get the hell out of there.

Chapter Nineteen

Sector Nine Freighter Clipper
800 Kilometers off Imperial Station
Zensoria, Osiron VI
Year 301 AC

"*Nightrunner*, you will stay where you are. At the first sign of engine ignition, or if we read any energy flow to weapons systems, you will be destroyed without warning." Gavereaux sat on *Clipper*'s bridge, relishing his ship's advantage. He enjoyed power plays, at least when *he* had the power, and he savored the fear he suspected those in the trapped ship were feeling. He was a bully by nature, as were most of those in positions of authority in the Union—and in most other nations as well.

"If you pick up so much as a spark going to the engines or weapons in that ship, you open fire. Understand?"

The agent sitting at the tactical station nodded. "Understood."

It wasn't a real tactical setup, of course, or at least it didn't look like one. *Clipper* had stronger weapons than a small freighter would be expected to carry, but Sector Nine generally pushed as far as it could get away with, and no farther. The goal had been to give *Clipper* the heaviest punch possible, without drawing dangerous attention or creating suspicion.

Gavereaux wasn't sure how his ship would fare in a head to head matchup with *Nightrunner*—if the free trader had uprated guns, too, it would be far too close to an even fight for his tastes. Fortunately, he had Lorillard's ship trapped, powered down and under his guns.

Just the way he liked it.

"Sir...*Embuscade* reports docking completed." A pause. "They had some difficulty connecting to the coupling. They took some damage to their stabilizers." The agent at the tactical station turned and looked back at Gavereaux. "They suffered three casualties due to integrity loss in two compartments. All three KIA, two of the Foudre Rouge and one of the ship's crew."

Gavereaux didn't like losing any of his soldiers. Twenty troopers plus one officer in command was a small enough force to secure a vast construct like the station, not to mention cleaning out any of *Nightrunner*'s crew that remained there.

But two won't make a difference. At least not in wiping out Lorillard's people. Securing the station was another matter, of course. It was huge, and probably dangerous. But he knew Gaston Villieneuve would send massive reinforcements to begin the true securing and exploitation of the system as soon as he received word of just what his people had found.

"Are the remaining Foudre Rouge ready to board the station?"

"Yes. They are prepped and set to go in on your command."

Gavereaux stared at the display, his eyes darting to the numbers on the side. *Nightrunner*'s reactor had been increasing its output, but now it had leveled off. *That's clever. Obey my orders, more or less...but hang on to the increased energy production you'd reached before that.*

He turned toward the tactical station. "Order the Foudre

Rouge in, but hold back one fire team in reserve. They are to find and secure the station's control center or main engineering space."

He turned back to his comm unit. "*Nightrunner*, you are to shut your reactor down to minimal levels, sufficient for life support only. You have one minute to comply." *There, an order you can't skirt by and pretend to obey.* He wasn't sure he was ready to open fire in sixty seconds—he didn't know what the crew of *Nightrunner* knew about the station, how much useful information they might possess, and he wasn't ready to throw that away. But he made damned sure to sound like his hand was already on the fire control. A good bluff was all in the delivery.

"Sir…Lieutenant Emile-2756 requests clarification on rules of engagement, specifically how his troopers should handle any of *Nightrunner*'s personnel they find in the station."

Gavereaux hesitated a few seconds, considering. He had whoever was actually on *Nightrunner* as good as captive in his own brig. They might be useful. But any still on the station…they might get away, find somewhere to hide, even sabotage some vital system. They were too dangerous…and nineteen soldiers wasn't enough to secure the station and guard prisoners.

"Shoot to kill. The Foudre Rouge are to terminate all contacts in the station immediately, but they are to take prisoners on *Nightrunner* if possible.

*   *   *

"We're stuck, like rats in a trap. Tyrell slammed his fist down on the control panel, pulling it back sharply as the pain told him he'd banged it down a bit too hard. He was angry—with himself, because he couldn't come up with a way out, and with the situation, too. *What the hell are the odds on some other mission being all the way out here when we are?*

Nightrunner had faced competition for relic sites before, but they were far out this time. Damned far. Running into another ship was a shock. Encountering two was off the charts.

He looked down, checking to make sure he hadn't damaged the captain's workstation. He was relieved to see the only thing hurt by the outburst had been his hand. He turned toward the second station on the bridge, toward his sole companion then on *Nightrunner*.

"Better cut the reactor, Doc. They've got us dead to rights." Tyrell hated being vulnerable, but he also knew the unidentified ship could blow *Nightrunner* to bits anytime it wanted to. That made playing for time the right way to go. Maybe there would be a chance to talk their way out of the whole mess.

Maybe...but my gut says it's a longshot. Still, dying in a few hours is better than dying now, if only for the chance something can happen in between.

The rest of the crew was still out there. He figured the variables at play might still come together in their favor, create an escape of some kind. He wasn't sure just how much be believed that, but whatever he thought, analysis didn't matter. Such vague hopes were all he had.

He figured there was a good chance Lorillard would have come up with some course of action if he'd been there. Or Andi. *Nightrunner*'s rookie crewmember had proven herself not only handy in a fight, but also damned smart. Tyrell was impressed as hell with her, as was everyone else on the ship. He had always felt something familiar in her mannerisms, the way she attacked problems, but he'd only recently figured out just who it was she reminded him of.

The captain.

Andi and Lorillard were incredibly similar in many ways. They agreed almost all the time, sometimes sounding almost like copies of each other. It had taken him a while to figure it out, but he'd come to a conclusion eventually, a realization of why they seemed so similar.

They were both natural leaders.

He'd teased Andi his share of times, given her the usual shit the rookie and the youngest crew member almost always took on ships like *Nightrunner*, but he'd also come to understand that he would willingly follow her…on missions, into battle, anywhere. She was Lorillard reborn as far as he was concerned, and the more he saw her in action, the more firmly he believed that.

He loved the captain, and his devotion and loyalty were absolute. But as he sat there, he found himself wishing Andi was onboard even more than Lorillard. Her mind was quicker, her tactics fresher. If anyone could figure a way out of the trap *Nightrunner* had found herself in, it was Andi.

But she was off in the guts of that massive station somewhere, along with the captain and the others. And he was sitting on the bridge, feeling more uncomfortable than he could ever remember, waiting and hoping his captors didn't decide to just blast *Nightrunner* anyway.

He searched his mind, tried to come up with a course of action, anything. But there was nothing.

Nothing but a single word, swirling around in his head, summing up his feeling on the whole situation.

Shit.

* * *

Andi ran down the corridor, her head slung low into her shoulders, her neck tense. It was a natural reaction to the almost deafening sound of the klaxon. The volume of the alarm varied with how close they were to the nearest speaker. Just then, it was earsplitting.

Andi's desperate action, her almost instinctive move to block the AI's connection to the security bots, had succeeded. For roughly three minutes.

That's how long it had taken for the alarm systems to go

off. She hadn't known if that meant the bots would be on their tail or not. At least she didn't know for perhaps another ninety seconds, until she heard the sounds of fire coming from behind them.

She'd felt an initial rush of satisfaction when they'd all escaped from the control room, but she knew they had a long way to go before they could reach anything resembling safety. Doubts crept into her mind as she fought to push them aside. Had she helped her comrades escape…or had she just managed to kill them all in some kind of perverse slow motion?

They didn't even have a plan, none save trying to get back to *Nightrunner*. But there were other ships in the system now. For all she knew, *Nightrunner* had already been blasted to atoms.

"We're never going to outrun those bots, Captain." The words burst from her lips, almost involuntarily. "We've got to take them out somehow."

A few seconds passed with no answer, but then Lorillard stopped abruptly. "You're right, Andi. We're never going to make it all way back to the ship." He turned, looking at one of the hatches along the corridor. "Sy, can you get any of these doors open?" A second or two passed. "Quickly?"

Sylene already had her tablet in her hand, even as she continued running. "My connection seems active, still." She seemed surprised. Andi was, too. She'd have thought the first thing the station AI would do was sever any unauthorized connections.

The thing is damaged, though. Some things still work, others don't…

Andi wasn't sure what practical use there was to that realization, but she was sure there was something.

Then, the hatch closest to her opened. A few seconds later, she noticed that all the doors she could see had slid open.

"I couldn't localize any one, not quickly enough at least.

So, I opened everything in this sector."

"Good, Sy…that's great." Lorillard turned to Andi. "You take Gregor and Yarra…move up to the next compartment. The rest of you, with me…other side of the corridor."

Andi wasn't sure splitting up was the right thing to do…until Lorillard continued.

"We'll try to draw them in here, Andi. You three can come in and hit them from behind."

She wasn't sure there really was a 'behind' with the security bots. Their center sections seemed to move three-hundred-sixty degrees. But she knew the captain was going for any tactical advantage they could get. And even the bots could only fully engage a threat in one direction at a time.

That meant Lorillard and the others were bait.

"Yarra, you've got those explosive charges, right?"

"Yeah, Cap." A short pause, then realization in her tone. "They're not really set up as grenades, though. I'm not sure how accurate they'd be if they were thrown."

"Give them to Andi." Lorillard knew, as the others did, that Andi had the sharpest eyes, the best aim. "You know what to do." He flashed a quick glance at her, and then he moved through the hatch, motioning for the others to follow.

Andi hesitated, for just a second, but then she could hear the bots getting closer. She waved to her two cohorts, and ran up to the next hatch, ducking inside the room.

It was a storage facility of some kind. There were shelves behind her, stacked high with large plastic boxes. She was curious about the contents, but she pushed such thoughts aside. The place didn't look like an armory and, frankly, nothing else but weapons would be of use to her just then.

She stood just inside the door, waiting. She was tense, sweaty, scared. She slung her rifle back over her shoulder, and she turned toward Yarra. "Let's get those charges ready."

Nightrunner's engineer just nodded, and she slid the pack

she carried off her shoulder, setting it down lightly. She reached inside, pulling out an irregularly shaped device, about thirty centimeters long. Andi was no engineer, but she knew a homemade bomb when she saw one.

She reached out and took the thing from her comrade. It was heavier than she'd expected, and poorly balanced. It was just about the worst thing she could imagine to use as a thrown weapon, but it was what they had.

"It's not an impact-detonation explosive, Andi…you're just going to have to set the timer, and make sure you throw it at exactly the right moment."

Great…that should be easy…

"I'm going to have to get close, and that timer's going to have to be dead on." She knew she'd have to run in and throw the thing almost immediately. The bots would detect her coming right away. Lorillard and the others would do what they could to distract them, but time was definitely not going to be on her side.

"How many of these do you have?" Andi already knew, but she wanted to be sure.

"Two. But there's no way you're going to handle both of them."

"No, not quickly enough, at least. You'll need to bring the second one. Come in behind me, and when the first one goes off, set that one for a three second detonation, and give it a good hurl at the other bot. Assuming I manage to take out the first one, of course."

That last bit was a moot point. If Andi's attack left both bots standing, they were all as good as dead anyway.

"Okay, Andi…" There was a little hesitation. Yarra had gotten them all out of some pretty bad fixes before, but that had been in the engine room. Her contributions had usually been her engineering skills. She'd never been part of *Nightrunner*'s 'muscle.'

"You can do it, Yarra. Just stay behind me…and stay focused." She would have had Gregor take the second bomb, but for all his strength and sheer power in a fight, he was somewhat of the lumbering giant when it came to throwing things. He had a legitimate claim to the title of worst shot on *Nightrunner* with a gun, and he was at his best in hand to hand combat.

"I'll be there, Andi."

She was always surprised how so many of the crew deferred to her when they were in action. They still gave her enough shit as the rookie on off times, but they lined up behind her when they were in danger.

She didn't understand it, what they seemed to see in her. She was scared shitless, doing all she could to keep herself from running down the hall screaming. She didn't belong there, and certainly not leading anyone. She was a fraud, nothing but an orphan who should be digging through the garbage in the Gut, looking for scraps to eat.

But her comrades clearly saw something in her, and even if it was stone cold fantasy, she knew she could use it. To help them all.

Andi stood just inside the door, listening. She could hear the bots approaching, though it would have been easier without the damned klaxons. She held her breath, trying to catch every sound. If they took the bait, moved into the compartment with the captain and the others, her plan was operative. If they kept coming, or they moved into the room she and her two cohorts were in, she'd have to improvise…and do it damned quickly.

The bots got louder as they moved closer. The security units might be tough in a fight, but they weren't likely to sneak up on anyone. For an instant, Andi thought they were going to pass right by the room where the captain and the others were waiting.

Then, she heard a burst of fire. Her stomach tightened, and for a second or two, she was sure the bots had opened up, that her friends were already dead. But she recognized the sound of that gun.

It was the captain's assault rifle. Lorillard had left nothing to chance. He'd had made sure the bots would follow his people into the room.

Andi knew that was her signal, too. She didn't know if the bots would open fire at once, or if they would try to secure some kind of surrender. She guessed the captain's gunfire had lessened the chance for negotiation…and that meant she had to go now!

She raced out of the room, holding the bomb uneasily in one hand. It was heavy, its shape difficult. But a two-handed throw would be rougher, less accurate.

Slower, too…and there was no time to waste.

She swung around in the hallway, almost leaping into the room. Her eyes moved back and forth, locking almost immediately on the closest of the bots. The two units were already reacting, and she could see the turrets turning toward her, even as she hurled the bomb.

She'd hit the arming switch as she was running in from the corridor, starting the three second countdown. She was cutting it close, maybe too close, but her mind had been awash in the sounds of the bots shooting at her friends, sounds that didn't exist. Yet. But she didn't waste any time for one simple reason.

She had none to waste.

She hurled the bomb, pushing with her arm, thrusting with all her strength…and then she dropped to the ground. There was no way to get far enough away. He momentum would, if anything, bring her closer to the targeted bot, and the explosion that was perhaps one and a half seconds away.

Her knees hit the ground hard, and a jolting pain raced up both of her legs. She was still dropping, her arms in front of her to block the impact, when the bomb exploded.

There had never been any doubt in her mind, the explosive would detonate. Yarra was nothing if not a capable engineer, and a skilled chemist as well. She knew her way around bombmaking gear the way Andi had known the tunnels and back alleys of the Gut.

Andi fell, more or less face first, until the force of the explosion pushed her back across the room, tumbling over and landing facedown. She managed reach out, to deflect most of the impact of the fall, but she couldn't see the bots, or the result of the explosion. She didn't know if she'd disabled the units, or at least one of them…or if, any second, she would feel autocannon rounds tearing into her body, ripping her into bloody chunks.

Chapter Twenty

Free Trader Nightrunner
Docked at Imperial Station
Orbiting Zensoria, Osiron VI
Year 301 AC

The clang was loud, and it reverberated through the ship. Tyrell ignored it at first, though he knew what it was. *Nightrunner* was powered down—mostly—but he'd managed to keep the passive scanners operational. He'd watched the one—what were they, rivals, enemies?—ship dock with the station, doing it rather more clumsily, he thought with some random flash of pride, than *Nightrunner* had managed.

Still, graceful docking or not, the ship was close, and enough time had passed for its occupants to reach *Nightrunner*'s docking point from inside the station. He ignored it, for a moment at least, but he'd never found that a useful way to deal with a problem.

And certainly not a problem that was likely to blast through the airlock if he didn't open up. He grabbed a rifle from the small storage locker in the corridor, and he moved toward the hatch. The weapon was pointless, he knew, useless for anything but maybe a suicide attempt, but going down unarmed seemed too much like…surrender.

He stopped at the small comm unit next to the inner

door. He flipped the switch. "This is Tyrell Stone, acting commander of *Nightrunner*. Who are you, and what do you want?" There was attitude in his voice, probably not the smartest way he could go, but on some level at least, the only way he could live with himself. He knew he was about to allow the enemy in, to surrender *Nightrunner*, something that would have seemed almost inconceivable even a few hours ago. But the enemy ship still had the vessel in its sights, ready to blow it away at any provocation. That made the composition of the force waiting outside largely irrelevant. There could be a hundred soldiers, or one old lady with a pot of soup. Either way, he would let them in, and when his delaying tactics ran out, he would turn over control of *Nightrunner* to them. There was no other alternative, at least none he could think of.

"Open the airlock immediately." No identification, no statement of intent. But the threat in his man's tone was clear enough.

Tyrell reached out to the controls, pausing for a couple seconds, as if waiting for some brilliant plan to appear in his head, something hatched from the frustrated helplessness that dominated his thoughts.

But there was nothing.

He heard another series of clangs, louder this time, more insistent. He couldn't imagine they were all that far from blasting their way in. That would serve nothing. The enemy would still take the ship, and if some chance did develop to seize it back, better it was in full working order, and without a gaping hole in its side.

He turned the dial, unlocking the airlock apparatus, and then he hit a series of three buttons. He heard a brief swish—the airlock was pressurized, but the atmospheric pressure in the station was slightly higher than the Megara standard 1,025 kPa maintained inside *Nightrunner*. As soon as the minor adjustment was complete, the outer door opened.

Tyrell heard the sound of heavy boots clanging on the metal floor. *Two of them*, he thought, about eighty percent sure he was right. A few seconds later, he heard the same clang as before, this time on the inner door.

He slid the rifle over his shoulder. If killing the two people in the airlock would have accomplished anything but *Nightrunner*'s almost certain destruction, he'd have gone for it. But that kind of resistance was pointless.

Nightrunner was the captain's. If anybody was going to get her blasted to dust, it would be Lorillard himself, and damned sure not Tyrell.

He reached out for the controls, and as he did, he leaned forward and looked through the small, clear window. There were two—men, he guessed—though they were so loaded up with combat armor and weapons, he wasn't sure.

Those are no frontier prospectors. *They're not even Spacer's District gangsters.*

He heard the clang again, and the impatience behind it. He reached out toward the controls, even as a single thought pounded in his head.

What the hell are these guys?

* * *

Andi could almost feel the heavy depleted uranium rounds tearing through her body, spilling her blood and her life onto the cold hardness of the deck. She'd come so far, lightyears from the filthy streets of the Gut, to a place with friends, comrades, men and women who fought at her side, who had her back.

Only to die out in the cold depths of dead imperial space.

But she wasn't dead. She wasn't even shot.

There was nothing. No fire, no bullets. No blood pouring from her body…at least not from anyplace it hadn't been already.

She hurt all over, there was no denying that. Aches and bruises and, she guessed, and more than likely a couple fractures as well. She'd done what she could to break the fall, but that had proven to be little enough, and she was pretty banged up. Still, she scrambled up, pushing through the pain, trying to get to her feet as quickly as she could—or as close to a standing position as she could manage.

There was still no shooting, at least not for a good five or ten more seconds. Then she heard the captain's gun again, an odd difference to the sound this time, almost like an echo.

She finally managed to get to her feet, more or less. She still had one knee on the ground, and, gritting her teeth against the pain, she pushed herself completely up.

She was standing, sore and hunched over, still trying to fully recover her balance. Not an ideal fighting position by any means, but at least it gave her a decent view of Lorillard's rifle, shoved deep into the side of the downed bot as he continued to fire.

Sparks and glowing chunks of half-molten metal flew all around the downed robot as the superfast projectiles slammed into it at such short range. One of them barely missed her, whipping by close enough that she could feel the heat.

Then, with a loud crack, the bot split in two, the now-separate sections falling to the deck. Andi didn't know enough about imperial security bots to be absolutely sure it was dead, but she'd have given odds of five or ten to one. In other words, a pretty damned good bet.

The best they were likely to get in the current circumstances.

Her eyes moved to the side. There was a greater worry, however…the other bot.

The explosion had pushed it hard, knocking it off its—feet wasn't the right word, but she didn't know what was—and slamming it into the wall. It was damaged, there wasn't much question about that, but she didn't have to look past its continued movement to realize it wasn't completely out of action.

"Watch out," she shouted, as she saw the thing turn itself over, opening fire as it brought the autocannon turret to bear. One of the dual barrels had been badly bent, and it blew apart when the firing started. But the other one functioned well enough, sending a deadly blast of projectiles across the room.

She watched as her comrades dove in different directions, off to each side, getting as far from the spray of gunfire as they could.

The aim was off, she realized with a small bit of relief, probably minor damage to the functional barrel. But the rate of fire was still withering, and that made the thing dangerous as hell. The bot was still on its side, struggling to rise. Once it righted itself, its arc of fire would no longer be restricted. It could sweep the room in a few seconds, and perfect aim or not, it would cut them all down like stacks of cordwood.

"Yarra…the other bomb. Now!"

The engineer looked terrified, frozen for an instant, transfixed, unmoving.

Andi had an urge to race over to her comrade, to take the explosive and throw it herself. But there wasn't time.

"Now, Yarra…now!" Andi raised her voice, dredging inside herself for the deepest, most authoritative tone she could manage. The sound that poured forth out of her mouth was so hard, so commanding, it startled even her.

It had an effect on the engineer, too. Yarra poked at the arming switch, still a little clumsily but well enough, and she hurled the bomb through the air toward the bot.

Her toss was two-handed, and quite a bit uglier to watch than Andi's had been.

But it was close.

Hopefully close enough, Andi thought, as she ducked down again, throwing her hands over her head to protect herself from the expected blast.

She hit the ground, the pain from her knees almost unbearable this time. Her face clenched, waiting for the explosion, as her eyes watered and teared from the agony of the impact.

Nothing.

Her mind raced. That *had* to have been three seconds. She felt her stomach heave, even as she got ready to pull herself back up, to do what she could to stop the bot before it shot them all.

Then the bomb exploded, giving Andi a lesson in just how *long* three seconds could be.

It was loud, louder even than the first one, and this time, a small chunk of—very hot, if not molten—steel grazed her arm, sending a fresh wave of pain up toward her shoulder. She howled, her effort to hold back the yell coming just an instant too late.

She glanced down at her arm. There was a long mark, maybe five centimeters, half deep cut, half bad burn. It hurt like hell, but somehow, she ignored it and brought her eyes back to the bot.

Yarra's bomb had exploded just to the side of the thing. It had taken damage from the blast, it seemed, and more, when it slammed hard into the wall. There was a large crack in the wall's previously perfect whiteness, and the bot lay on the deck just below.

Andi could see chunks of the thing missing, blasted parts laying on the ground all around it.

She could also see that it was still moving.

The turret was completely knocked out, at least, but she had no idea what other weapons the thing had. And she wasn't going to wait to find out.

She pulled her rifle from her back, even as she gritted her teeth and forced herself up to her feet once again, with no less pain than last time. She flipped the weapon to full auto, and her eyes moved to the bot, searching for what seemed the most vulnerable spot. She'd taken one step forward when she heard the captain's voice.

"Hold up, Andi, I've got this." He moved forward, jamming the muzzle of his hypervelocity rifle into a crevice between the two main sections of the thing. He fired, one small burst at a time, perhaps four or five in total, until the bot split in half, as its twin had done.

Add finishing off damaged imperial security bots to the crew's skillset…

Lorillard stared down at the thing, even as Andi did the same, the two of them checking to be sure it was dead. Then, he looked up, his eyes finding his youngest crew member. "These things are tough as hell…" He pulled up his rifle. "Makes this thing almost seem worth the not so small fortune I paid for it."

Chapter Twenty-One

Free Trader Nightrunner
Docked at Imperial Station
Orbiting Zensoria, Osiron VI
Year 301 AC

The soldiers stepped into the corridor, each of them turning and facing a different direction, huge assault rifles held out in front of them. They were big, stocky, but not as large as Tyrell had thought. It was their combat armor bulking them up.

"Drop your weapon. Hands behind your head." The command was simple, to the point. And the tone left little doubt the soldier would blast Tyrell into strawberry jam if he didn't comply at once.

He slid the rifle from his shoulder, letting it drop to the floor. Then he put his hands around his head, clasping his fingers together in the back.

"Pistol and knife, too." The soldier's tone was unchanged, but somehow it seemed even more threatening. After stepping toward the back of the ship and looking around the empty space, the second man returned. He stood there, his rifle pointed at Tyrell.

"Okay, okay...take it easy..." Tyrell moved one hand down from his head, slowly, trying any way he could not to provoke the soldiers. He reached around and unclasped the belt that held both of his remaining weapons. It slid slowly off his waist, and fell to the deck.

The one soldier gestured to the other, a roll of his head. The second man moved forward and collected Tyrell's weapons. He stepped back, setting the two guns and the knife down on the deck behind him.

"How many aboard?" The same tone. The same voice, exactly, though Tyrell could have sworn it had been the other one speaking before.

He felt the urge to lie, to say he was alone. But that would be stupid. There was zero chance the two soldiers would accept his word and not search the ship. Tyrell had no moral problem with lying, not to an enemy especially. But it was stupid telling a lie when you were certain to be caught almost immediately. All he could do was get himself—or Doc—killed.

"One other. Forward, on the bridge." He gestured with his head down the corridor.

"Go, secure the bridge." It was the other soldier again. The two of them were freaking him out. He couldn't tell them apart, and Tyrell had always considered himself an expert at dissecting peoples' words, their affectations. He'd been the best poker player on *Nightrunner* before Andi had arrived, and he could still give her a run for the title.

But these two soldiers sounded like twins. No, more than twins. They sounded *exactly* the same.

"Come." The remaining trooper gestured toward the back of the ship.

Tyrell turned and walked slowly. He was alone with the soldier. If he could jump his captor, take him by surprise…but no, he knew it wouldn't work. The soldier was behind him, a good meter away, his extremely nasty looking rifle aimed right at Tyrell.

He sighed and walked back slowly, sitting in one of the chairs around the large table in the middle of the room. The soldier stood just inside the doorway, his weapon unwavering as it pointed right at Tyrell. A moment later, Doc came in, the second soldier moving behind him, almost exactly as the other had done.

Tyrell glanced at Doc, hoping his expression sent a message to his friend. 'Be cool, wait.' It was all they could do.

"Do not get up, do not move. If you disobey, you will be shot."

A wave of responses shot through Tyrell's mind, smart-assed remarks, claims he had to go to the bathroom, other ideas at trickery. But he held his tongue, saying only, "Understood."

The two soldiers took positions on opposite sides of the table. Then, one at a time, they reached up with one hand, the other remaining on their rifles, and they pulled off their helmets.

The man in the back of the room stood just under two meters, at least in his boots. He had close-cropped, sandy-brown hair, and dark brown eyes.

The other soldier stood a little less than two meters, with short, sandy-colored hair and brown eyes.

Tyrell's head snapped back and forth twice, maybe three times before what he saw really registered.

The two men weren't just similar.

They were *identical.*

* * *

Andi stood, trying to hide the fact that she was breathing deeply, struggling to maintain her calm. Her hands were clenched tightly into fists, but that was because her palms had been shaking. She was loyal to her comrades, she trusted them, as much as she was capable of trusting anyone, but she wasn't about to let them see how unnerved she was.

She'd been in desperate fights before, struggled with all her strength, with her life on the line. But she'd never faced anything like the imperial security robots.

She realized, with a cold certainty, the almost random nature of the crew's survival to that point. If they hadn't brought the two charges, if Yarra or the captain or whoever had added them to the equipment roster hadn't done so, they'd all likely be dead by now. That was what hit her the hardest, the utter randomness of it all. She wished she could say she'd seen the need for the two bombs, save perhaps for getting through a stubborn door. But she hadn't. The things were clunky and heavy, hardly suited for use as weapons. If anyone had asked her, she was pretty sure she'd have said, 'leave the damned things.'

And, yet, they were the very weapons that had saved them. At least for the moment. They were still far from anything remotely resembling safety.

"Everybody in one piece...more or less?" Lorillard had moved toward the middle of the room, or at least to a spot that put him in the center of the assembled crew. The left arm of his tunic was wet and red with blood, and he had cuts and scrapes visible on his face and his hands.

They all knew, 'one piece' was a relative term, and despite an assortment of injuries, they sounded off almost in unison, declaring they were fine.

"We've got to get going, get back to the ship."

The ship. Andi hadn't forgotten, not exactly, but there was noting quite like something a meter or two away trying to kill you to take your mind off other worries.

Nightrunner was armed, and capable of holding its own against most frontier prospecting ships. That didn't address the apparent fact, of course, that there were *two* other vessels out there. Andi didn't trust the station's AI, but then she didn't doubt what it had told them either. And even one on one, *Nightrunner* wasn't going to beat anything out there with just Tyrell and Doc onboard.

She was nauseous thinking about it, imagining getting back to where the ship was—*where it had been*—only to find it gone…or worse.

"Cap, this stuff on these shelves is pretty incredible. High end processors and boards, like nothing I've ever seen." Gregor was turned facing away from the others. He'd pulled the top off of one of the boxes on the shelves.

Lorillard turned in response. "Gregor, we've got more important things to worry about than gathering loot." The captain seemed annoyed, and as Andi listened, she too, felt a flash of anger at her giant comrade. They'd be lucky to get out alive, and even luckier to find the ship, and their two friends there, where they'd left them. How could Gregor be thinking of the haul just then?

"It will only take a minute, Cap…and what if anybody gets hurt, or the ship is damaged? We might not get a chance to get back here, especially if we have to run for it. It's why we came, after all. Why we risked our necks. It's right here. Should we just leave it all?"

Andi's anger dissipated. She wasn't sure how she felt, but Gregor's words made sense to her. They didn't sound at all like the raw greed she'd imagined when he'd first spoken. *Nightrunner*'s crew had some resources, of course, but if they had to deal with injuries and damage to the ship, any proceeds from scavenged electronics would certainly be a welcome addition to the mix.

There was a darker thought as well, one Andi didn't like to consider. If any of the crew were killed, their share from any mission profits might help out any loved ones they left behind. Prospectors weren't generally family types, and Andi knew some of the crew were true loners, save for their comrades on *Nightrunner*. But some of them had ties outside the strange world they occupied at the edge of the Badlands. Sylene had a little brother, at least, one to whom Andi knew she sent money. Tyrell had parents back on whatever world he'd come from, and Jammar, too.

The only one she had no idea at all about was the captain.

"Alright…fill up a couple bags. Take whatever looks best, but do it quickly. You've got two minutes, and then we're out of here.

Gregor nodded, and then he turned toward the shelves, waving for Jammar and Barret to come with him. They all pulled sacks from the small packs they wore. Two of them were moderate in size, but Gregor's was huge. The three of them began filling the bags, grabbing handfuls of sensitive-looking electronics and jamming them inside the bags. There was no time for precision, and imperial old tech was valuable enough even when it was in pieces. Andi had looked on with distaste at first, but then she found herself unable to prevent her mind from guessing at the value of the components.

She didn't have much of a benchmark, not for a haul like this. It was the biggest score she'd seen, and by a huge margin. She hated herself for it, but she couldn't get the thought of what that much money could buy out of her mind. It was stupid, foolish—she knew they were far, far from getting anything at all back and managing to sell it—but she couldn't keep her thoughts from it. She might have given herself a break, acknowledged that her life of grinding poverty had more to do with it than foolishness or lack of focus on the mission. But she didn't.

Andi didn't give breaks, and least of all, to herself.

She almost pulled the extra bag she had in her own pack, and joined her three comrades, but some discipline inside her stopped that cold. She was a fighter, at least she'd been trained in combat by one who had been a true warrior. She would do her best for her comrades in that capacity, not carrying one more bag of loot.

"Alright, let's get moving. Whatever you've got in there will be enough. With any luck, we'll get a chance to come back for more." Andi didn't think Lorillard really believed that last part.

At least, she didn't. They were in big trouble. She realized that, and there wasn't' a doubt in her mind that the captain did, too.

Gregor and the others responded to Lorillard's orders at once, throwing their sacks over their shoulders, and lining up in a rough fashion.

"Everybody, check your weapons, make sure you're ready for whatever comes." Lorillard didn't elaborate, but they all knew there were very likely more than two security bots on the vast station. How many remained operational was more of a guess, but caution was definitely in order. Bots or no bots, there were two other ships in the system, and they could land at any time and board, just as *Nightrunner*'s crew had.

They might have boarded already.

Lorillard didn't say anything else. He just nodded once, and then he went to the doorway and looked out cautiously into the corridor.

Andi watched, suspecting the captain was wondering the same thing she was. What were they going to run into on the way back to the ship? And would their vessel still be there, intact, when they arrived?

Lorillard looked once more in each direction, and then, he waved for the others to follow, and he stepped out, heading back the way they had come.

Back to *Nightrunner.*

Chapter Twenty-Two

Free Trader Nightrunner
Docked at Imperial Station
Orbiting Zensoria, Osiron VI
Year 301 AC

"*Clipper* command, do you read? *Clipper* command, do you read?" The soldier had been sitting at the comm station for half and hour or more. Tyrell had watched, his surprise growing with every passing minute. There was no sign of anger or frustration in the man's voice, despite the seemingly endless wall of static that had responded to his every attempt to contact his superiors.

Tyrell knew the soldier wasn't going to push his signal through. He'd spent an hour trying to reach the rest of *Nightrunner*'s crew, but he'd lost contact almost the instant they'd climbed through the airlock and out into the system. He'd blamed the problem at first, solely on the materials from which the station had been constructed. *Nightrunner* and its crew was no stranger to old imperial tech, and the difficulties modern scanners had in penetrating many of the materials was fairly well known.

But there was something more at work, he knew. *Clipper* hadn't had any problem contacting *Nightrunner* earlier, to issue its threats and command the crew to drop their power output. *Something* had changed. There was more at work than sophisticated ancient materials.

The station was jamming them now.

Tyrell wasn't *Nightrunner*'s greatest tactician, but it didn't take too much analysis to guess that the landing party had done something, triggered some kind of response from the defensive systems within. Was that good or bad? He didn't know, but as he thought about it, he could feel 'good' slipping slowly away as an option. The station was by far the most intact imperial artifact he had ever seen, and the thought of any of its defensive capabilities turned against *Nightrunner* or the landing party left him with a cold feeling inside.

"*Clipper* command, do you read? This is Epsilon-90874D, reporting in, requesting further instructions."

Tyrell had almost tuned the soldier out. After all, how many times could he listen to '*Clipper* command, do you read?' But the soldier's last statement gave him information, at least something new about his captors. They didn't know what to do next. They'd been expecting some kind of orders, but the imperial jamming had prevented those from coming through. That had to be useful, an opportunity. But he couldn't figure out how to exploit it.

He'd spent the entire time since the two soldiers had taken charge of *Nightrunner* trying to devise some way to strike back, to regain control. He looked down at the small set of shackles that tied him to one of the ship's structural supports. The chains were small and light, but he'd taken every chance his captors had given them to test the things with all his strength, to no avail. They were strong. He doubted even Gregor could have broken free of the things.

Doc was also chained to one of the supports, and there was nothing within reach of either of them. Tyrell had more or less come to the conclusion that there was nothing he could do, that retaking *Nightrunner* would have to wait until the rest of the crew returned.

If they returned.

And, if they did, what would happen? His comrades were handy in a fight, but they wouldn't be up against their like, other Badlands prospectors. The guns and armor the soldiers carried were military grade, all the way, and the view he'd gotten of the two to them had left no doubt.

They were Foudre Rouge.

Tyrell didn't know much about the Union's shock troops—save for general knowledge and legends—but he'd never really believed they were clones. At least until an hour before. The two soldiers in *Nightrunner* were exact copies of each other.

They *had* to be Union soldiers. And that meant he—and the rest of his comrades—weren't up against their normal rivals, other prospecting teams.

They were facing Sector Nine out there…and the more he realized that, the more he was certain he *had* to find a way to break out.

Because, otherwise, none of them had a chance in hell of getting home.

* * *

Andi hurriedly scrambled to a halt at the captain's command, wobbling a bit before she righted herself. She was behind Gregor, which meant she couldn't see anything but the vast expanse of his back.

She didn't know what was going on. Lorillard was at the head of the line. He'd been about to climb through the hatch, back out into the first corridor they'd traversed. She'd almost let herself become hopeful they would make it back without incident.

Almost.

Then the captain had ducked back, and snapped off a sharp, "Halt!"

Andi peered around Gregor's bulk, trying to get a

glimpse of something, anything to tell her what was going on. She saw Lorillard pulling the hypervelocity assault rifle off his back.

That told her a lot of what she needed to know, and she followed suit, bringing her own—admittedly less powerful—weapon to bear.

"Who the hell are they, Cap?" It was Anna's voice. She had been second in line, and Andi caught a glimpse of her peering around into corridor.

And instant later, she heard gunfire. Not the loud crack of weapons like her own, but the higher-pitched whine of guns like the captain's. That was a surprise. She'd never seen another civilian with a weapon like that before. They were not only difficult to find, they were massively illegal and incredibly expensive, especially on the black market.

Who the hell would have one of those?

Her palms grew moist, clammy. They were up against an enemy with front line military gear. What the hell was going on?

Then she heard Lorillard, finally answering Anna's question.

"Those are Foudre Rouge," he said. The words hit Andi hard, but even more jarring was the sound of fear in the captain's voice.

"Back, all of you. Now!" Lorillard had turned himself, and he was waving almost frantically, gesturing for them all to head back down the corridor. "Get into the side compartments, and get ready. Get ready to fight!"

Andi had never heard Lorillard as shaken as he sounded just then. She was scared to death, but she was also alert, focused. She could almost feel the adrenalin flooding her bloodstream, and memories of all the training, the practice—the times she'd killed—flowed into her brain. She was ready to face any enemy.

Andi Lafarge didn't back down from a fight.

But Foudre Rouge…

She didn't know much about the Union's clone soldiers, at least not from personal experience. But the Marine had told her about the Foudre Rouge, and that moment had been the only time she'd seen real fear on his face. Her mentor had shared many things with her, spoken of his adventures, his comrades back in the day, the worlds he'd seen.

But he'd only talked about the Union's elite soldiers once in the three years she'd known him, and only then when he'd been in the middle of a particularly bad Blast trip.

Much of what he'd said had been difficult to follow, yells and screams as she'd watched him reliving some past battle. But then he'd calmed some, became more coherent. He'd told her of the deadly warriors, the times he and his Marines had faced them. The Foudre Rouge were clones, he'd said. Everyone had heard that, of course, though she wondered how many truly believed it. She wasn't sure *she* had until the Marine told her.

They were created from over a hundred different cell lines, each one developed for a specific purpose—command, scouting, combat. They were raised from birth in quarantined crèches, conditioned for loyalty to the state, to ignore fear, to follow orders with suicidal disregard for any dangers.

They were trained from childhood. The completed rigid physical development routines, ate fixed diets, learned the use of a dozen different weapons and styles of combat.

Facing them would be nothing like a battle with other frontier adventurers. Their training, physical capabilities, equipment, were all far superior to anything *Nightrunner*'s crew had faced.

But Andi shoved those concerns aside. You didn't always get to choose your battles. There was no way out. The fight was on them. The Foudre Rouge lay between them and escape. They had to kill the enemy, or the enemy would kill them.

That was an easy choice for Andi, if one that left her feeling a bit nauseous.

She turned and raced back the corridor. She'd seen an open compartment not too far back. The hatch was big, large enough for at least two of them to take position. She knew enough from the Marine's training that the positional advantage, at least, lay with them. They'd have time—she hoped—to get into place. Then, the Foudre Rouge would have to advance down the corridor, a tight, confined space, exposed to fire the entire time.

She ducked back into the room, reaching out, grabbing the back of Gregor's tunic and pulling the giant in after her. She didn't want any of her comrades to get caught out in the hallway, but Gregor was the slowest of them all, and he would have been almost impossible for the enemy to miss.

All his great bulk and muscular physique would be just so much raw meat against hypervelocity rounds.

She leaned against the side of the doorway, bringing her rifle to bear, doing all she could to keep as much cover as she could. Her eyes were focused on the end of the corridor. All the others had passed by. She took a quick look behind, just to confirm they'd all gotten into one room or another. She could see the captain, just behind her position, and on the other side of the hall. His rifle was out. It was their best weapon by far, but she wondered how much ammunition he had left. The depleted uranium projectiles weren't that much easier to get than the gun itself. Nor much cheaper.

At least nobody's still out in the corridor.

She swung her head forward again, staring at the corner up ahead with laser-like intensity. It had been some time since she'd been in so intense a combat situation, and she'd never faced an enemy like the one now approaching. She felt a flutter or two in her stomach, but mostly, she was grim, ready. Death had been snapping at her heels her whole life. She still feared it, of course, but not exactly the way most people did.

She waited, concentrating on her breathing, her eyes focused.

Then it happened.

She saw movement, right at the edge of the corner. The soldier didn't swing around and come racing down the corridor. She only saw a thin sliver of his body, mostly his arm, and the side of his head. She almost leaned out to take an aimed shot.

But her instincts told her what was coming.

She jerked herself back inside the room…just in time, as a burst of hypervelocity rounds ripped down the corridor, ten or more of them slamming into the edges of the doorway, right where she'd been a second before.

She was still trying to convince herself she'd avoided any hits when she heard a loud, deep yell behind her.

Gregor!

She spun around, just as her comrade dropped back from the doorway, falling to one knee as he reached out and put his hand on his right arm.

Andi could see the blood spurting all around, seeping out between his fingers as he clasped at the wound. For an instant, she almost panicked, but then she got a better look. It was bad enough—and no doubt painful as hell—but it was survivable. Gregor was tough as nails, and she figured, he'd not only survive the injury, he'd be back in the fight as soon as he managed to get some kind of rag or strap tied around his arm.

She felt the urge to race over and help him, but she knew that was impossible. The two of them were in the forwardmost room, and if Foudre Rouge made it down the corridor and burst inside, they'd both be as good as dead.

She twisted her body, swallowing hard as she swung her rifle around, and leaned out, ever so slightly into the hall. She opened fire, targeting the very edge of the corner, the place where the Foudre Rouge soldier had been seconds before. Her shots were louder, deeper, than the high-pitched hypervelocity rounds.

She caught a glimpse of a shadow, one of the troopers just around the corner, held back by her fire. She was burning through her ammunition, a precious resource that would quickly run out, but if she stopped, the Union soldier would come back around and open fire again himself.

Her mind raced, images of the Marine, talks they'd had in their small hovel, the lessons he'd tried to give her in battle tactics. Andi had always been more interested in learning how to shoot and how to fight. Now, stuck in a stalemate along the corridor, she wished she'd paid more attention to small unit tactics.

She ducked back as her rifle fired the last rounds in the magazine. She popped the clip as quickly as she could, and slammed another one in place, but she knew it wouldn't be fast enough.

She waited for the enemy to open fire again…but there was nothing. For an instant, she felt elation. Maybe she'd caught the Foudre Rouge napping. But she rejected that, almost immediately.

Then she heard the sounds of boots on the deck outside.

A fresh flow of adrenalin filled her with new energy, and even as she swung around, bringing her weapon to bear back in the corridor, she saw the Union soldiers, at least five or six of them, running toward her position. The closest one was no more than two meters away when she opened fire.

Her first shot was on target, but it struck dead center on the man's chest armor. She'd have bet the impact had hurt, but it hadn't penetrated, hadn't stopped the trooper's advance.

She had one last shot, even as the Foudre Rouge soldier brought his own rifle toward her. She knew the clone wasn't going to miss, not at that range. She had two choices, and a fraction of a second to decide. Take that last shot…or duck back, and prepare to defend herself in the compartment.

There was no time for thought, for analysis. It was a decision made on instinct, and almost reflexively, she fired again, this time aiming for the soldier's shoulder, for the gap between the sections of his armor.

The man lurched back, a spray of blood announcing that she'd scored a hit. The clone didn't yell, didn't show any signs of pain, but he fell onto the man behind him, sending a wave of disorder down the small column.

Andi fired again, at the next soldier. Another hit, this time in the leg. She wasn't sure if the shot had penetrated, or if the bullet ricocheted off the armor. The first trooper, now prone in front of her new target, blocked her view.

She ducked back, though whether it had been a response to something she'd seen, or if instinct had just intervened, she didn't know. But the corridor erupted into hypervelocity fire as two or three of the soldiers farther back opened up over the prone forms of their comrades.

Andi turned quickly and looked at Gregor. He returned her gaze, a silent message. He was fine, ready to fight.

She looked all around the room—again—but there was still no real cover. Finally, she moved to the wall next to the door, pressing her back hard against the polished white surface. She gestured for Gregor to do the same on the other side, though his bulk was harder to hide than her lean form.

She set her rifle down—too unwieldy for the close range fighting she expected—and she drew her pistol. She took a deep breath and held it for a few seconds, just as she heard boots outside…one of the Foudre Rouge.

The enemy was on the other side of the wall, ready to burst into the room.

Chapter Twenty-Three

Andi stood next to the doorway, her back pressed hard against the wall. She'd discarded her rifle, and she held her pistol in one hand and her knife in the other. Her heart was pounding, loud and hard, like a drum just inside her ears. She was struggling to keep her hands from shaking as she waited for the enemy she knew was coming.

She stared at the open space, the doorway leading into the room. The Foudre Rouge were no Gut street toughs, no drug racket thugs. They were elite soldiers, trained since birth to fight. They wouldn't make any stupid mistakes or give her any careless openings.

That realization left her unsure what to do. There seemed no way to win the fight, to defeat the adversaries she was facing. All she could do was fight, with everything she had. That had always been enough…though she'd always known someday that rationale would fail her.

She listened. Her ears had always been sensitive, able to pick up the faintest sounds, and the Union soldiers, however capable they were in combat, were clearly not trained for sneaking around quietly. She was sure the first

Foudre Rouge trooper was right outside the door. She'd heard his boots on the deck outside, his breath as he stood just on the other side of the wall from her.

There was nothing, though, no movement, no sign of anything coming through the door, not for a few seconds. The soldier knew she was there, of course. She'd shot one of his comrades. He understood she was a real threat.

She waited, the tension stretching out the passing seconds, the tightness inside her intensifying, the sweat on her forehead sliding down her face. But she didn't move, didn't waver. She barely breathed, waiting for what she knew was coming.

She looked across at Gregor, nodding slightly to her comrade. She wasn't sure he understood her meaning. He wasn't stupid, not by any means, but he wasn't a tactical wizard either. The door was only wide enough for one soldier at a time, and whoever came through first could only focus attention on one side or another.

That meant one of them would have to scramble, do whatever it took to stay alive…and the other would have to strike.

Her stomach tensed, like some giant invisible hand had grabbed it and squeezed hard. She could feel the enemy, sense the air moving as the soldier pushed forward slowly, cautiously. She had an urge to leap out and attack, to try to catch the Foudre Rouge as he was coming through. But she knew she had to stay in place. A desperate, hurriedly-aimed attack was as likely as to result in a shot bouncing ineffectually from the soldier's armor. Her pistol didn't have the hitting power of an assault rifle, and she'd seen the Foudre Rouge protective gear turn away shots from the heavier weapons.

Her shot—or Gregor's—*had* to be precise, targeted at one of the enemy's weak spots.

Or they were both dead.

She brought up her arm, slowly, as quietly as she could,

preparing herself for the fight relentlessly approaching. She did what she could to push away the fear, the voice inside telling her this could be her last fight. She knew that was true, perhaps even probable, but she ignored it anyway.

Then, suddenly, the seeming slow motion all around her erupted into rapid action. The Foudre Rouge soldier moved forward, his assault rifle extended out in front of him. He seemed to be coming straight in—which would have been perfect—but then he turned suddenly, bringing his weapon to bear.

On Gregor.

The giant lurched hard to the side, leaving a spray of blood from his still-untreated shoulder wound as he did. He was fast—for himself at least—but not fast enough. The enemy soldier's rifle came around, tracking Gregor's movement, fixing on the giant's chest.

Two shots, in rapid succession.

But they weren't the high-pitched whine of the Foudre Rouge assault rifles.

Andi stood, out a few centimeters from the wall now, her eyes fixed in a cold stare on her victim. The Union soldier lurched back, as both of Andi's shots struck him, in the vulnerable spot where his breastplate met his heavily-padded legs.

She'd fired from absurdly close range, not more than ten centimeters, but she still wasn't sure, at first, if she managed to really injure the soldier or if the impacts of the shots had merely caused pain and distracted him.

Then, she saw the blood. Not a trickle, nor a small patch slowly expanding, but great gouts pouring out from where her bullets had struck.

The soldier was turning around, bringing his weapon to bear on her…but he never made it. He dropped to one knee, even as he let one hand slip from his rifle to reach back where he'd been shot. The left leg of his uniform was soaked through with blood.

Andi was already moving, trying to position herself away from the shot she expected, even as she aimed the pistol again. Her eyes darted quickly to the door, to the next Foudre Rouge, already coming through. She felt an urge to try to shoot at the second soldier, but the Marine had been clear in his teachings about the need to prioritize threats. The Foudre Rouge coming through was a deadly danger, but the one already in the room, wounded as he was, was the deadlier threat.

Her eyes moved all over his form, looking for another weak spot, someplace she could fire again, even as he raised his own rifle toward her, one handed.

Then she heard a loud crack, and the trooper fell forward, landing right next to her with a sickening thud. She hadn't placed the sound, not at first. It wasn't a gunshot, it was...something else. But it was only when the trooper hit the ground that she saw Gregor standing there, holding his rifle like a club.

The giant had slammed the butt of his weapon down hard, right at the bottom of the soldier's helmet. Andi knew how strong her comrade was, and she imagined the trooper's neck had snapped like a dry twig under that deadly impact.

She felt a rush of exhilaration, and even relief, but she knew it was misplaced. The battle was far from over, and she could see at least two more of the Union soldiers coming through, pushing into the room.

She was away from the wall now, out in the open. Things were going to get ugly, and fast.

She dove across the room, the quick change of direction an attempt to throw off the enemy, to create half a second of confusion. She hit the ground, and managed an almost perfect combat roll—something else the Marine had taught her. She came back up into a prone position, her pistol out in front of her. She fired, three times in rapid succession. Two of the shots ricocheted off the target's armor. The last one drew blood, but she quickly realized it was just a flesh wound.

Then, she saw a blur, Gregor launching himself across the room, slamming into the lead Foudre Rouge trooper. She saw them both move across the room and fall hard, and she winced at the pain she knew her wounded comrade must have felt.

But there was no time for such things. There was another soldier, already in the room. She looked up, her eyes focusing on the enemy's assault rifle, just as he aimed it at her.

She was done. She knew it. There was nowhere to go, no cover, no way out. She'd fought well, but she'd lost.

She heard the sounds of the shots, the strange, high-pitched whine of the hyper-velocity projectiles, and she caught the burnt ozone smell from the weapon.

She was dead, she knew it. She was at most two meters from the Foudre Rouge. The soldier couldn't possibly have missed from that range, and at the speed of those deadly chunks of metal, they would tear her body to bloody chunks.

But she was still there. No pain, nothing.

Just the Union soldier falling, landing face down in front of her, his head surrounded by a rapidly expanding pool of blood.

And the captain standing behind, his rifle in his hands, and his eyes shifting from his clearly dead target to the inside of the room, and his two crew members there.

It was the second time a friend had saved Andi's life.

* * *

"What the hell is going on? They were receiving us before." Gavereaux sat on *Embuscade's* bridge, and he slammed his balled fist down on the armrest of his chair. The Foudre Rouge soldiers *had* to have reached *Nightrunner* at least an

hour before. Most of the others had to be deep inside the
station. He just couldn't understand why he wasn't hearing
from anyone.

Should he blast the ship to plasma? Even if his people
had not successfully taken the ship, any crew members there
should have responded. *Nightrunner*'s crew had yielded
before. Were they up to something now? Should he wait,
send more soldiers…open fire?

Firing would require returning to *Clipper*. He'd taken the
small shuttle over to *Embuscade* when he'd lost his comm
link with the Foudre Rouge gunship. He'd wanted to closely
supervise the effort to secure the station, and he'd left
explicit orders for *Clipper* to do nothing unless *Nightrunner*
broke free of its docking and made a run for it.

In that event, he'd been clear. Destroy them.

"Sir, we're picking up strange energy readings coming
from the station. It's likely that is the source of the jamming.
I can't tell much…the scanners are hardly more operational
than the comm."

"I don't understand. We were able to communicate,
between *Clipper* and *Embuscade* and *Clipper* and *Nightrunner*.
Now, nothing." The station's resistance to any comm or
scanning signals had been frustrating enough, but the active
jamming outside the confines of the great construct was
driving Gavereaux to the edge.

"Perhaps something set off a set of defensive protocols,
sir…and activated the jamming."

Gavereaux shook his head. He was frustrated, incredibly
so. But he was beginning to realize something else. The
degree to which the station was operable was nothing short
of astonishing. He'd known this mission offered him the
chance at tremendous personal gain, but now his mind
began to race. The value of the tech in the station was
beyond appraisal, almost beyond imagining. Once the
research teams got there and really started figuring the thing
out, the change would come quickly. The Union would not

only close the science gap with the hated Confederation, it would massively surpass its rival, and every other nation on the Rim.

It might take five years, even ten, to adapt the technology, and to build enough advanced weapons, but with the secrets inside that station, the Union would likely conquer the Confederation outright, and then the rest of the Rim. Its dominance would be complete, its forces unstoppable.

And he would be at the seat of power, the hero who had brought back the technology of the old empire.

It was heady stuff, and thoughts of such things kept distracting him. He had the resources to deal with a crew of rogue Badlands prospectors, he was sure of that. But he was still nervous. Captain Lorillard was a capable man, one who could be dangerous. He didn't really see how *Nightrunner*'s pack of misfits could deal with twenty Foudre Rouge, plus the rest of his people, but he knew he'd feel better when he'd captured them all. Or put them down.

They had to die, of course, all of them, at least eventually. He couldn't allow even a chance someone could get back to Dannith with word of what they'd found. But until he had a better idea of what was actually inside the massive station, he wanted a few of them alive. They'd been inside longer, and he wanted to know what they had found.

He waited another few minutes, growing even more frustrated as he listened to another call to *Nightrunner* go unanswered. He moved back and forth, restless, anxious. Unsure what to do.

He couldn't just sit there, not any longer. That left two choices.

Open fire, blast *Nightrunner* to plasma. *Which means shuttling back to Clipper with the order…*

Or send more Foudre Rouge to *Nightrunner*, with orders to return and report in person on the status of the prospectors' ship. He only had four of the soldiers left after the two he'd already dispatched to *Nightrunner* and the teams he had sent into the station. If he ordered another pair in, his reserves would be down to two.

He thought about it, even as another attempt to contact *Nightrunner* resulted in nothing but static. He almost decided to head back to *Clipper*—or to send someone else—and order the lasers to open fire. That would kill two of his soldiers, of course, assuming they actually *were* in *Nightrunner* and just cut off by the jamming. But Foudre Rouge were expendable—they were created to be expended—and certainly a few of the clone soldiers were no concern at all in a mission as crucial as this one.

But Lorillard's crew...they know what they're doing...and they're better at handling old tech than anyone I've got...

That was the hard truth, and he knew it. He needed them, for a little longer. He needed them to help secure the station, deal with any still-functional security systems. Then, he could get word back to Montmirail, and urge that reinforcements be dispatched at once to the Osiron system, to the desolate bit of nowhere that had suddenly become the most important place in the galaxy.

Damn...

He turned, frustrated, and he snapped out another order.

"Send two more Foudre Rouge to *Nightrunner*, at once. They are to investigate and return to report the current status."

"Yes, sir."

Gavereaux took a deep breath and tried to remain calm. He had *Nightrunner* under his guns, and he had Foudre Rouge soldiers inside the station. He told himself he had no reason to be overly concerned, nor to be afraid of Lorillard and his pack of pirates.

But he was anyway.

Chapter Twenty-Four

Somewhere Inside Imperial Station
Orbiting Zensoria, Osiron VI
Year 301 AC

"Thanks just doesn't seem like enough, Cap." Andi had managed to control her hyperventilation—barely—but her voice was still a cracking squeak. Danger was one thing, but she'd been less than a second from death.

Probably a lot less. But she didn't think there was much utility in trying to figure how minute a fraction of a second it had been.

"We're a team, Andi. You know that." Lorillard managed a smile, a bit of celebration that he'd saved two of his crew, she suspected. But the tension in his voice told her the complete story. Lorillard was more than concerned or scared. There was something else there.

"What do we do, Cap? Head back to the ship? These sacks of swag are probably worth more than everything we've found in the last five years combined." Gregor was sitting on the floor, next to the body of the Foudre Rouge trooper he'd killed. The Union soldier's head was laying at a grotesque angle, and his helmet had rolled off his head, revealing open, but lifeless, eyes. Anna was crouched down next to Gregor, slicing open the already torn section of his sleeve, trying to get at his wound.

Andi had no doubt what Lorillard's response would be, and she agreed. She was completely onboard with Gregor. They had enough already to make the mission a great success—and they still didn't know the status of *Nightrunner*, or their prospects for getting out of the system. It was time to get the hell out and regroup. They could always come back, possibly with a few other crews, and finish the job.

But Lorillard surprised her.

"No, we can't go. Not yet."

"Captain, seriously? We need to get back, see what's going on with the ship…and we have no idea how many more of these guys are prowling around here. We'll be lucky even to get back to *Nightrunner*." Jammar this time, the words heavy with his thick Physalian accent.

"These are *Foudre Rouge*, Jammar. The Union's elite soldiers." Lorillard's tone was deadly serious, as he pointed toward the corpses. "This is not some other crew trying to horn in on our find. If it was, I'd offer whoever it was a straight out split on all of it. Honestly, we could use the help, and there's plenty to go around. But that's not what we're dealing with here."

Andi listened. She thought she knew where he was going with his words, but she wasn't sure she cared. Sure, the Union was the Confederation's enemy. Everybody knew that, even lost souls in places like the Gut. But, to her, the Confederation had been no friend either. She'd been born in a horrific slum, in a place that was allowed to ignore all the stated ideals Confederation politicians spoke of so passionately—and hypocritically—because it produced massive wealth and production. No one wanted to rock that boat, and if a few million people had to live in misery, well that was a reasonable price to pay to keep the freighters full and running.

Even after she'd escaped the nightmare of the Gut and joined *Nightrunner*'s crew, the Confed navy had been something to avoid, its patrol ships periodically cracking down on prospecting in the Badlands. As far as she was concerned, they all deserved each other.

"I hear you, Cap, but what the hell can we do against Union soldiers…except slip away if we're lucky?" Jammar didn't address the fact that the Union soldiers on the station suggested the ships out there were also Union. Andi had been fixated on reaching *Nightrunner*, and making a run for it, but now the worries about the ship, about what might have happened already, fanned hot.

"We have to do something, Jammar, before we can leave." The rest of the crew were all in the room by then, and Lorillard turned and looked at them all. "We can't allow the Union to gain control of this station, to exploit the technology in here. Have you even considered the implications of a true study of this place, what hundreds, or thousands, of scientists and engineers could do in here? The balance of power on the Rim will be shattered. The Confederation might even be defeated. It might fall."

Andi had been fairly resistant to concerns about the Confederation, but the thought of it falling entirely, of being taken over by the Union, *was* upsetting. She wasn't sure she understood why, at least not completely, but she was sure of it.

"Do you really think the Union would invade, use this technology to completely destroy the Confederation?" Andi had never thought of the Union-Confederation struggle in those terms. She'd always imagined the wars as a fight for border systems, and on the Confederation's part, to regain the eight planets that had been lost in the first conflict, the War of Shame. She had her share of bitterness for the Confederation, but she found the thought of it being *gone* decidedly unsettling.

"The Union's system in based on power, Andi, and nothing but. Every member of their government exists for one reason, to claw and scratch and climb his way to more political power. I know you came from a terrible place, and it's shameful such things exist in the Confederation, but that is *not* how most Confeds live. You've seen that since you escaped. You know it's true. But in the Union, most people live like that, or not far above it. And they exist every day in fear, terrified anything they say or do might bring Sector Nine down on them. Whatever misery you experienced—and whatever anger all of you have at the harassment we've had to deal with—you will never truly know how lucky you were to be born in the Confederation."

Andi shook her head slowly. She respected the captain, and she trusted him as much as she was capable of trusting anyone. But she couldn't think of herself as lucky to be born where she had been, not in the Gut. "I don't know, Cap…I don't know how much worse it could have been."

"You got out, Andi. You found somewhere to go, and you came to us. As bad as things were for you, your chances of doing that in the Union would have been one in a million. It's almost impossible to escape from there." He turned and looked at the others. He was becoming upset, as edgy and uncontrolled as any of them had ever seen him.

"I understand what you are saying, Captain, I do. But how can you be so sure? How can you know so much about the Union, about their soldiers…and Sector Nine?"

Lorillard was silent for a few seconds, and she could see in his face, his thoughts were elsewhere. Then, his eyes moved to her, locking onto her gaze.

"I know, Andi, because I was born in the Union, in a place I suspect was very much like your Gut. I know because my family tried to escape…and I was the only one who made it out. I saw my mother killed, shot down in the street. I ran, even as the Sector Nine operatives caught up with my sisters and my father." He paused, and she could feel the pain in his words, the bitterness in the memories welling up inside him. "I almost stopped, turned and went back…but I was too scared. I managed to get around a corner and sneak down into the sewers. I was down there for months, I don't even know how long, and finally, I worked my way out, stowing away on a freighter. I had a couple of close escapes after that, but I made it. I was that one in a million."

Andi was silent, fighting back tears as she listened. She'd long had a sort of arrogance, she realized, a certainty that she had experienced the worst, come from the most deprived circumstances…endured the most pain. Now, that cold assurance began to crumble.

"I don't know what happened to my father and my two sisters." Lorillard took a ragged breath. "I tell myself they fought, tried to escape, that at least they were killed then and there." Another pause. "I've heard stories about what happens in Sector Nine facilities, the torture, the brutality. I manage to believe they were killed outright, most of the time…but I still wake up some nights, soaked in sweat, the bloodied face of my little sister screaming inside my head."

The room was silent. Andi knew they didn't have time to waste, but she couldn't move, couldn't speak. Not for a moment anyway.

Lorillard's words had hit her hard, both in sympathy for her friend, and in the loss of the self-pity she'd long reserved for herself, the belief that no one had been born into worse circumstances, faced greater hardships than she had.

It made her think of the Confederation in a different way, too. The Gut was an abomination, a shame upon any nation that had such concentrations of filth and human suffering. But Lorillard was right. Andi had seen other parts of the Confederation, now. Dannith was a rundown, unspectacular planet, but its millions enjoyed a standard of living billions of Union workers would envy. Even Port Royal City's Spacer's District, worn and sleazy as it was, lacked the all-encompassing poverty and desolation of the Gut.

Andi had never seen Megara, never visited any of the Core worlds, nor even the more enlightened systems in the Iron Belt. She'd never seen the agricultural planets out near the Far Rim. But despite a few unpleasant encounters with Confederation naval patrols, she had to admit, once she'd escaped from Parsephon, she'd enjoyed a considerable amount of personal freedom...a benefit she suddenly realized was rare and precious in the universe, and something she hadn't fully appreciated.

"Okay, Cap...say you're right. Say we can't leave the place to the Union. How are we going to prevent that? We have no idea how many Union soldiers are wandering around. And, if there are Union ships out there, and if they haven't already blasted *Nightrunner*, what's to stop them from getting word back to their people? For all we know, there's a Union navy taskforce on its way. Even if we escaped, and raced back to Dannith to report this—and assuming the navy took us seriously and didn't just lock us up—there is no way to be sure the Union wouldn't have the place all wrapped up by then."

Lorillard maintained Andi's gaze for a few seconds. Then he sighed and turned toward Sylene. "Sy, any chance you can get back into the data system, activate some kind of defensive response?"

"The main AI is cut off from some of the subsections, Cap, most likely because of severed lines in damaged parts of the station." Sylene pulled out her tablet. "I'll never work my way into the control units in those sections, not in the time we've got...but I may be able to trigger security alerts. If there are functional bots or other defensive systems in this section, the local AIs might just activate them, even without contact from the main AI."

Lorillard looked back at Sylene, and he asked a question, even though the look on his face suggested he already knew the answer. "Can you direct the system to target the Foudre Rouge, and leave us alone?"

Her head was shaking before he'd even finished. "Sorry, Cap…it'd take me months to even find my way around these systems. I don't know the architecture, and I have no idea what internal defenses are programmed into the routines. I'm just planning to make a clumsy attempt to trigger a response, hoping the system will come back with a full-scale sectional alert."

"So, the Foudre Rouge will be dodging security bots and other defensive systems, assuming any remain operational…but so will we?"

"That's about it, Cap. Best I can do…if I can even do that." A pause. "Sorry."

Lorillard sucked in a deep breath. His face was twisted into a frustrated scowl. It was clear he didn't know what to do next.

"Maybe we can destroy it, Captain."

The words had burst out of Andi's mouth, without thought, without the chance to hold them back.

"Destroy what?" Lorillard looked confused, but then, a strange look crept onto his face. Understanding…and shock. "The station? The whole thing?"

A wave of grunts and stunned comments worked its way around the assembled crew. But Lorillard was silent.

"Yes, the whole thing." She turned and looked at her comrades, most of them staring at her like she had three heads. "Why not? What else can we do?" It felt strange, all of a sudden, standing there, awash in a strange way with patriotism, or at least feeling an urgent and unexpected need to help defend the Confederation from the Union. She hardly recognized herself, and from deep within, a part of her looked up, horrified at the very suggestion of destroying something of such unimaginable value. But she remained rigid, determined. "If the Union's out there, they're going to take control anyway…so we're not going to get anything out of this that we can't carry out now."

"But this is an extraordinary find, Andi. It's like nothing

we've seen before. Like nothing anyone has seen, for almost three centuries." Yarra this time, speaking as Andi expected from the gifted—and knowledge hungry—engineer.

"And the value here…even if we can't handle it ourselves, the Confederation authorities would have to reward us for leading them to something like this." Barret turned and looked around at the others, half of whom at least, were nodding their agreement.

Andi was swept up by her sudden realization of just how important the Confederation's survival truly was, but there was enough of a cynic in her to take the other side, too. "They'd have to? Really? You don't think they'd come out here, take control of the place, and still lock our asses in some cell? Even to keep us quiet?" Her conversion to patriot was clearly still an uncomfortable, and somewhat conditional, one.

But it was real.

"Even so, what chance is there of getting back in time, connecting with someone high enough in the command structure, and convincing them to send a force out here…before the Union does the same? They're ahead of us. They've orchestrated this whole thing, even us being here." Andi didn't know that last part for sure, but suddenly it made perfect sense to her. They'd been suckered in from the beginning, sent forward like cannon fodder, to unmask the dangers. "For all we know, they've got half a dozen battleships on the way, maybe one transit away."

She paused for a second. That last comment had even given her a scare.

"There's no way to save the station, and you all know it. We either find a way to destroy it…or we give it to the Union. Assuming we can even get out of here. We don't even know if *Nightrunner* is still there, docked, waiting for us." She held back any references to the ship being destroyed. She tended toward the dark, but even she had some restraint in that direction.

The others began speaking again, one voice over the next. There was more confusion than there had been, but still clearly some resistance to destroying the greatest find ever discovered in the Badlands.

Finally, one voice, loud and clear, cut through the others, silencing them all.

"Andi is right." Lorillard took two steps forward, toward the middle of the room, the others forming a rough circle around their leader. "We can't allow the Union to take control…we can't even allow the possibility of that happening. It's unthinkable." He hesitated, and then he continued, his voice, if anything, deeper, grimmer. "We can leave, but not with this station still here. It is difficult to imagine destroying such a technological wonder, I know, but if we do not, we risk seeing untold billions subjugated as virtual slaves, and what light remains on the Rim extinguished, perhaps forever."

The others were silent as they stood around their leader. Seconds passed, perhaps a minute. Then, Yarra spoke. "You may be right, Captain, but even if you are, how the hell are we going to destroy this thing?"

Chapter Twenty-Five

Somewhere Inside Imperial Station
Orbiting Zensoria, Osiron VI
Year 301 AC

"There it is. At least, that's where I'd say it is." A pause. "Of course, this is all guesswork, Captain. I can't even be sure the files I'm accessing are accurate. I could be pulling up plans of the old commander's vacation house as easily as a schematic of the station." Sylene had been staring at the screen of her tablet for upwards of twenty minutes, while Anna tended Gregor's wound and Andi and Jackal stood guard at the door. Lorillard had spent most of that time pacing back and forth, clearly worried about the time Sylene's research was taking.

"Your guesswork has always been enough for me, Sy…besides, we don't have any other options. We were lucky to get the time we did, but if we stay here much longer, we're not going to get to that location *or* back to the ship. Not with Foudre Rouge out there on top of whatever security systems remain active." Lorillard turned and looked out across the room. "Everything still clear, Andi?"

Andi leaned her head back out one more time, checking in both directions, still as surprised as it seemed Lorillard was that nothing had come their way. "So far, Cap." She

216

stood and listened for a few seconds, but there was nothing. "All clear."

Lorillard turned toward Anna. "How's he doing?" From the time it had taken for her to bandage the wound, combined with the series of grunts and a couple angry yelps, it had been apparent that Gregor's wound was worse than they'd thought, or at least harder to dress.

"Yeah, Cap. He's good to go. I had a hard time digging out the bits of cloth that got jammed in there, and cleaning the thing out, but he's all tied up now, nice and tight."

"*You* had a hard time? I thought I was being interrogated." Gregor was strong, and he had the constitution of a bull, but Andi had always been amused at the giant's fairly low tolerance for pain. He was a reliable comrade, and handy in a fight, but he was also a little bit of a baby. She didn't think he'd have lasted a week in the Gut.

"Alright, let's get ready." Lorillard had, wisely to Andi's view, decided to ignore the interplay between the two of them. "Here's what we're going to do. I think we've got the reactor core location. It's a good bit from here, but accessible." Andi knew that was an overstatement, at least by most accepted definitions of 'accessible.' Lorillard had very little idea what lay between their current location and the reactor core. "There's a big fusion unit down there at the very least, and, more probably, an antimatter system."

Andi knew blowing a fusion reactor wasn't terribly difficult. Any interruption in the magnetic fields containing the reaction—at least one occurring faster than the operating system could respond with a crash shutdown—would release a miniature sun, and turn the station, and anything still docked to it, into plasma and hard radiation.

An antimatter system would be even easier. Just cutting the power to the magnetic bottles holding the precious and volatile substance would do the job. There was no reaction necessary, and even a completely shutdown unit was vulnerable, as long as it had any fuel left. It wouldn't take much antimatter to blast the station to atoms. A kilogram would do the job just fine, and probably a lot less than that.

"Jammar, Jackal, Barret, Anna...you all head back to the ship." Andi caught the cadence in Lorillard's voice as he mentioned the ship, the worry he was trying to hide. Still, she thought it was the right way to go. "Head back to where we *hope* the ship is still docked," wouldn't be the best morale booster just then.

Lorillard glanced over at Gregor. The giant was haggard looking, but Andi knew he still had some fight left in him. Still, the captain finally said, "Gregor, too. Go back with the others, and have Doc take a look at that shoulder."

He turned toward Andi. "You better go back, too, Andi."

The words were like a gut punch. Andi would have been just as happy back on *Nightrunner* heading home on a quiet and uneventful journey. But there was no place safe just then, and she wasn't the sort to shy back from the forward action. She was still on the fence as to whether she cared as much as Lorillard about destroying the station. It seemed like a terrible waste, of technological advancement certainly, but even more important to her, of almost limitless wealth. She'd dreamt of the kind of money and power that would shield her from danger, allow her to live as she wished, to ignore the laws and rules thrust upon her with the blatant disregard of people like the O'Bannons. And the station's vast technology offered just that, and more.

But she trusted Lorillard's judgment, and somewhere a bit deeper, beyond her resentments and the drive to attain great wealth, she understood that the Confederation was a far better alternative to the Union. At some level, she realized that it was unthinkable to allow the Union, with its Foudre Rouge terror troops and its blood-soaked Sector Nine agents and torturers, to gain a massive technological advantage.

"Captain, I think I could..."

"You're the best pilot we've got, Andi...after me, of course." Andi smiled at the brief touch of humor. "You've got to go back, just in case." Lorillard didn't elaborate. He didn't have to. Prowling around, looking for the station's reactor core and rigging it to blow up or malfunction...it didn't make anybody's list of safe endeavors. Andi didn't want to think about losing someone else, and certainly not Lorillard. She didn't want to think about it, but she didn't have a choice. Her rational mind was trying to calculate the odds, and she didn't like any of the results she was coming up with.

"Sy, I know you didn't sign up for the really hardcore stuff, but I don't know what it's going to take to trigger the reactor. It'd sure be a help to be able to access the information systems."

Sylene nodded almost immediately, if a bit nervously. "I'm with you, Cap...but I'm far from sure I'll be able to help. The local system AIs are one thing. The reactor's got to have its own, probably with a ton of security." A pause. "But I know how important this is..."

"Thank you, Sy." Lorillard nodded gently as he spoke. Then he turned toward the others. "Yarra, I could use you, too. No one knows their way around this imperial tech like you do. I'm hesitant to pull you from *Nightrunner*, in case the ship needs repairs..." He paused. Andi had no doubt they all had various nightmare scenarios about what they'd find when they got back to the ship. "...but we just can't leave this station for the Union to gain control."

"Count me in, Cap." There was no hesitation in Yarra's voice, not at first. Then: "Though, I wouldn't exactly say I know my way around imperial tech like *this*." She waved her arms, gesturing all around.

"You're the best we've got, Yarra...and, I'd say, one of the best out there, anywhere. I've been waiting for years for you to come tell me you were leaving because some megacorp waved a huge research job in front of you."

"A desk would drive me crazy, Cap. How could I give up all this…" Again, she waved her arms around her.

"Alright, we've spent enough time here. Let's get going. And watch out. We have no idea what is still operational on this hulk…or how many Foudre Rouge are out there."

* * *

"What the hell is going on in that station?" Gavereaux was angry, frustrated. He had no comm at all, not even to *Nightrunner*—nor the two Foudre Rouge he'd sent to that, presumably captured, ship—and certainly not to any of the parties he'd sent inside. The old imperial material from which the station had been constructed was mysterious, and impenetrable to any of his scanning or communications systems, and that effect was backed up by some seriously high-powered jamming. He'd lost touch with every Foudre Rouge team he'd sent in before they'd gotten twenty meters inside.

There was nothing to do but wait.

"We still have no comm, either into the station, or outside. Scanners are blocked almost at the hull of the artifact, but we retain limited readings out here. Enough to keep watch on *Nightrunner*. For now, at least."

Gavereaux nodded, but the last sentence the agent had added troubled him. It was natural to expect constancy, but now he wondered how long he should wait. He'd had comm outside the station when *Clipper* had first arrived. Then, the jamming had started. Could he lose the scanning capability he still had? He couldn't allow *Nightrunner* to slip away from him. The secrecy of the station, especially keeping word of its location from Confederation authorities, was paramount.

He leaned back in his chair, his eyes fixed on the small display, on the hazy image of Captain Lorillard's ship. He looked over at the numbers on the side, checking the power readings. The scanning capability he had seemed steady.

He turned and looked over at the weapons display. The lasers were fully charged, the fire locks still firm. He looked back at *Nightrunner*, and inside his head, a debate raged.

Lorillard's crew could be useful—very useful—in analyzing the station. They'd be particularly helpful when he got them back to Union space, when proper Sector Nine interrogators got a go at them.

Don't get ahead of yourself…you need to keep this station a secret. That's the first priority, the only one now…

He could hear his own voice, two versions of it, arguing, shouting at each other. Should he wait, be patient? There was no real reason to believe his Foudre Rouge had not taken control of *Nightrunner*. He simply couldn't reach them on the comm, and he was letting it get to him.

The other voice was just as strong, just as relentless. Lorillard was an experienced and capable captain, and his crew were among the best on the Badlands frontier. Underestimating them was asking for trouble. They were potentially valuable, yes, but if he let them get away, escape from the system…

He turned toward the comm station, but he remained silent. If he'd been on *Clipper*, or if he'd had a comm link with the other ship, he'd have given the order he felt floating at the back of his throat.

The command to open fire.

*   *   *

There was another clang on the airlock door, loud, an urgency to its sound. Tyrell looked over. At least he knew what it was. The two soldiers seemed less certain, both gripping their weapons tightly the instant they heard it, exchanging tense glances.

The one Foudre Rouge, the superior—marginally so, at least to Tyrell's observation—moved across the room and aimed his rifle at the hatch. He gestured to the other while snapping out a quick series of commands. It sounded like incoherent babble to Barret, as had most of the interchange between the two soldiers. Barret was no expert on Foudre Rouge, but he thought he'd heard mention before of the secret battle language of the Union's clone soldiers. He'd always thought that was a myth. After all, it sounded made up, and there was no shortage of bizarre legends about the hated Union troopers in Confederation media.

Now, he suspected, he'd just seen hard evidence of its existence.

The second soldier moved up to the door, slowly, cautiously. He was attentive, but Tyrell couldn't read any hint of actual fear. He'd seen tension, caution, focus, in the soldiers holding him captive, but not the slightest inkling of anything resembling actual fear. He'd heard the Union clone soldiers were put through rigorous training from childhood, and that they were conditioned from ear to ear to be obedient and fearless warriors.

Another legend proven correct? He had a hard time imagining any human being not feeling fear...but it definitely looked like the Union fighters had buried it pretty damned deep, if they hadn't eradicated it entirely.

The Foudre Rouge soldier looked at the comm panel for a few seconds, and then he reached out, tapped at the controls.

Nothing.

Barret watched, wondering how much difference there could be between Union and Confederation intercoms. He felt a feeling of superiority, a sense that the Union soldiers were stupid, incapable. Then, he stopped those thoughts cold. He could see—and feel—the competence of the enemy fighters...and the danger they represented.

Then, almost as if to emphasize his realization, the trooper managed to activate the unit.

"Identify." It was short, brusque, just like all the other

mannerisms he'd seen in the Foudre Rouge. He'd always considered them an enemy, at least in a general, quasi-patriotic sense. Now, he understood why they were so feared.

A response came back, the voice hard, cold, the words gibberish. Battle language again.

Tyrell sighed softly. *More Foudre Rouge.* He'd let himself hope the other members of the crew had returned, and it was somewhat of a letdown to realize that, instead of reinforcements, he had more enemy troops to deal with.

It was a relief, too, in its own way. He'd been scared to death at what might happen if the others came back unaware.

The door slid open, and two more of the enemy soldiers came in. Barret had been plotting, trying to convince himself he and Doc had a chance against the two soldiers—assuming, of course, they could get out of their shackles. He'd gamed it out in his head half a dozen times, and every one of them had ended poorly. Against four enemies, it wasn't even worth considering.

The soldiers spoke in their battle language for perhaps another half a minute. Then, they stood rigidly for an instant, exchanging something that looked vaguely like a salute. Then, the two who'd just arrived turned and slipped back out the door.

Tyrell watched, surprised and relieved to see the new arrivals depart so swiftly.

His tactical situation had improved. He was back down to two Foudre Rouge.

And, he was back to plotting desperate ways to strike out, to try to reclaim control of *Nightrunner.*

Chapter Twenty-Six

Somewhere Inside Imperial Station
Orbiting Zensoria, Osiron VI
Year 301 AC

Andi walked down the corridor, far more speedily, perhaps, than caution dictated. She was anxious to get back...and find out just what was going on with *Nightrunner*.

She'd ended up in the front of the small column, and the others had slipped into position behind her. It was nothing she'd ordered or requested, nor anything they'd discussed. She didn't have a leadership slot, certainly nothing official—something she certainly didn't think she rated—but the rest of the crew members seemed content to follow her anyhow. They were all edgy she knew.

At best. At worst, they were terrified.

Maybe it's the calm demeanor you project.

Though, what a load of shit that is...

The truth was, she was as scared as any of them. Terrified for herself, of course, and for those of her comrades following her down the corridor. For the captain, too, and the others with him, deep in the station somewhere, taking a risk so desperate, the mere thought of it made her want to double over and vomit. Scared for *Nightrunner*, too, and what might happen, or have already happened, to the ship.

There was something else, too, something unfamiliar. She was afraid for the Confederation, about what would happen if the Union, already almost twice as large in systems and population, gained the technological edge as well.

She surprised herself at how good an actor she was. *Or how good a liar.* She had managed to keep the fear and the tension from her voice, and she suddenly realized the others were looking to her for strength. She couldn't understand it—she was twenty years old, and for all she'd been through, she didn't know a damned thing about leading people.

She wondered how much of conventional leadership came down in the end, not to some X factor or list of abilities, but rather to the simple ability to bullshit. To lie.

To pretend to be someone you weren't.

Her hands were clasped around her assault rifle. The weapon didn't match the piece of military-grade goodness she'd watched Lorillard use, but it was effective enough in combat.

Just remember, if it comes to a fight, aim for the weak spots in the Foudre Rouge armor…

She'd seen firsthand that the Union breastplates could turn away even a direct hit to the chest from a gun like hers, at least at ranges longer than a meter or two. And, from the looks of the Foudre Rouge, she didn't think giving one of them a second chance was a very good idea.

She took a deep breath and pressed on, moving down the almost featureless corridor. She stopped for an instant and looked up ahead. They were almost back to the ship— at least to where she hoped the ship would still be. There hadn't been any enemy contacts, and she was beginning to allow herself to hope they would make it back without incident.

Then, she froze.

She'd heard something, from behind them. Well down the corridor and around the corner. It was out of sight, and fairly distant, but she knew what it was. She knew immediately.

She would recognize the sound of Foudre Rouge boots on the steel deck until the day she died.

Three of them…maybe four…

"Against the wall, everybody." She turned and whispered the command, gesturing for the benefit of any who couldn't make out her soft-spoken words. "And quiet!"

She pressed her own back against the wall and stayed silent. She was listening, trying with all she had to pick up even the slightest hints at any sounds. She caught the boots again, softer this time, farther. She sighed with relief. She was pretty sure the enemy soldiers were moving away.

Still, she wasn't taking any chances. She thrust her arm out again, waving back toward the wall, signaling her people—and they were behaving just that way, as *her* people—to stay where they were.

She listened again, holding where she was and keeping her comrades in place until two minutes had passed without another sound. Then, she turned and said, "Alright, I think we're clear. Let's get back to *Nightrunner*. Now." The thought in her head—the one she knew was in everybody's head—added a quick, *if it's there*, to what she had said, but she kept that part to herself. They all knew the danger, but there was nothing to be gained by indulging such worries. If *Nightrunner* was gone, or even worse, if the ship had been destroyed, they'd decide what to do then. When they knew.

Endless worries and speculations before then weren't going to accomplish a damned thing…except maybe to dim their focus, get them killed by something they could handle if they were sharp enough.

She moved forward again, cautious as before. The near-encounter with the enemy troops had both pushed her to move faster *and* to be quieter. As before, the two contrary impulses mostly canceled each other out.

There was something else on her mind, however,

something gnawing at her worse than her fears of what lay ahead of them. The best she could place them, the Foudre Rouge she'd heard seemed to be heading in the same direction as the captain and the others. She felt the urge to turn around, to follow, and possibly to engage the enemy soldiers. To keep them from finding the captain, or intercepting his party on their way back.

But she couldn't go back, not yet. She knew Lorillard had entrusted her with getting the rest of the crew back to the ship, and she wasn't going to fail him. They'd been gone for too long anyway. If *Nightrunner was* in some kind of trouble, they had to get there and deal with it.

She was worried about the captain, and Yarra and Sylene too, but the best she could do for them was to make sure the ship was ready to go if—when, she pushed herself to believe—they got back.

She looked down the corridor, and she saw the dark metal of the ship's docking tube hatch. They had made it back, and *Nightrunner* was just where they'd left her. She let the worry and even some of the fear for the captain go for a few seconds, allowing a wave of relief to flow through her.

And then that was gone in an instant.

She saw—something—inside, through the small hyper-plastic window in the hatch.

Something moving.

She couldn't tell what it was. *Maybe it's Tyrell or Doc,* she told herself, but the feeling in her gut made it clear she didn't believe that.

Her hands tightened on the rifle, and she could hear the coarseness of her own breathing as she took one step forward, and then another.

Then, the door began to slide open.

Andi's insides tightened, as though some massive hand had grabbed her body and squeezed. *Maybe it* is *Tyrell or Doc. Maybe they saw us coming, or the scanners managed to penetrate this far down the corridor.* That all sounded good enough, even plausible, but she didn't buy it.

She didn't believe any of it.

She looked around, almost frantically. There was no place in the hallway to hide, nowhere even to grab some cover. If there were hostiles coming through the landing tube just ahead, it was going to be a quick and dirty fight, right out in the open.

She was already bringing her rifle up, her eyes focusing on the sights, as the hatch slid completely open…and a Foudre Rouge trooper stood there ominously, his lateness in bringing his own weapon to bear suggesting he was no less surprised to see Andi and the others, than they were to see him.

Then, everything went to shit.

Fast.

*　*　*

"Sy, when we get there, I need you to figure out the data networks as quickly as possible. My first choice is to do something that way, trigger an error that will cut power to the magnetic fields or something else that causes a critical malfunction."

"Cap…I have to be honest with you, I don't think…"

"I know, Sy…I know. You may not be able to do it, especially not in the few minutes we'll have down there. But, do your best. It's all any of us can do." He turned his head to the other side. "That's where you come in, Yarra. You know your way around reactors a hundred times better than me. If Sy can't do what we need in the software systems, we're going to have to trigger a structural failure. I know we used the two big charges we brought, but we've still got some parts, plus guns, ammo, equipment. Once we find a sensitive point, we're going to have to rig some kind of explosive device powerful enough to get the job done."

"Captain, it could take days to even get a feel for a

system like the one that has to be powering this place. No, not days. Weeks. Months." A pause. "I'm not sure I'll be able to do anything any quicker than Sy can inside the datanets. I'm not sure I'll be able to do anything at all."

"Both of you, I understand. We're up against it on this one…but we can't leave without rigging this thing to self-destruct." He looked at Sylene. "I know you've got family back in the Confederation. Do you want to see Foudre Rouge landing wherever they live, blasting away the Marines and other defenders with unstoppable weapons? Because if the Union gets control of this place, even for long enough to have research teams tear it apart, that's what you'll be looking at. Maybe in five years. Maybe ten. But believe me, I know the mentality of those who run the Union, and if they can get a dominant edge in technology, they *will* use it.

They will use it to turn everyone else on the Rim into their slaves."

"We'll get it done, Cap. Somehow." Yarra nodded as she spoke, as though it helped her believe her own words.

"Yeah…somehow." Sylene sounded no more than half convinced, but that was an improvement.

Lorillard turned back, facing forward, and he continued down the long corridor. He had no hard data on how far they'd come, but a review of Sylene's schematics combined with his own experience, gave him something less than certainty and more than a gut check. Seven hundred meters, maybe eight hundred. They should be close. There was an intersection up ahead, and the corridor to the right should take them to the reactor.

At least if Sylene's data was correct. He trusted her implicitly, but he also knew the task he'd given her had been close to impossible. She'd done the near impossible before, but it was a dangerous thing to count on.

If we fail, we die, and if we die, the Confederation might die, too.

Lorillard knew his people were a band of misfits, that most of them had some level of resentment toward the

Confederation authorities, anger and bitterness that obscured their view of the realities at stake. He'd been born in a totalitarian nightmare, and he'd suffered and fought and sacrificed to escape from it.

He had friends and loved ones who hadn't made it out, who had died trying, or who were still there, living the sustenance level life of a Union peasant or factory worker. He couldn't leave the station to Sector Nine and the Foudre Rouge. He *wouldn't*, whatever it took.

Whatever the sacrifice.

"Cap, I think I hear something…" Yarra stopped and turned around. Then, she said, "Boots, Cap…there's someone coming down the corridor."

Shit.

Lorillard knew whoever, or whatever, it was, the news wasn't good. The only friendlies within a hundred lightyears—and really, the only friendlies anywhere as far as he was concerned—were heading back toward *Nightrunner*.

He'd been concerned about security bots, but the mechanical guardians didn't wear boots. And, that left only one possibility he could think of.

Foudre Rouge.

Chapter Twenty-Seven

Near Free Trader Nightrunner
Inside Imperial Station
Orbiting Zensoria, Osiron VI
Year 301 AC

Andi's finger tightened on the trigger, and her rifle spat forth fire and death. She was the first to shoot, on either side, and she beat her enemy by a good half second or more. But hers was the inferior weapon, and her target was heavily armored, far more protected than she was.

The bullets ripped down the corridor, a cloud of destruction, most of the shots slamming into the Union soldier's breastplate. Chunks of metal ricocheted all around with a series of loud cracks, slamming into the walls and the landing tube door. Andi knew the Foudre Rouge's armor had stopped most of her bullets, but she couldn't tell if any of her shots had actually struck the soldier himself.

Even as she maintained fire, her mind roughly counting down the last couple seconds to the end of her clip, her adversary opened up. Heavy rounds zipped by her, traveling much faster than her own, their sounds higher-pitched, and somehow more terrifying. They slammed into the stark white of the walls, and two or three went by close enough that she could *feel* them.

A few of the shots, the ones hitting on the most direct vectors, cracked the nearly indestructible material of the walls, but most of them came in at sharper angles, and bounced off, continuing on new vectors, with drastically reduced velocities.

It was one of those nearly spent rounds that hit her.

The impact pushed her back, hard enough to upset her balance, and send her stumbling to the ground. Even as she fell, she could see the forward Foudre Rouge trooper down the corridor dropping hard as well, his rifle skittering to the floor, even as his body hit the deck with a loud thud.

Andi lay where she was, feeling around for the wound on her body, the point of impact she couldn't feel, save for a painful bruise on her side. But there was nothing. *That's impossible. Whatever hit you knocked you right off your feet...*

She felt all over, with increasing intensity. Then, her hand moved over her pack. There was something there, hard, metal. *The first aid kit.*

She always carried the med kit in her pack, one of the vestiges that still remained of her rookie status on *Nightrunner.* The small, steel case was dented now, she could feel that through the soft material of her pack. It was a miracle. The Foudre Rouge's bullet would have torn right through the thin metal of the medkit, and into her body, without question...if a full speed shot had hit her.

The wall had saved her, the ricochet. It had slowed the projectile enough. *Perhaps just enough,* she thought with a grimace, as she turned and felt a jolt of pain from the bruise the impact had left.

She was surprised at the inaccuracy of her enemy's fire. That wasn't what she'd been led to expect from Foudre Rouge. Then, she realized. She owed her enemy's poor aim to her own bullet, the one that had taken him down. That half second advantage she'd had, it had been the razor's edge for her. The difference between life and death.

She was still down on the floor, leaning forward,

propping herself up with one arm. Pain radiated out from her side, worse than she'd thought at first. She'd been spared the bullet ripping into her flesh, but the force of the shot had pushed the first aid kit hard into her hip. It was a bad bruise at least, and, she thought as she winced from the pain, maybe a fractured pelvis.

But it was still better than a kill shot to the head.

The air was full of fire in both directions. She heard a thud behind her, but she forced herself to remain focused. She tried to bring her rifle back to bear, but she couldn't manage it. She dropped the weapon and whipped out her pistol. The small gun was weaker than the rifle, and she knew she'd have to put her shot in just the right place to do any real damage to an armored opponent.

She flashed a glance down the corridor. The Foudre Rouge she'd shot was down, not moving. She didn't know if he was dead, but he didn't seem to be an imminent threat, either. The soldier who'd been behind—the only other one she could see—was prone now, on one knee, also apparently wounded—the work of one of her comrades—but still firing.

She heard a shout from behind her, and then a blast of fire that caught the Union soldier in a storm of bullets. His armor turned most of the shots, but at least three of her comrades were firing, plus her with the pistol, and the Foudre Rouge finally succumbed to the storm of bullets and dropped his rifle. He stumbled forward, holding himself up for a few seconds, and then, still in the middle of the fire tearing down the corridor, he fell on his back to the deck, pierced by at least two or three more shots.

Andi gritted her teeth, and she leapt up. The pain was bad, though perhaps a bit less than she'd expected. She stared down the corridor satisfying herself the enemy soldiers were at least out of action. Then, she spun around.

Tears welled up in her eyes almost immediately. Gregor was doubled over, breathing heavily. The already wounded giant had taken another round, this one in the thigh. His hands were down on his leg, trying to hold back the hemorrhaging, but blood spurted out between his fingers, quickly turning his light khaki pants bright red.

But Gregor's wound wasn't the one that gripped Andi's spine and nearly tore her self-control from her.

Anna was on her knees, near the back of the small column. Her arms were out, cradling Jammar's unmoving body. Andi tried to hold onto some hope, even a shred, but one look at her shipmate removed all doubt. Her friend had been hit three times, or four, she couldn't be sure, all in the head. There was nothing left of his face but a grisly mess of blood and shattered bone.

He was dead, there was no doubt. The first of *Nightrunner's* crew to die since she'd joined the ship.

And only the second one ever. She'd heard stories about Cara, a few times at least, when the crew was in a particularly somber mood, about how she had died. But she hadn't known Cara, and as much as she empathized with the pain the others still felt at the loss, she'd never been able to drum up much emotion for someone she'd never known. Her closest affiliation with *Nightrunner's* lost soul had been discomfort with the way the others had said things like, 'she's in Cara's bunk,' or 'she can stow her gear in Cara's locker.'

Mercifully, such things had stopped quickly, and as the crew had accepted her, they'd stopped making those kinds of remarks. Now she had her own pain of the *Nightrunner* family's loss, fresh, biting.

Jammar was her comrade, her shipmate, her friend. She looked down at him, for as long as she could bear, and then she averted her gaze from the wreckage of his face, locking eyes with Anna for an instant. The woman was still cradling Jammar's body, tears pouring down her face now. Andi's sadness fed off the sight of her friend's crying, as well as the image of her dead comrade, and the water welled up in her own eyes. It poured out, first one long streak rolling down her face, and then a dam breaking, almost as if some part of her thought tears might wash away the sadness. She detested displaying weakness, but in that moment, she was helpless to stop it.

There was rage, too. She was going to gut the next Foudre Rouge she saw, and she was going to watch the bastard die. Whatever it took.

She didn't know when that would be as she made the silent oath to herself, but in the end, she only had to wait a minute, maybe less.

She shook off the despair and stood up, grabbing her rifle as she did. She pushed thoughts of Jammer away. There was no time, not now. The two Foudre Rouge her people had fought had come out of the ship.

She knew what that meant, and what it might mean for the two crew members they'd left behind. She *had* to get into the ship immediately, had to see if Doc and Tyrell were alive or dead.

And, she had to kill any more damned Foudre Rouge who were in there.

She pushed forward, her heart beating like a drum, through the open hatch and down the tube. She stumbled in on the pliable material of the tube's 'floor,' and she pulled one hand from her rifle to reach out to the side wall and steady herself. She wobbled a bit, but she held her balance, enough, and she made her way down toward the familiar dark gray of *Nightrunner*'s airlock hatch.

She'd forgotten all aspects of leadership that had been passing through her mind, and she barely noticed as her friends followed her in.

She was driven just then by anger, by hatred. By the need to kill.

Andi Lafarge hadn't spent a lot of time on inner reflection, on wondering who she truly was. But it didn't take too much of that to come to one realization.

She had one hell of a nasty temper.

Just as she reached the inner door, it opened...and another Foudre Rouge trooper stood there, staring right at her.

She was two meters away, perhaps less. She almost brought her rifle up, but then something inside her took hold. There wasn't time for that. She launched herself right into the Union soldier, hitting him in the midsection before he could bring his own weapon to bear.

Andi felt a wave of pain as her shoulder rammed into the Foudre Rouge's hard, armored breastplate. Her enemy had been caught somewhat by surprise, and the force of her impact cost him his balance. He fell over backwards, Andi coming down on top of him as they both went down.

Even as she was falling, her mind was racing, her hand moving to her side, pulling her blade from its sheath. Her enemy was armored, proof against even the sharpest knife over most of his body. But even high-tech armor had its weak spots, the areas where protection had been sacrificed to mobility. She sucked in a deep breath and jammed the blade hard, aiming for the soldier's side, for the narrow line where the breastplate met the top of the thigh armor.

She felt resistance as her blow hit, and for a fleeting instant, she thought she had missed her mark, that her killing strike would bounce harmlessly off the armor.

But then, she felt the razor-sharp blade cutting through something softer...and then she felt warm wetness on her hand.

She jerked hard, driven forward by the feel of her enemy's blood, cutting with the knife, driving it deeper, struggling with all her strength to slice open his stricken body.

To gut him like a fish.

She was still cutting and stabbing when she realized her enemy had stopped struggling. She pushed herself back, and scrambled back to her feet. She was wobbly, dizzy, and the bruise on her thigh hurt like hell. But as she looked down, she realized immediately, the soldier was dead. She had killed her enemy—again—and she felt exhilaration.

For a second.

Then thoughts of Jammer came flooding back, the words of the oath she'd sworn to herself, and carried out almost immediately. And no more than a second later, she saw another figure standing just inside the airlock, at the edge of *Nightrunner*'s wardroom, staring right at her. Another Foudre Rouge.

He held a rifle, and it was moving it up, pointing right at her head.

Chapter Twenty-Eight

Reactor Core, Imperial Station
Orbiting Zensoria, Osiron VI
Year 301 AC

"This is definitely it, Cap. I can't say I understand much of this, at least at first glance, but I can tell you without any doubt...this *is* an antimatter reactor." Yarra stood, and despite the fatigue, the fear, the desperation, she was clearly mesmerized by the technology she saw in front of her.

The room was a marvel, enormous and full of all sorts of incredibly advanced technology. There were devices and stations that defied Lorillard's efforts at identification, and even the things that looked more or less normal had a...difference...to them. And everything was spotless, gleaming and looking like it was all brand new.

Lorillard stood behind Yarra, looking around with a good deal more confusion in his expression. There were three large cylinders down at the far end of the vast room, the biggest structures by far. The whole place felt a little strange, almost a tingle in the air. He tried to decide if he was just imagining that or if it was some kind of energy or radiation, but in the end, he came up with a coin toss.

He flashed a glance back to Sylene, who was edgily standing guard at the door they'd used to enter. She was the least likely choice for guard duty, not only among the three of them, but also the entire crew. But Lorillard had wanted to get a quick look himself, and he'd left her to keep watch. He'd hoped Sylene would be able to hack into the control system, but she'd run into a wall almost immediately.

They'd run into one security bot on the way. They'd escaped without injury, thanks to a lucky shot by Yarra, but the bot's appearance shattered the fragile hope that the station's defensive system was out of operational units. Lorillard had allowed himself to hope for a safe and quiet trip back to the ship, but he had a strange feeling in his gut. He wasn't sure what it was, nerves, fear, intuition, but he was sure something was going to go wrong. He'd always gone into missions cautiously, but the sense of doom clouding his mind just then was something new.

He turned back and looked down to the far end of the room. It was at least three hundred meters long, and maybe a lot more. Lorillard had never had a particularly good sense for judging distances by eye. "Those tanks…" He reached out and pointed toward the closest one, a perfectly circular construction, bright silver without a mark on it, nor even any signs of dirt or age. It looked like it had just been dropped there, though Lorillard knew the thing had been in place for centuries. "…they hold antimatter?"

"Yes."

Lorillard hadn't expected so direct an answer.

"There are magnetic fields inside, confining the antimatter, keeping it from contact with any matter."

"Any matter at all? Is that even possible?"

"We've got…I mean the Confederation has…limited quantities of antimatter stored in similar fashion. Storage is a problem, of course, but the biggest thing preventing the use of antimatter for power generation on the Rim is the cost of production. It's temperamental stuff, no doubt, but if we had the technology to produce the material in large qualities at a reasonable cost, I suspect we could manage the rest of it." She paused and gestured toward the tanks. "I'm only guessing at how those operate, but the few specs I've read from Confederation research projects call for the energy created by leakage, and subsequent annihilation of escaping particles, to be funneled back into the maintenance of the magnetic fields."

"So, you think those things basically sustain themselves?"

"Well, something like that. The reclaimed leakage in Confed units doesn't produce enough energy by itself, but the idea—and I'm not sure if it's ever been implemented on any Confed systems—is to supplement the leakage with low level reactor function. So, in theory, the storage facilities are not relying on any outside energy sources. As long as there is antimatter in the tanks—and they continue functioning— the fields are maintained. Considering the consequences of even the briefest power failure, that makes a lot of sense, of course."

"How long can that last? These things are centuries old, and if one of them had failed, even for an instant, this place would be long gone, no?"

"That's true, Cap. From what I know, one of the hurdles, other than production of antimatter, is attaining success rates high enough to work in a situation where even the slightest blip will destroy the entire system. I'm sure there are multiple layers to these setups…systems and backup systems. For example, a million to one chance of failure backed up by a million to one backstop, is a trillion to one. I'm not sure what parameters were standard in imperial days, but considering these things are three hundred years old—minimum—and they look like they were just unpacked from a freighter, I'd say they were pretty tight."

"And, that's what we've got to overcome. We've got to create that failure that layers of old imperial tech were designed to stop."

"Cap…this is amazing. Research here could advance our science by centuries. Destroying it…"

"I don't like it any better than you, Yarra." Lorillard
knew where she'd been going. His own mind was already
there. "But that's not one of the choices. We either destroy
this thing, and all the tech on it, or we let the Union take
control. You can guarantee they've got ships on their way
now, and all we can do if we leave is try to convince the
authorities we're not crazy. By the time the navy sends any
real forces out there, the Union will have this whole system
fortified, and garrisoned with their ships. The amazing
advancements you see…they will get them, not us, not the
Confederation. And they will use them against us." He
paused, and he looked down at the deck. "They will use
them to conquer the Rim.' Another pause. "No, there is no
other way. We *have* to destroy all this, and we have to do it
now."

He glanced back toward Sylene. Everything seemed
quiet, but he couldn't help but feel like they were already on
borrowed time.

"Check these systems out, will you? Figure out how we
can rig them to fail. There's no choice." He stared silently at
her, and he added, "You know it, too, Yarra. You know we
have to do it."

The engineer looked back, seeming for a moment like
she might argue. But she just nodded, and Lorillard felt the
realization, the capitulation she was feeling.

"Okay, Cap, but I'm not sure what I'll be able to do.
Blowing up those tanks would do it, but I can't even begin
to guess what kind of charge that would take. We've got
some components. I might be able to put together some
kind of bomb…but it's going to be a guess as to whether it's
powerful enough."

"Do it." Lorillard nodded as he spoke. Then, he turned
toward Sylene. "Sy, come over here and try again, see what
you can do with these data systems. I'll stand guard."

Lorillard was the commander, the leader…but he knew
he was damned close to useless just then, save for holding a

gun at the door.

Sylene nodded. "Sure thing, Cap." He could tell from her voice she was no more optimistic than Yarra about tackling the sophisticated imperial tech. Still, she didn't argue with him. She just turned and walked over, and she stood in place for a long while, her eyes moving over the workstations and the displays.

Lorillard walked the rest of the way to the door, and he positioned himself behind the wall, just enough of him leaning in the open to keep an eye on the corridor. There was nothing, no sounds, no signs at all of any enemies. But, somehow, he knew trouble was coming. He was as sure of it as he'd ever been of anything.

He just hoped Yarra and Sy could get something figured out, and rigged up, before whatever was coming hit the fan.

*　*　*

Andi stared at her death. She'd had close scrapes before, desperate escapes, but this time she knew she was finished. She could see the enemy's rifle, follow as it completed its movement, the Foudre Rouge locking on to her. There was no way out, no move she could make, no way to evade, not at so close a range.

She wasn't the sort to give up, though, not ever, and she raced to bring her own gun to bear, ready to fight to the very end. If she had to die, it would not be meekly yielding. Still, she was behind her adversary, too late to save the situation.

The struggle with the first trooper had taken too long, or perhaps she had wasted a crucial half second celebrating her kill. Either way, she stared at her killer, knowing with cold certainty, she was as good as dead.

But the Foudre Rouge didn't fire. He just stood where he was, for perhaps a second, even as Andi held her own fire. Then her adversary stumbled forward a few steps.

She saw Tyrell standing behind him, the remains of a shattered chair in his hands. He was twisted out in a strange pose, and she wondered if he was wounded. Then, she realized he was shackled to the table. She wasn't even sure how he'd managed to reach out far enough to attack the Union soldier…but he had.

And he'd saved her life doing it.

The Foudre Rouge troopers had armor protecting their backs and helmets covering most of their heads and the backs of their necks. But it was clear, if only from the tinge of red she could see on the bent shards of the metal chair remaining in Tyrell's hands, that he had managed to land his blow right between helmet and armor.

Her eyes darted to the side, and her body leapt into action, without conscious direction. It was instinct, almost one hundred percent, but she knew the enemy was still alive. Tyrell's blow had distracted him, and probably injured him, but he wasn't dead.

He wasn't out of action either. She had a few seconds, but if she wasted them, she'd throw the chance her shipmate gave her away. The injured enemy could still kill all of them.

The Union soldier spun around to the rear, a reaction, Andi figured, to the attack. Tyrell was already lunging back, ducking for cover the best he could behind the table. The Foudre Rouge had held onto his rifle, and he opened fire. Andi saw a round catch her shipmate in the leg, just as he was diving behind what skimpy protection the table offered.

She stayed focused, pulling up her own rifle, bringing it to bear. She was less than two meters away, close enough, she wagered with herself, that even her less powerful rounds would rip through her enemy's armor. No need to hunt for seams and weak spots.

Not from a meter away.

Her clip was low, she knew, no more than five or six shots left. She had to make them count. She could hear the others coming through behind her, her comrades, no doubt rushing to join the fight. But she knew they would be too late. The struggle was down to the Foudre Rouge and her, and only one of them could survive. Even as that realization flashed through her mind, she could see the enemy starting to turn back toward her.

Should she try to disable him, capture him? Was there information he could provide? She suspected it would be extraordinarily difficult to break a Foudre Rouge soldier—though she fancied she could do it—not to mention to subdue and capture one. But there was no question. He *would* be a valuable prisoner, especially considering all the unanswered questions they faced.

She decided. She should injure him, try to take him captive.

Then, she emptied her rifle into the center of his breastplate anyway, confirming her belief that the rounds would penetrate at such short range. Blood welled up from the gaping holes in the soldier's armor, and he fell back almost immediately. She leaned forward and looked, but she knew already with almost total certainty.

He was dead.

So much for taking a prisoner…

Chapter Twenty-Nine

Somewhere Inside Imperial Station
Orbiting Zensoria, Osiron VI
Year 301 AC

"No, Andi...you can't go back there. Not alone." Anna was standing in front of her, making an impassioned plea. *Nightrunner's* crew had no ranks, no established hierarchy save that the captain was their leader. But since the landing party had returned, and even during the trip back, they'd all been deferring to Andi's decisions.

Even Anna's objections to her leaving the ship were efforts to convince her, and not any attempt o impose seniority or majority rule on her actions.

"I have to go, Anna. The captain and the others are there. They've got to know there are more Foudre Rouge out there. There are only three of them..." Andi didn't mention that Sylene and Yarra were probably the two weakest members of the crew in a fight. Captain Lorillard could take care of himself pretty well, but the party as a whole hadn't been formed for battle.

"Just you? If they're in trouble, we all should go." It was clear from her tone, the idea scared her to death. But Andi didn't doubt Anna would go along with her.

"Who? Gregor?" The giant was twice wounded, and

even as they spoke, Doc was still working on him, an effort set to an almost musical score of the big man yelping in pain and shouting at his caretaker.

"Tyrell's hurt." She paused, and then continued, her voice soft, somber. "Jammar's dead."

There was a moment of silence, as they both stared down at the deck. Then, Andi continued. "Yarra's out there with the Cap, which means you and Barret are the closest we've got to anyone who can get the ship ready to blast." She didn't mention the fact that *Nightrunner* was under the guns of one of the Union ships, and likely trapped where she was...or, at least, left with no options save a desperate and dangerous escape attempt. That didn't matter. Everything she was saying was true. Still, there was dishonesty to it all. Her motivation had little enough to do with such concerns, and more with her desire to keep the rest of her comrades safe. She was ready to rush back into the depths of the station in a desperate attempt to help the captain and Yarra and Sylene, to take whatever risks that entailed...but she wasn't ready to let any of her other shipmates go with her.

"I'll go with you, then. Barret can prep the ship without me."

Andi held back a sigh. Anna had always been reasonably handy in a fight. But she was also the closest thing *Nightrunner* had to a pilot with both the captain and her gone. "You need to preflight the ship, and get her ready to go as soon as I get back." *And to fly her out of here if I don't get back...*

How the hell am I going to tell them to leave if we don't return by some time or another?

Even bringing that up would start a new debate about the others coming with her. She couldn't discuss that with them.

She wasn't going to bring it up. She'd leave an alert on the AI instead, set for two hours after she left. If she wasn't back by then, the chances were, she wasn't coming back.

"Do you trust me, Anna?" The words blurt out of her mouth, a sudden idea of how to get her friends to do what she wanted. "Do you, all of you?" She turned and looked at the others in the wardroom.

She got a wave of responses, nods, and quiet acknowledgements. She knew they trusted her, that they respected her abilities and judgment.

"Then, please, listen to me. I can go in faster by myself, try to get the captain and the others. I'll bring extra ammo and a medkit. And, I'll get back here as quickly as possible."

She turned and walked over to the storage locker, pulling out a large sack, and filling it with clips, and the smaller of the two medkits on the shelf.

Then, she walked back to her quarters for a minute, the only place on the ship where she could get a moment's privacy, enough time to program the AI to tell them all to leave. She kept it short and simple, fighting the urge to leave individual messages to each of them. She just didn't have the time.

She stood up, took a deep breath and tried to push the fear from her face. Then, she walked out into the narrow corridor, and back into the wardroom.

"Okay, you all know what to do. I'll be back, and I'll bring the others with me." She wished she felt as confident about that as she'd managed to sound.

There were some uncomfortable looks, and she could feel more than one of them teetering on the edge of arguing with her. She had to go, before any of them pushed through the uncertainty and decided to follow after her.

She stepped into the airlock, and out into the damaged—but still functional tube. She worked her way through, almost losing her footing a couple times, and she jumped out into the corridor inside the station. The first place she'd seen when the landing party had first set out, so many hours before.

The place she'd battled her way back to *Nightrunner*.

Where Jammar had died.

There was no time for any of that, not now. She had to find the captain and the others.

* * *

"I think we may have something, Cap."

Lorillard was standing next to the doorway, his rifle out and at the ready. He'd heard something, a few sounds from far down the corridor. He didn't know what it was, or how much of an imminent danger it represented, but he hadn't told the others. He hated himself for hiding it, but he needed them focused. His entire crew, save for himself, had been born in the Confederation, into various circumstances, certainly, but still within the borders of the most enlightened nation on the Rim. He'd been born in the Union, and he knew in a way the others never truly could, just how vital it was to keep the enemy forces from harvesting the technology in the station.

"What is it?" He turned and glanced over at Sylene. *Nightrunner*'s computer expert had walked about halfway toward the door before she'd spoken.

"Yarra's working on a bomb. It's a dicey thing, but she's pretty sure it will work, and also that it's strong enough to knock the containment out of one of those cylinders."

Lorillard didn't know if that was true or not—though he was inclined to believe his engineer when she said something—but he was absolutely sure any breach in magnetic containment, on any of the tanks in the room, would reduce the station to atoms.

"How long?"

"Half an hour? Maybe forty minutes?"

"Faster would be better." Lorillard couldn't hear the sounds anymore, but he figured they were likely running out of time.

"We'll try, Cap. I think I can rig a timed detonator from scraps of what we've got in our packs. It won't be sophisticated, but I'm pretty sure it will work."

"Then don't waste time explaining to me. Go get it done." The words were a little more strident than he'd intended, but he wanted to get her farther from the door. Worrying about what was out there—and there weren't many good options—wasn't going to do anything to speed her work.

She nodded and went back to the other side of the room. He watched for a moment, his eyes moving from Sylene to Yarra. The engineer was hunched over, surrounded by bits and pieces of equipment from their packs. He shook his head slightly, struggling to believe something so important had come down to cobbling together a device as crude as a patchwork bomb. They could have brought any number of professionally-manufactured explosives, but such devices were the last things he'd have expected to need. They had come to salvage, to recover…not to destroy. Lorillard was an old space hand, molded and scarred by years in the deeps, but he'd never ceased to be amazed at fortune's unpredictability.

He was tense, scared of course, not only for himself, but even more because he'd brought two of his people this far in, put them at such great risk. But he knew there had been no choice, even that, if the price to destroy the station was all of their deaths, he would accept that cost. The Confederation had given him a life, one he could never have had in the Union. He simply couldn't let it fall, nor even seriously risk such a disastrous development.

No cost was too high to pay.

He turned back, peering around the edge of the opening, looking for anything. Movement, shadows, more sounds. But there was nothing, at least nothing he could detect.

But they weren't alone. He knew that. And his gut had rarely been wrong.

* * *

Andi's finger tightened, and the assault rifle opened up, firing at full auto. She'd resupplied herself on *Nightrunner*, but she was still hesitant to burn too quickly through her ammo. Such concerns didn't matter, though, not just then. The two Foudre Rouge were just ahead of her. She'd heard them, tracked them, moved slowly up behind…and then one of them turned.

She had seconds. Not even seconds. Just an instant. Then, the two soldiers in front of her would open up and the torrent of bullets would tear her body to shreds.

She felt the urge to look behind her. She'd been pretty sure she'd heard something coming up as well, from the sound of it, probably another security bot. She thought she'd eluded it, but she had no question the sound of the fire would bring it quickly.

The bot wasn't a major concern, of course, not if the Foudre Rouge cut her down in the next two seconds.

Her fire felt rushed, erratic, but then she could see that even her gut instincts had become attuned to fighting the heavily armored enemy. She was close—maybe ten meters or so—and her rounds ripped through the gap between the rear soldier's chest and backplate, and his leg armor. At least half a dozen shots had connected, and maybe more, and the Foudre Rouge dropped hard, blood spraying out all around.

One down…

The second trooper was almost around, his rifle moving toward her. She fired again, five or six more shots, and then her clip ran dry.

The bullets ricocheted off the Foudre Rouge's armor. The soldier's movement and Andi's rushed aiming had combined to deny her a repeat of the first attack's success. Even as her enemy prepared to fire, her legs acted on their own, lunging hard to the side, sending her diving through an open hatchway just to her right.

It was fortune as much as anything that had positioned her next to a compartment when the enemy heard her, and she had pushed off as hard as she could, knowing each fraction of a second could be the difference between life and death.

She hit the ground—hard—and she felt pain radiating through her body. Her hip, not broken as she had earlier feared, but pretty banged up nevertheless, hurt like hell, and her knees slammed hard onto the steel floor.

She arched her back, struggling to flip herself around, even as she reached for another clip. It was a clumsy maneuver, and her fingers almost lost the small cartridge. But she pulled it loose and slammed it in place, even as she brought the weapon to bear on the doorway. She was in the open, and the enemy trooper would likely stay behind the wall, in cover. There was a word to describe her chances.

Shit.

She knew the Foudre Rouge would be there any second, and she waited, determined to take her best shot. She *had* to take out the trooper, somehow. Even if he shot her too, if she died right there, maybe killing her adversary would open the way for the captain and the others to get back.

Andi was no selfless paragon. She wanted to live. Badly. But she knew the difference between dying for nothing and dying for something.

And saving three of her friends was definitely something.

But the trooper didn't come into the room after her. She was confused for a few seconds, and then she heard it. Gunfire out in the corridor…coming from both directions.

Her first thought was that one of her comrades had followed her despite her best efforts. But the sound of the weapon was wrong. It was higher-pitched, more so even than Lorillard's gun or the weapons of the Foudre Rouge.

And the rate of fire was higher.

Suddenly, she knew.

It had been the security bot…it had caught up to her.

More accurately, she had led it to the Foudre Rouge, which it seemed to regard as just as much an enemy as it did her.

It was good news. It had saved her life.

It's also going to kill me in a few seconds, unless…

She reached inside her bag, pulling out one of the grenades she'd grabbed from *Nightrunner*'s weapons locker. They were strong, frags with enough power—maybe—to take down one of the station security bots.

She had no certainty there was only one out there, nor sure the grenade would get the job done, but it was a damned sight better option than lying there waiting for the thing to find her.

She forced herself to her feet. She was wobbly, weak, but she pushed on. If the bot hadn't detected her before, it couldn't have missed the sounds of her climbing to her feet. She lurched toward the door, planning on leaping out into the corridor, but then she stopped, and her eyes focused on the opening.

She would wait, and try to catch the thing as it entered the room. It would have to find her, lock on to her. She just might have a chance.

She waited, breathing once, then twice.

And then it was there. Just like the units she'd seen earlier, but in far better condition. A hundred thoughts ripped through her mind in a wild torrent, but she ignored them all. She just hurled the grenade, almost without a thought, and then she dove to the side, throwing her hands over the back of her head to shield her from the blast.

Chapter Thirty

Somewhere Inside Imperial Station
Orbiting Zensoria, Osiron VI
Year 301 AC

Lorillard's rifle snapped up. He'd heard something this time, for sure. Gunfire, a good distance away…sounding very much like some kind of exchange. He felt the urge to run down the corridor, to investigate, and he took a step forward to do just that.

Who the hell could be fighting down there?

He stopped abruptly as he saw shadows extending from around the far corner.

He knew what they were immediately, and he ducked back, taking as much cover as he could behind the doorway.

Foudre Rouge.

His blood ran cold. To the Confeds in his crew, the Union soldiers were terrifying enough, but Lorillard had seen them in action, not against similarly-armed Confed Marines in pitched battles, but shooting down rioting crowds, smashing open doors, hauling away prisoners who were never seen again.

They were merciless killing machines, utterly obedient to their masters, trained from birth for combat. The perfect warrior to form the steel fist of a brutal totalitarian regime.

He had a fear for them no one else on *Nightrunner* could understand.

And now they were coming. Coming for him, and for his people. It took all he had to hold back the panic, to control the shivering his fear was trying to unleash.

He turned his head abruptly. "We're out of time! Whatever you've got, it's going to have to work." Even as he said it, he knew what he was really telling them.

'You're going to die in a few minutes, so rig this place to blow before that happens.'

He hated that he was giving up on his people, accepting that they were going to die there with him. But there was no way they were getting past the Foudre Rouge. He might take down one, with a massive assist from luck, maybe even two.

But he could hear then approaching now, and he figured from the sounds, there were four at least.

That meant the fight was hopeless. The only thing his people could do was to blow the station while they could.

If they could. He had no idea if Yarra's bomb was ready.

"I need a few more minutes, Cap." He could hear the tension, the near-panic in the engineer's voice.

"We don't have it, Yarra."

"We'd better get it then, Cap…'cause this thing ain't gonna blow, not yet. I've got to set the detonator into the explosive. Two minutes. Get me two minutes."

He nodded, a pointless gesture since he was facing the other direction, and he suspected her eyes were focused on her work. He didn't know if he could get those two minutes, but he was damned sure going to try.

He stared down the corridor, trying to focus, to aim for the spot where the enemy troopers would emerge. He had to get the first one, at least, take some advantage from whatever facsimile of surprise he would have. But even as he tried to clear his mind, a thought wandered in. He wondered if Yarra had realized yet, that they were all dead, that she was rigging that bomb to blow up herself as well as the station.

Another second passed, perhaps two. Then he saw it. The slightest movement, nothing more than a helmeted head peering around the corner. He knew the shot would be difficult, that it would require almost perfect aim.

He fired, without delay, even without thought, a burst of three rounds. For an instant, he wasn't sure if he'd hit his target or not. The head had jerked back out of sight…but then an instant later, the Foudre Rouge fell forward, into the corridor, trailing a spray of bright red blood.

Lorillard felt a rush of exhilaration, but there was no confidence accompanying it. He'd managed a head shot— the enemy's head was all he'd had in his field of view—but he couldn't be sure the soldier was dead. He fired again, two more bursts, this time hitting the still target three or four times.

Even as he finished off the first soldier, another one popped around the corner. He heard the high-pitch of the enemy's weapon, similar to the sound of his own. The hypersonic rounds ripped down the corridor faster than his eyes could track, even than his mind could imagine. He was jerking back, trying to dodge the enemy's fire, but he wasn't quick enough.

For a second, he thought his arm had been torn clean off. But a quick glance confirmed the appendage, badly torn apart, was at least still there.

He stumbled backwards from the door, somehow maintaining enough control to push himself away from the opening, out of the enemy's direct line of sight.

He dropped to one knee, letting the rifle drop at his side, as his hand swung around, reaching out, trying to staunch the flow of blood from his ruined arm.

No…you can't give up…you need another minute at least. He glanced again at his arm, the remnants of his once-light gray sleeve completely covered in deep red. He was bleeding to death, he realized that almost immediately.

But can I last another minute…

He pulled his hand away, and blood spurted out from the wound with a renewed force. He winced for an instant—the pain was almost unbearable—but he was focused on what he had to do. He'd been born into misery, watched his friends and family waste away working twelve hour shifts in filthy factories, seen those who protested, complained about their lots, dragged away forever. He hated the Union, and everything it stood for. He couldn't let them move toward total control of the Rim, subject billions more to the tyranny and despair he'd endured.

He would avenge his family, the comrades who'd set out to escape with him, those who'd never made it. He needed to live, for another minute at least.

He needed to fight, to find the strength somewhere. He had to hold that door…somehow.

He scooped up the rifle, struggling to bring it to bear with one hand. His one arm was half-severed and useless. He shifted to the side, trying to get some help balancing the gun from gravity, and he aimed the best he could toward the doorway. He could hear the enemy coming, the sounds of their boots on the metal deck.

It was down to seconds now, seconds that might decide the very fate of the entire Rim.

* * *

Blackness, hazy thoughts, confusion. She lay on the deck, against the wall. There was blood streaming down her face. She could feel it. She reached up, her fingers feeling around, finding a nasty cut on her forehead. A few more seconds went by, and then suddenly, she was aware.

She struggled to leap up to her feet, ignoring the pain from half a dozen small wounds. She reached for her pistol as she rose, but it was gone. She felt a panic inside her. She was unarmed. Almost. Her hand went to the sheath at her waist, pulled out her knife. It wasn't much in a fight against an imperial security bot, but it was all she had.

Her eyes scanned the room, looking for her enemy, even as she expected a burst of fire to take her down at any second. But there was nothing.

Nothing except the scattered debris, the bot torn into four large sections, plus a few dozen small bits. The wreckage was twisted and blackened, and all of it was motionless.

The grenade had done it.

It had almost done her, too. She tried to turn to the side, but her mobility was all but gone. Everything hurt. Part of her wanted to drop back to the deck, to lie still so the pain—some of it, at least—would stop.

But her mind was clear again, and she knew she wasn't done. She still had a job to do.

She looked around, finding the pistol laying a couple meters away, against the wall. She scooped it up, along with her rifle and her sack. Then, she stepped back out into the corridor. She glanced down at the dead Foudre Rouge, killed by the bot. But she only looked for an instant.

She'd already lost time. There was no more to waste.

She moved down the corridor, picking up her pace, limping painfully with each rushed step. She was driven by determination, by loyalty to her comrades…and by the rage flowing through her body.

Nightrunner's crew had been set up. She'd known that already, of course, in some way, but the thoughts had only just truly coalesced.

They'd been sent out to die, to open the way for Sector Nine to come in and move into the station. The fury she felt at such treachery was like a force of nature, and it reinvigorated her battered body. There was no pain, no injury that would stop her. They would have to kill her…and if they didn't, she was damned sure going to kill them.

Every one of them.

She pushed herself forward, listening carefully. There were more bots out there, she was sure enough about that, and there were Foudre Rouge, too. She didn't know where, but she knew she had to hear them before they heard her.

She had to get to the captain and the others. She had to help them get out of the trap they were in.

She quickened her pace, and she spun around a corner. She'd seen the layout Sylene had pulled up from the station's data system, and she remembered it. At least she was pretty sure she did. She'd always had a nearly perfect memory, and now she was betting on it.

She was betting her life.

She pushed forward, ignoring the pain and fatigue, and then she stopped dead.

She wasn't sure if she'd heard something first, or if some kind of sixth sense had intervened.

Whatever it was, any doubt vanished an instant later.

Gunfire...

She was close to the reactor—at least to the spot on the schematic Yarra had guessed marked the power plant's location. Her whole body tensed. There was a fight going on up ahead, and she *knew* her comrades were in the middle of it.

She broke into a dead run, her rifle ready, and she whipped around another corner and stopped again.

There were shadowy figures ahead of her, down the corridor. They were distracted, focused on something else. She saw one of them drop, and another lean around and open fire.

Then, they all started to move forward, around the corner, firing as they went.

She didn't have a doubt, none at all. They were moving on her shipmates.

Sy's not much in a fight, and Yarra's not much better...

It was one of the things that had driven her to ignore the

captain's orders, to race to find and aid her comrades. Lorillard was the only real fighter in the group. And he was outgunned and trapped.

She lurched forward, recklessly, knowing she was out of time. She opened up at full auto, running as she sprayed her fire up and down on the last Foudre Rouge trooper in the small enemy column. It would be luck, she knew, to catch him in a vulnerable spot with such crude aiming, but fortune had served her well before. It had taken her far from the filthy streets of the Gut. Had it done that only to see her die in the depths of dead space, a hundred lightyears from any inhabited planet?

She was going to find out.

Her fire ceased as her clip ran out, but she could see her target was already falling. She'd unloaded fifty rounds into him, and from the volume of blood she could see, she knew at least a few of those had gotten through the armor.

Her hand reached back behind her, into her bag, grabbing a reload. She jammed it into place, and then she raced down the corridor, chasing the other Foudre Rouge and lost in a wild frenzy of combat and killing.

Chapter Thirty-One

Lorillard's fire was erratic, the rifle shaking in his single-handed grip, sending shots all around in all directions. Still, the first Foudre Rouge in the room fell back, struck by several of the hypervelocity rounds. At such short range, the military-grade projectiles tore through the trooper's armor with ease, leaving a gaping hole in the dead man's chest.

The kickback was too much, though, and the weapon finally wrested itself free from Lorillard's tenuous grasp. The gun skittered across the floor, and the captain lost what little balance he'd regained, and he fell to the cold steel of the deck.

He struggled to remain in action, even as he rolled over, sliding around in the expanding pool of his own blood that surrounded him. He could feel weakness, fatigue. He knew he was dead if he didn't at least slow the bleeding, but there was no time. Another Foudre Rouge soldier was turning toward him even then, bringing his rifle around.

Lorillard pulled his pistol from its holster, and he fired, wildly, emptying the cartridge in a couple seconds. He managed to hit, with at least one or two shots, but the handgun wasn't the military level weapon his rifle was, and the weaker rounds just pinged off his enemy's armor.

Lorillard was vaguely aware of the others, Sylene and Yarra, scrambling for weapons themselves, but he knew they would be too late.

The Foudre Rouge was already aiming, about to fire, when Lorillard saw...something.

Movement, behind the enemy soldier. He thought it was another Foudre Rouge at first, but even the fleeting glimpse he'd managed was enough to tell him it wasn't.

Then, the fire began.

He gritted his teeth, preparing himself for the shots that would finish him, but the shooting he heard was different, not the high-pitched whine of the enemy's hypervelocity rounds.

The trooper reacted, suddenly, pulling his weapon away from Lorillard, spinning around frantically. He got about halfway when he dropped to one knee. He held the weapon up, for another second, perhaps, and then it slipped from his hand.

He was hit, Lorillard realized. Badly.

The Foudre Rouge reached down to his belt, fumbling for the pistol holstered at his side. But before he could draw the weapon, a shadow came up behind him. A figure emerged, moving into view.

Andi Lafarge. Bloodied, battered...but with a look on her face that froze Lorillard's blood.

She reached around, tore off the wounded trooper's helmet, sending it crashing to the deck. Then he saw the knife in her hand, watched as it slashed across the Union trooper's throat, too fast for eyes to follow. The soldier wobbled for an instant, and then he fell forward, face down, as the blood poured from his throat, pooling out around his still form.

Andi stood there a moment, looking like the angel of death personified. She was cold, ruthless, without pity or mercy, her blade, now stained red, clutched tightly in her hand. She remained, unmoving, apparently unfeeling, for a few seconds.

Then, Lorillard caught her gaze, and her eyes fixed on him. She looked at his arm, the terrible wound, the blood. Suddenly, there was something there, emotion, empathy.

Tears.

* * *

Andi's eyes fixed on Lorillard, and she almost felt her heart stop. She'd killed the last Foudre Rouge, cut through the flesh of his throat with more malice and fury than she'd imagined possible. She'd felt a spark inside, the feeling of victory. She'd made it. She'd taken out the enemy, at least all those that were there at the moment. She'd gotten there in time.

Or had she?

She looked down at the captain…and at the blood all around him.

She raced over, dropping to her knees in the circle of viscous blood surrounding him. She felt the sickly-warm wetness through the knees of her pants, even as he hands moved to his stricken arm, slowly pulling at the matted fabric, stained deepest red, that covered it.

"Andi, what are you…"

"This is going to hurt, Cap…" She ignored Lorillard's question. She'd disobeyed his orders, yes, and they could have a long talk about it once they got back to the ship. She pulled at the fabric, trying to extract the strands that had been driven into the wound. She pushed back as she almost wretched at the sight of the injury. Between almost rhythmic spurts of blood, she could see muscle torn open and shards of bone visible. Lorillard's arm wasn't wounded. It was destroyed.

That's okay, she told herself. *He can get a good prosthesis when we get back to Dannith.*

But even as the thought drifted through her mind, she knew that would never happen. Lorillard wasn't going to make it back to Dannith. He wasn't going to make it back to *Nightrunner.*

She hadn't given up completely, or at least her mind was still shouting at itself, insisting there was hope. Rational thought and blind loyalty squared off in her head, ready to fight for her next actions, but even as they did, she knew there was no hope.

Lorillard groaned with every pull of fabric, every attempt she made to push flaps of flesh back into place. She reached down, cut off a section of her tunic with the knife, and she began to wrap it around Lorillard's arm. Her eyes darted around, staring at the pools of blood, trying to get an idea of just how much he'd lost already. Even as she fashioned the makeshift tourniquet, she knew, somewhere deep inside, that she was too late.

"Andi…" The captain's voice was weak, his tone hollow. "It's too late…I know that. You know…"

"Captain, just lay back. I'll take care of…" Her voice was choked by the tears she was barely holding back, and even as Lorillard interrupted her, she pulled hard on the strip of cloth, tying it off just above the deepest wound.

"Andi…aaaagghhh…" Lorillard's comment was choked off by his cries of pain as Andi affixed the tourniquet. "Andi," he said again, the difficulty growing with each word he spoke. "…too late…not going to make it…"

Andi heard sounds off to the side, Sylene and Yarra rushing over, dropping down next to her, tears filling both their eyes as they gazed at their stricken leader.

"Bomb…ready?" Lorillard gritted his teeth as he struggled to turn his head toward the engineer.

"Yes, Captain…it's ready." Andi wasn't sure what was going on, but she could tell from Yarra's tone something was wrong. "But the timer…" She held up a small device. It was torn open, twisted into an irregular shape. At least one of the Foudre Rouge's bullets had struck it.

"Bomb still work?" Lorillard rasped for breath as he spoke.

"Yes, but…" A short pause. "But there's no way to set it now. It will detonate as soon as the switch is turned."

Andi's stomach clenched fiercely. She knew what Lorillard was going to say before a word escaped his lips. Worse, she knew there was no other choice.

"Leave it with me…and get out…of here. Now."

"No, Captain…we can't…" Andi's voice lost all its sternness and all of the strength that had been there so recently. It was a plea now, the desperate cries of a child. "We can't leave you." And even as she said it, she knew they had to do just that.

"No time to…argue. Not…going to…make it anyway…" Lorillard sucked in a deep and painful breath, and he exhaled, a thin spray of blood coming up with the air. "Too im…portant…to fail…" He angled his head, looked right at Andi. "Please…don't want to…die for…nothing…"

Yarra wiped her hand across her face, and she sniffled hard, struggling to banish the tears, at least for a few seconds. "We have to get you closer to the cylinder, Captain…" She got the words out, and Andi was grateful.

She was grateful because she didn't have to.

"Help me…up…" Lorillard extended his good arm toward Yarra. The engineer reached out, taking hold under the captain's armpit. Lorillard flashed a glance at Andi, one that pled with her for her help.

She knew what he wanted her to do, and she dreaded it. She leaned forward, sliding her hand under his shattered arm, and she lifted, as gently as possible. She could feel that he was trying to hold back his cries, but they burst out anyway, the sound of pure agony.

Andi's face was sloppy with tears, even as she pulled harder, and with Yarra's help, got him up, at least to a semblance of on his feet. He wobbled, and his grunted and spat out blood, but somehow, they managed to make their way across the room, toward the closest of the great cylinders.

Sylene followed behind them, sobbing as quietly as she could. She had scooped up the device that Yarra had set down when she'd helped the captain up, and followed the others slowly, perhaps a meter behind.

Andi felt like time was being stretched, that each small step took an hour, a day, a week. But finally, they reached their destination, and they gently set Lorillard down, leaning him up against the cool, silver metal of the cylinder.

"Sure this…will…work…" He was haggard, his words soft, hoarse. The walk across the room seemed to have drained most of the energy he'd still had. He was staring out, looking at his friends, but it didn't look to Andi like he was seeing them.

Yarra took the device from Sylene, and she put it in Lorillard's lap. He reached out, almost like a blind man feeling around for something. His hand found it, his fingers moving gently over it.

Yarra took his hand and moved it gently toward a large switch.

"Just…flip…switch?"

The engineer sucked in a breath, struggling to clear the tears. "Flip it and then move your fingers and let it go. Flipping it sets the final arming. Releasing it and letting it snap back detonates."

Lorillard looked up, still appearing dazed…but something appeared on his lips, thin and barely comprehensible, but definitely there.

A smile.

"A dead…man…switch…appropriate…" His words were slurred a little, but they were still clear enough.

Lorillard took another breath, and he clenched his face for an instant, fighting back against the pain. "Go…all of…you. Now…"

He turned his head slightly, and for an instant, his eyes seemed clear again. "Please…go…escape. For me…"

Yarra leaned down and put her arm around his neck, the closest she could come to a hug without hurting him. Sylene did the same right after. Neither one of them could force out any words, at least nothing intelligible through their sobbing.

Andi froze for a second. She'd found her mother dead in the street. She'd found the Marine dying. She'd felt pain from both of those losses that still tore at her like a keen blade. But she'd never left a friend or loved one to die.

She was a stone-cold killer in her own right, but it was taking all she had to keep herself from falling to pieces. She knelt down, and she leaned in toward Lorillard's face. She kissed him on the cheek.

"Get them…home…Andi…counting…on you…get my…people…home…"

She nodded, unable to stop crying long enough to force out any more words.

"Take…rifle…yours now…"

And almost lost her composure. The captain's rifle was a treasure in its own right, something almost impossible to obtain outside the military. She'd always been envious of the thing, wishing she had one of her own. Now, that all came back on her, a wave of guilt and sorrow that almost overwhelmed her.

"Will hold…as long…as I…can…" A pause. "Message for you…on AI…when you…get back. Listen…as soon…as you…can…"

Andi just nodded, sniffling hard as the years rolled down her face.

"Now…go…go…"

She stood up and pulled her eyes from the captain,

exchanging glances with her two comrades. Then she turned around and walked across the room, Sylene and Yarra right behind her.

She picked up the pace, speeding up to a moderate jog. She didn't know how long Lorillard could last, but when he flipped that switch, she and the others had to be back in *Nightrunner*, and away from the station.

Leaving the captain behind...to die...it was the hardest thing she'd ever had to do.

But one thing would be worse, even more unthinkable.

Failing his final request.

Chapter Thirty-Two

Free Trader Nightrunner
Docked at Imperial Station
Orbiting Zensoria, Osiron VI
Year 301 AC

Andi pulled herself though the docking tube and into the airlock. She turned and reached out, helping Yarra and then Sylene. Once they were all in, she poked at the controls, closing the outside door, and initiating the minor adjustment in air pressure.

They were all exhausted. They'd run back, at least as far as they'd been able to. Sylene had been the weak link there, but she'd pushed herself to the edge, and they'd only slowed down after she'd collapsed to the deck in a panting heap, retching up a bit of foam from her otherwise empty stomach before she pulled herself together and pressed on.

Andi had no idea how long they had to make good their escape. How long the captain could hold on. It was difficult, even, to think about it, about wondering how long her friend could last before he killed himself. She knew her tourniquet had bought some time, at least. Still, there was always the chance a Foudre Rouge or security bot would find Lorillard. If that happened before *Nightrunner* took off, they were all dead.

Or, if Lorillard's endurance gave out before they got the ship away from the station. They'd be just as dead that way. Worse, perhaps, if Lorillard was caught by surprise, or if he slipped into unconsciousness before he triggered the explosive, the Confederation itself would be in jeopardy.

The door slid open, and she leapt inside, turning almost immediately and heading toward the bridge. The rest of the crew was in the room, and they leapt up, shouting out almost at once in a wild cacophony of questions.

"What happened?"

"Where is the captain?"

"What do we do next?"

She ignored them all. She didn't have time to explain…and she didn't think she had it in her to tell them about the captain. Not just then.

She turned her head back. "Yarra…get down to the engine room. Make sure everything is prepped, and get ready for…for whatever we have to do."

Andi knew *Nightrunner* was still under the guns of one of the enemy ships. That was a disadvantageous position at best, and certain death at worst. But death couldn't be any more certain than it would be if they stayed docked to the station until the bomb went off.

She raced across the bridge toward her station, and she stopped by the captain's chair. The idea of taking Lorillard's seat, of acknowledging that she was, in fact, taking his place, even just for the escape attempt, hit her like a punch to the gut. But there was no time for emotion, for any weakness. And the captain's station had more sophisticated piloting controls than hers.

She plopped down in Lorillard's chair, struggling not to think about it, as her hands moved over the workstation. In a few seconds, she had everything ready. Everything but power from the reactor.

She reached down to activate the comm, but Yarra beat her to it. The engineer's voice crackled out of the small speaker. "Everything's a go down here, Andi...but the reactor's on minimal output. It'll take five minutes to power up, minimum, and they'll probably be able to pick that up on their scanners, even through all the jamming.

Shit...

Andi looked around the bridge, as though searching for some magical control somewhere, some button or switch that would solve the problem. But there was nothing.

Unless...

"What about an emergency restart? Blast the thing up to full in a couple seconds." Andi was no engineer. She wasn't even sure an emergency restart was a real thing. But she knew that's what they needed.

"We could lose the reactor, Andi. It could blow and kill us all..."

"We're going to get blown up if we stay here anyway. And, we're going to get shot down if we give the enemy time to react. Unless you have any better ideas, Yarra...do it."

The last two words had come out in a different tone, one of command. She hadn't intended it that way, but then she heard Yarra's sharp—and obedient—response.

"Yes, Andi...give me half a minute." No argument, no hesitation.

She looked down at the controls, her fingers moving swiftly, revising the departure course. She wasn't going to give the enemy any extra chances to take *Nightrunner* down, even if that meant pulling out of the docking collar like a drunken spacer. The vector she plotted was tight, but it should clear the appendage of the station that extended just to *Nightrunner*'s port side.

She wished she had something better than *should*, but that's the best her gut gave her.

"Ready, Andi. You'll either have full power in three or four seconds, or..." There was no need to finish the statement.

"Okay, Yarra…on my mark." She paused. "And, Yarra…as soon as we've got power, I need you to get the lasers online." Andi would be just as content to make a straight line run to get the hell out of the system, but her instincts told her it was going to take some fighting to save *Nightrunner* and its people.

Her people.

She couldn't fail the captain, couldn't deny his final request. She *wouldn't* fail.

"Got it, Andi." Yarra was holding it together, barely maybe, but still together. Andi couldn't expect more.

"Okay…go!" Even as she snapped out the command, her hands moved out to the controls. She took a deep breath and held it.

She could feel vibrations beneath her feet as *Nightrunner*'s power plant went suddenly to full output. The engines roared as she fed the energy flow in, her other hand tapping the control to cut loose the docking tube. It was an expensive piece of equipment to just leave behind, but the last thing she had was time for was hauling it back in.

She tried to hold her focus, keep her mind from the deadly danger. The enemy ship waiting to attack didn't even register on that list yet, not as long as she knew that any second, Lorillard might trigger the station's destruction—and *Nightrunner*'s along with it. That was concern number one, at least until Andi could get the ship away. Number two—though possibly a candidate for number one—was the worry the vessel's reactor might react badly to the abuse Yarra was even then heaping on it. Nuclear reactors weren't the safest things to push to their limits.

The ship shook hard, and she fired the docking jets, pushing *Nightrunner* away from its mooring. The vessel shook once, hard, as it popped away from the station. Then, she reached out and grabbed the main throttle.

You'll know in a second if Yarra got the power up and running…

She pulled back hard, and *Nightrunner* lurched wildly, a

wave of g forces slamming into her as the thrusters blasted at full.

Yarra had done it!

That didn't mean a catastrophic failure couldn't still happen, but every second that passed reduced the chances. Even Andi's non-engineer mind knew that.

She stared down at the controls, suddenly feeling inexperienced, out of her depth. It was one thing to pilot the ship with the captain there, watching, looking over her. But now, she was alone.

She jerked the nav controls hard, changing the thrust vector abruptly. Then she did it again, moving to yet another angle. She had to get away from the station, but she couldn't be careless with her vectors. The ship was under the guns of one of the Union vessels, and an instant's carelessness could forfeit all the gains of the sudden reactor restart. She was banking on the sudden full acceleration to buy the time to pull away before the enemy could fire. But it would be evasive maneuvers that kept *Nightrunner* alive as the surprise of her sudden move faded.

The scanners were full of static, but she could see the hazy image of the Union ship, already responding to *Nightrunner*'s unexpected action. *Nightrunner* was already a hundred kilometers from the station and accelerating at full power. But the Union vessel was following, trying to match her wild maneuvers. It wouldn't take long for the vessel to update its fire locks. A few seconds later, she saw streaks moving across the screen. She knew just what they were.

Laser fire. The enemy was shooting at them.

Nightrunner lurched hard again, as Andi remembered what Lorillard had told her about evading enemy fire. Unpredictability was the key, more so than velocity, allowing just enough intuition to combine with the AI's algorithms to throw off the enemy's targeting.

She was no expert, not yet, but she was a quick learner. *Nightrunner* was shifting around wildly, altering its vector as unpredictably as she could manage. She wasn't sure what a flight school instructor might have said about her flying, but she was damned sure her Union pursuers would have a hard time reestablishing a lock, especially with the station's jamming interfering with the scanners. Still confidence was one thing, and hope another, and she wasn't sure exactly where she sat on that spectrum.

And neither one of them was a guarantee.

She would lose at least some of her protection, she knew. As they pulled away from the station, at some point, they would clear the jamming.

Assuming the station doesn't…

Every readout on her board suddenly shot wildly to maximum readings. Her eyes caught the hull temperature, watching in frozen horror as it topped out no more than a hundred degrees from the alloy's melting point. The rad levels were like nothing she'd seen before, and she hoped the ship's shielding was in good shape—and thick enough to protect them, or at least to hold back a lethal dose.

She reached out, grabbed the controls, changing *Nightrunner*'s vector again, bringing the ship away from the station. From where the station had been.

She knew immediately what had happened. Yarra's hastily-assembled bomb had worked, and it had breached the antimatter storage. The station hadn't just exploded, it had vanished in the unimaginable fury of massive matter-antimatter annihilation.

Nightrunner was hundreds of kilometers away, but the energy from the titanic explosion bathed the ship in radiation, and came a hair's breadth from vaporizing the hull.

She clutched at the controls, rerouting burnt out circuits, struggling to maintain control of the damaged ship. The station's explosion hadn't destroyed *Nightrunner*, but it had taken out more than one system. Navigation was partly out…she was controlling things entirely manually. Half the positioning jets were down, too, making it harder to change vectors, and reducing her options for evasion.

But the lasers were still functional, at least according to her display. And the jamming was gone.

Clear space to target lasers was a weapon that cut both ways.

She hit the controls to charge up *Nightrunner*'s guns. The scanners, what remained of them, were suffering interference from the radiation, but with the active jamming gone, she figured she had a good chance of targeting a shot.

Besides, she was sick of running. If those bastards were going to come after her, she was going to make them pay for it. She wasn't sitting helplessly under their guns anymore. She was out in the open, her own weapons ready.

And she was powered by a cold, frozen fury. Her first instincts after the station blew was to maintain control of the ship, deal with the enemy vessel.

But now, the reality had set in. The station wasn't the only thing that was gone now.

Jim Lorillard was dead.

She had lost another mentor. Another friend.

And, she wanted blood for it.

She gripped the main nav control, nudging the ship's vector, bringing its guns to bear. The enemy was still coming on, and with each passing second, the clarity of her scans improved as the range declined. The sensor units were damaged, mostly monitoring antennas overloaded on the hull, but what she had was probably good enough.

And *probably* would have to do…

She was no gunner, even less so than a pilot. But there was no time to get anyone else on the bridge. She'd have to do it herself.

She brought up the firing display, hooked in the AI. Targeting a ship hundreds of kilometers away, moving at the velocities common in space travel, was almost impossible without computer assistance. Instinct played a role, too, mostly in guessing at enemy evasive moves and choosing the moment to fire.

Andi flipped on the gunnery units and held her breath for a few seconds, until the targeting computer booted up. For an instant, she was afraid it was down, just like the nav unit. But then, the assisted targeting screen came up, and her controls locked onto the guns.

She saw a pair of long streaks of light whip down her display. The enemy had fired again, the last shot coming within ten kilometers of *Nightrunner*. That wasn't near enough to do any damage, but it was definitely close enough to make the hairs on her neck stand up. Whoever was on those guns had a head start on her.

She pressed the firing stud, and breathed a sigh of relief when the weapons actually fired. The shot was wide, no closer than fifty kilometers from the target, but she hadn't even been sure until then the lasers were truly operational.

She jerked her hand hard to the side, almost an afterthought. Combining evasive moves and targeting was far from easy. They were almost opposites, and without the nav AI, she had to stay on it closely. She didn't know what she was facing in terms of human gunners, but she was sure enough, if she let her guard down the Union AI would plant a laser blast right into *Nightrunner*'s guts.

She brought the ship around again, firing, coming closer this time, within fifteen kilometers. It was better, but not good enough. The target ship was less than two hundred meters bow to stern, and hitting something that size across hundreds of kilometers of open space was precision shooting.

She fired again. This time, she almost let herself believe she'd hit. The final review showed one of her shots coming within five kilometers.

She could hear her heart pounding, her killer instinct rising, taking control. She was close, another adjustment, just the right instant to fire and…

Nightrunner shook hard, and the ship went into a series of spirals, turning over and over, half a dozen times before Andi managed to stabilize it. Her hands moved frantically over the workstation, checking on damage, adjusting the ship's vector, rerouting non-responsive systems. The hit hadn't been critical, she was almost certain of that after she'd done her first check.

But it wouldn't take critical damage to doom *Nightrunner* in the fight. The loss of *any* vital system, even for a moment or two, would be fatal for them all.

"Yarra, how's the reactor?" The static on the speaker told her the internal comm systems had been damaged. She wasn't sure the engineer had gotten her message, at least not until a distorted and difficult to hear response came through.

Not for the first time, Andi was grateful for her sharp hearing. "No significant damage," had been the answer. And that meant they were still in the fight.

She brought the ship around yet again, and her eyes narrowed on the targeting screen. The enemy was closing, and Andi knew she was running out of time. They'd almost gotten *Nightrunner* once, and if she gave them any more time, they'd finish the job.

She had to take them out, and she had to do it immediately.

She breathed deeply, regularly, trying in every way to connect her mind to her task. She saw the enemy ship, on the display *and* in her mind. She put herself in her adversary's position, imagined what she would do to evade herself.

Her hands gripped tightly on the controls, her finger gently over the firing stud. She angled it slightly changing her vector, ignoring the flash as the enemy fired again, coming dangerously close.

She'd gambled long enough, gotten as much time as she could hope for. The gunner on the enemy ship was skilled and capable, that was obvious. She had to take him out…or he would get her.

She let her mind slide, almost into a trancelike state. Her finger tightened…and then she angled her shot one last time, working almost on pure instinct, and she fired.

The lasers whined as they discharged the output of *Nightrunner*'s reactors into two great lances of deadly, focused light. Then, she saw it, blinking two or three times, and looking again in her disbelief.

A direct hit. Both beams had struck the enemy amidships. The vessel hung in space for a few tense, excruciating seconds, and then it vanished in thermonuclear fury.

Yes! Andi felt a moment of triumph, of relief. But it didn't last. She was far from home, the ship was damaged, the crew was battered, and half of them were badly wounded.

And Jammar and the captain were dead.

Nightrunner might get back home—though she was far from sure of that. Getting back to Dannith relied more on Yarra's ability to keep the almost shattered vessel flying—but even if they made it, their family had suffered terrible losses. Whatever they got for the tech in the ship's hold, whatever they did next, none of them would ever be the same again.

She leaned back and rubbed her eyes with her hands. Then, she saw something, a small symbol on the barely-functioning scanner. A ship, moving toward the transit point.

The other Union vessel…they must have gotten away from the station in time…

She felt a flash of panic, and then the urge—the need—to chase after them, to destroy them as she had their comrades. Hatred coursed through her veins, but her reason fought to regain control. The enemy ship was too far away, on too sharp a vector, too close to jumping out of the system. *Nightrunner* couldn't catch them…and it she did manage to come into range, the ship was in no shape for another fight.

Get my people home…Lorillard's words echoed in her ears, and they settled in her soul like a sacred oath. The captain had trusted her with the others, and she wouldn't fail him. She couldn't live with herself if she did.

She leaned forward and tapped the comm back on. "Yarra, give the reactor and the engines a quick check, and then we'll plot a course out of here."

She took a deep breath and exhaled loudly.

"It's time to go home."

Chapter Thirty-Three

Free Trader Nightrunner
Docked at Samis Shipyard
Orbiting Ventica VII
Year 301 AC

Andi sat in her quarters, her old, small, cramped stateroom wedged up against the cargo hold. She hadn't moved to the captain's cabin, not yet. The very idea still seemed...unthinkable...though she had every right to do just that.

She'd listened to Lorillard's last message to her at least five times before the words had truly sunken in. He'd left her all sorts of instructions for accessing the numbered accounts and distributing the crew's stashed savings. Most shockingly, he'd bequeathed his position to her, bade her take his place, at the helm...and as *Nightrunner*'s commander.

And as the ship's owner.

His will had been with the other documents he'd left behind, and it granted her full ownership of *Nightrunner*.

She'd been stunned. She still was. It didn't seem real. How was it even possible?

He'd explained himself, briefly. She was the most like him, the likeliest of his people to successfully take command after his death, to ensure the others could stay together, those who could still stomach it, at least. He'd come to trust her, and he'd never thought of *Nightrunner* as his, so much as the groups. He didn't want to see the ship sold, the proceeds divided. He wanted the legacy of his people, his team to live on.

Andi felt as utterly unready for the responsibility as she'd ever been for anything. But rejecting the captain's last request was unthinkable. She would step into his shoes, do her best to lead the crew, to move things forward and emerge from the black shadow of his death. She didn't know if she could manage it, but she would try her best.

Still, it was likely to be a good long while before she moved into the captain's quarters. She had to clean them out first, and going through Lorillard's things loomed over her future like a dark and terrifying nightmare.

First things first. She had to get *Nightrunner* ready for action. The ship had made it back, barely, but that had only been the result of Yarra's near wizardry. The engineer had fixed malfunction after malfunction and rerouted a hundred failed circuits. She'd rebuilt half the ship's system, replacing damaged and destroyed mechanisms with ingenious, if jury-rigged, replacements that had gotten the vessel back to port.

Just.

Now it was time to get real repairs done. There were any number of shipyards orbiting Dannith, but Lorillard had left her one more gift. Discretion. A location and a contact…and a way to get *Nightrunner* back in top condition away from prying eyes.

The shipyard orbited a moon around the system's deepest gas giant, a position that defied all effort at explanation in her mind, until it hit her like a sledgehammer.

The remote location *was* the yard's main selling point. It was a place for ships to go when their owners wanted to avoid undesirable attention. Vessels came back from the Badlands in need of repairs all the time, of course, but

Nightrunner had fought a battle, and it had been bathed in the radiation from a massive antimatter explosion. The fewer questions anyone asked, the better. Which was why Andi had docked with the shipyard before going anywhere near Dannith. Even at a twenty percent premium over rates at a normal orbital yard, she thought it was well worth it.

She got up and stared at herself in the mirror. She was twenty years old—almost twenty-one—and she often looked even younger. But now, she was wearing a trim suit that looked almost like a uniform, and her hair was pulled back under a dull gray hat. It was as old and as professional as Andi Lafarge could make herself look, and she turned and walked down the corridor and out the hatch.

There were three men standing outside the ship waiting for her. She only had one name, the one Lorillard had left her in his final message.

"Is one of you, Durango?" It had seemed an odd name, but was the only one she had.

"I'm Durango. Who are you, and where is Captain Lorillard?" It was clear *Nightrunner* had been there before.

"Captain Lorillard is dead." She managed to say it without her eyes watering and her voice cracking, barely. It was just about the first time she'd managed it. She knew it would get easier, and in some way that made her feel guilty. *Will the captain be any less dead in a year than he is now? Any less important to you?*

"I'm *Nightrunner*'s owner now. She reached into her pocket and pulled out a datachip, proof that Lorillard had left the ship to her.

"It looks like you had a rough time of it." His eyes moved over the ship's hull, his gaze freezing for a second here and there as he surveyed the situation. "Well, we can fix her, but I can tell you now, it's going to cost a bundle."

"We've got artifacts…but we'll have to get back to Dannith to sell them. Is there a shuttle or something we can take to the planet?"

"We'll shuttle you back, alright. This job's gonna take a few months, and we don't have any hotels out here. But no need for you to go to Dannith to sell your swag. I can hook you up here, and you'll get a fairer price than any thieves in the Spacer's District will offer. It's in our interest to help folks move their old tech…since that's where most of our billing get paid from."

Andi nodded cautiously. She didn't trust Durango, not even close, but she liked the man at first impression, and she appreciated his directness. Besides, Lorillard *had* trusted him, and that counted for a lot.

"Okay, set it up. We've got circuit boards and processors, and a good number of them…in better shape than what you normally see. So, whoever you bring better have deep pockets, because this is no little bag of imperial novelties."

Durango nodded, and he looked at her with what seemed like the beginnings of respect. "Fair enough. I'll have my man here tomorrow, nine sharp. That work for you?"

Andi nodded.

"Good, then I'll get my people started on a price for you…if you don't mind a dozen boys crawling around your ship."

She just nodded again. Then she turned and walked back inside.

* * *

Andi crept quietly up to the door. There'd been a single man posted outside the closed tavern, and dispatching him had been no trouble at all. Andi always enjoyed knifework, at least when she was in the mood that gripped her just then.

She scoffed at Darvin's arrogance and stupidity. It was beyond unwise for a man who dealt in deceit and treachery to trust his safety to one disinterested guard, groggy and half asleep at his post. That would prove to be a disastrous oversight.

At least the guard had been half asleep until she'd gotten there. He was completely asleep now. Andi's lip was crooked, the hint of a grim smile there. She had once been plagued with mixed feelings about being a killer, but no longer. The men she had killed—and so far, her victims had all been male—were a virtual rogue's gallery of creatures who deserved death. There was no room for self-recrimination or hesitancy in terminating enemies, she had resolved herself to that reality. At least, not in a universe so overflowingly filled with people who needed to die.

She could hear voices inside. She'd have preferred to move against the Dannite information broker alone. *He* was the one she'd come for. Anyone else in there would be collateral damage.

Still, she liked the odds it would be somebody else who richly deserved what she was bringing, and not some innocent in the wrong place at the wrong time. The thought she might be wrong, that the individual talking to Darvin might be an innocent, or at least one who didn't rate death, troubled her for a few seconds.

But not enough to stop her.

She moved forward, pressing each foot down lightly, taking care not to make any sound on the old, wood floor. A creak or a hard step could give her away. That wouldn't necessarily mean she had failed. She suspected she could take Darvin in a straight up fight easily enough, but she preferred to maintain surprise, to ambush the fool, an appropriate response to the way the bastard had set up Captain Lorillard, and the rest of her comrades.

She could hear laughing. The sound only fueled the icy cold rage inside her, the grim determination to take her vengeance, right then and there. It was something she needed, something that couldn't wait any longer. Lorillard was dead, and Jammar as well. Some of the others had left, taken the moderate fortunes they'd managed to collect, and fled from the brutality of frontier prospecting. She understood. It was hard to lose so many friends, to press on after such losses. She thought nothing less of any of them, and she wished them well in their lives, thoughts that were tempered only by the pain that they too, were gone in their own way, leaving a pang of loss nearly as cutting as the ones left by the dead.

This is for all of you…

Andi couldn't walk away. Not from the frontier, not from prospecting. And damned sure, not from the revenge she'd vowed to gain for her lost friends.

She stood right outside the door, peering in, catching the hint of a shadow on one of the walls. She focused, her mind like a laser, creating a view of the room. It was partial, and likely not entirely accurate, but it was what she had.

She pulled the pistol from its holster, gripped it tightly.

It was time.

She lunged through the door, turning to the right almost immediately, her eyes finding the table, with two men sitting opposite each other. They'd been talking…but now they were reacting, reaching for weapons.

Andi's arm came up, finding the first target. She's picked out Darvin as the greatest danger. He was closest to facing her, and he'd seen her first. His own hand was reaching, almost certainly for some kind of weapon.

She fired her pistol, and Darvin's shoulder exploded in a spray of blood. Even as her primary target dropped his weapon and screamed in agony, she was moving, bringing her weapon to bear on the second man. Sector Nine, she told herself as her eyes settled on him. *Probably bringing this miserable traitor the last of his reward for setting us up.*

No…you are delivering the last of his reward for that.

She fired twice, both shots taking the man in the head, shattering his skull and sending blood and brain across the room, splattering against the wall like some grotesque work of art.

It *was* art, she knew. *Her* art.

Darvin had fallen to his knees next to the chair. He was screaming in pain, and his face was covered with a mask of tears. Every shout of pain, every stream of tears, invigorated Andi.

Revenge was nothing new to her. She'd been wronged before, and she'd taken her vengeance for it. But the rage inside her was stronger, more concentrated than any she'd felt before. She'd loved the Marine like a father, but the old man was as guilty in his own death than anyone else. The system that created a world like Parsephon, that had killed her real father, thrown her mother out into the street to scratch out survival as well as she could, and ultimately die there…it enraged her, but there was a facelessness to it, a strange inevitability that made it seem almost like a natural occurrence.

But this was much clearer. Her comrades had died because of the man kneeling in front of her. He had set them up, willingly and deliberately, sent them to the depths of the Badlands to die.

His bill had come due.

She stepped forward, standing over him, kicking away the gun he was making a weak effort to reach.

"You sent us out there to die, Darvin. And you succeeded, at least in part. But when you set people up, lure them into a trap…it's a bad idea to leave any of them alive." Even she was surprised at the venom in her voice. She could see Jim Lorillard's face hovering in front of her, and the whimpers and grunts of her enemy, every sign he gave of the pain and fear he was feeling, filled her with a satisfied energy. She had no pity for the miserable creature lying in front of her, no remorse.

No mercy.

"No…please…I didn't know…" He was trying to move his body, to wriggle along the floor, away from the mad woman standing over him.

"You disappoint me, Darvin. You're a miserable scrap of human waste, but I thought at least you'd be a good liar. Better than the stooge you hired to give us the job." She paused, taking a second to savor her victim's fear. "Yeah, you didn't expect that to protect you, did you? You banked on us being pretty stupid. That was a mistake. It only took an hour to find the fool, and he spilled his guts—in more ways than one—in just a few minutes. He gave you up before I even *really* hurt him." She stepped forward again, offsetting the half meter or so Darvin had managed to slide away.

"Please...please..."

"This is for Captain Lorillard..." She paused, just for a second or two. Then she shot him dead center in the kneecap.

Darvin screamed in pain, an almost deafening, howl of pure agony. He lurched to the side, grabbing at the shattered knee, his face soaked with tears.

Andi fired again, right at his second knee. "And that is for all that the others have been through." She listened to his cries, his pathetic screams. To her, the sounds were a symphony, the music of pure satisfaction, of perfect justice...if such a thing could exist.

Andi stepped forward again, standing directly over Darvin. "I'd enjoy continuing this at some length, you miserable piece of shit, but I'm afraid I have other things to do." Not exactly true, but Andi had no intention of losing her tactical sense amid her orgy of vengeance. Darvin had more men than the one she'd put down at the door, and she could only guess how many Sector Nine maggots were crawling around Dannith's Spacer's District. She had resolved never to forget one of the enemy ships had escaped. The station was gone, so there was no danger of the Union gaining control of its tech, but Sector Nine tended to hold grudges, and she wasn't sure just how much they knew about her and the rest of the crew. That made it time to get out of there.

Not to mention conventional law enforcement, at least what there was of it in the District. She was meting out justice, she had no doubt at all of that. But the police might not agree. It was time to finish things.

"So, I'm afraid we're going to have to wrap this up now, Darvin." She raised the pistol, aiming it dead center on his forehead. "This one, you miserable pile of excrement...this one is for me."

She pulled the trigger, her finger moving slowly, as she relished every instant of the kill.

Chapter Thirty-Four

Central Business District, Port Royal City
Planet Dannith, Ventica III
Year 301 AC

Andi walked out of the bank, somber, feeling as though her mind was in a dozen places at once. She'd listened to Captain Lorillard's message, the recorded instructions he'd left her in the event of his death. Some of it had been meant just for her, to help her to carry her new responsibilities, the burdens he had left her, along with great opportunities. She'd come to admire and respect the captain, and in spite of the—strange—way Andi had become part of the crew, she'd known for some time that Lorillard returned the respect. He'd become another mentor to him, of a sort. The Marine had taught her how to fight, to survive, but his lessons had been confined to the streets of the Gut. Now, she had spent two years prowling the darkness of the Badlands, scouring the ruins of the old empire. The Marine had prepared her, begun her education, but Lorillard had completed it, at least enough to bequeath the ship to her, and with it, responsibility for the others.

And something else. Andi had been stunned to discover Lorillard had a child, a daughter. The message hadn't gone into any real detail about their history, save that Lorillard was sure she had no use for him. It was clear they were estranged, and that he hadn't seen her in many years. But he had never forgotten her, and the only thing he'd requested of Andi, save for taking care of the crew, was to see that his money, the gains of almost a decade's adventures on the Badlands frontier, got to her, somehow.

Andi knew nothing about such things, but she solved that by seeking out one of Dannith's most prestigious attorneys…at least most prestigious among those who dealt in the shadowy gray area usually frequented by Badlands prospectors, and their technically illegal profits.

She'd set up a trust, the lawyer's suggestion, and a safeguard against Lorillard's daughter refusing the money, or giving it away out of anger and resentment. The captain had been her friend. He wanted his daughter to have that money, and if not her, perhaps any grandchildren he might one day have. Andi was determined to see that it was so. There was no way to force Lorillard's daughter to use it, of course, but the trust would always be there for her, anytime she wanted it.

Whatever her disputes with her father, he had left her a wealthy woman. The captain had never made a massive score—save the one they had just obliterated—but he'd accumulated considerable gains over the years, and he had spent little beyond the costs of repairing and upgrading *Nightrunner*.

Andi had done more than set up a trust. She'd used her time in the bank to multiple ends. She had transferred funds from the numbered accounts directly to Sylene and Tyrell, both of whom had decided the nightmare they'd just come through, and the losses they had suffered, were just too much. They weren't monstrously rich, perhaps, but they both had enough to retire in reasonable comfort. Andi had also dealt with Jammar's money. There was a file in the ship's AI, with instructions all of them had left in the event of their deaths. Jammar had parents on Garillon, a world out near the Far Rim. Andi didn't know much about it, but she suspected it was a pretty poor planet, and she had no doubt the money would make her comrade's parents very well off indeed, at least by local standards.

Though, she suspected it would be a poor swap for their son. Andi didn't know anything about Jammar's relationship with his parents, but she remembered enough about her own mother, and the almost sole focus she had placed on protecting Andi, whatever the cost. She tired to imagine how her mother would have fared if it had been Andi who died, leaving her mother staring down at her young daughter's corpse.

She'd shed some tears for Jammar's parents when she'd read the file entry about them, though she suspected they were, in fact, mostly for herself. She'd come a long way from Parsephon, but there was still something deep inside, a self-loathing of sorts. She was driven to create a better circumstance for herself, but there was always guilt there when her own advancement contrasted with her memories of her mother dead in the street, or the Marine, as his life slipped away. She'd some to realize just how much of the rage that drove her had come from those thoughts, from the realizations that the people she'd cared the most for were gone, and no matter how much success she found, there was nothing she could do for them.

The rest of the crew had decided to stay with the ship, which left her with half a crew, at least. Even Gregor had insisted he would return, as soon as he got out of the hospital. Andi wondered what the giant would look like with his new prosthetic arm. She'd been to see him twice, but as of the last time, the doctors still hadn't attached it yet. It had been a special order, of course. Few hospitals stocked such things in the giant's size.

She'd had one more task in the bank. She'd converted almost every credit she had herself into portable platinum coins. Durango's contact had given them a very fair price for their swag, and she'd seen the proceeds added to the crew's accounts. All save her share.

The repairs on the ship had cost her every milli-credit she'd cleared from the mission, plus most of what she'd already had from past missions. She'd just withdrawn the last of it—a transaction that wouldn't have been possible, at least with the needed confidentially, at another bank. But Lorillard had chosen institutions well, as he'd done with everything else she'd seen over the past two years.

She had enough money left to fill up the fuel tanks and the food lockers. Maybe. She needed another mission, a fresh job, one that would allow her to replenish her cash and put her on less shaky ground, and she needed it fast. She was wealthy, of course, at least on paper. The ship was valuable, even more so to the right buyer who would appreciate some of the special features Lorillard had installed over the years. But aside from *Nightrunner*, she hardly had a couple of coins to rub together.

That was nothing new, but somehow, she didn't think a Badlands prospector and a ship owner was going to make up any cash shortfalls by lifting packages on the streets or robbing plush houses. She didn't need that anymore. There was money to be made, she knew that.

But it wasn't on Dannith. It wasn't anywhere in the Confederation.

It was out there, somewhere.

Out in the Badlands.

* * *

"I'm going to miss you." Andi's face was somber, her sadness on display. She'd become close with all of her comrades, but she'd forged a special bond with Sylene. They were nothing alike, of course. Sy was highly educated, Andi was a street rat from the Gut. Sylene had never been much in a fight, and Andi had become a practiced killer. But there had been something between them, a chemistry of sorts, and they'd quickly gone from shipmates to best friends, almost sisters.

And now, Sy was leaving. Andi understood. Her friend had served a long while under Captain Lorillard, but she'd never really been suited to the life. Losing the captain and Jammar, and coming so close to death herself…it had just been too much for her. They'd been back for months now, and Andi had noticed Sylene's hands still shook uncontrollably. She'd almost tried to convince her friend to stay, but she knew Sy didn't belong out there, certainly not anymore. As much as it hurt her to see her friend go, if she convinced her to stay, that pain would one day be a hundred times worse, mourning her comrade's death instead of her departure.

"I'm going to miss you, too, Andi. But we'll see each other again, hopefully soon."

Andi just nodded. That was the kind of thing people said, and she understood why, but that didn't make it any more likely. It felt better for people to tell themselves what they wanted to believe. There was often only pain in facing reality. But Sy was heading for the planet Callisto, halfway across the Confederation. Andi had her new responsibilities, and she couldn't imagine when she'd ever get the chance to go there.

She wasn't sure she'd never see Sylene again, but she also knew the goodbye was, for all intents and purposes, as good as a final farewell.

"My brother is here, Andi. You remember, I told you about him."

"Yes, of course." Andi hadn't even though yet about recruiting replacements for the crew, but when that painful duty came on her, she figured she would be tougher even, than Lorillard had been on her. Anybody who wanted a place on her ship had to prove he or she was worthy. She'd make them walk over hot coals, just to see if they could take it.

But not this time. She didn't know anything much about Sy's brother, save that he'd been in some kind of military training back on their homeworld, when whatever scandal had destroyed her career, had also rippled out and derailed his. Andi could tell how deeply responsible Sylene felt for her younger brother, and she hadn't found it in herself to do anything but promise she'd take him aboard the ship, sight unseen.

"Come in now…" Sylene turned and shouted toward the other room.

A man walked through the doorway a few seconds later. He was young, tall, reasonably muscular. He looked like a good match for the crew, save for the unbearably eager expression on his face.

Remember yourself back in the Shooting Star and hold back your judgments…

"This is Captain Andromeda Lafarge. She has agreed to take you on the crew…because I asked her to. Never forget that. If I hear you've been anything but loyal and dependable, I will come back here and deal with you myself."

"I will, Sis…I promise." He turned toward Andi. "Captain, thank you so much for the chance. I promise I will do whatever you need me to do. I won't fail you, whatever it takes."

Andi nodded, but before she could say anything, Sylene spoke again.

"Andi, this is my brother. Vigorsky Merrick…but everybody calls him Vig."

* * *

"It looks great, Durango. Better than I'd dared to hope. Not cheap, by any means, but a solid job." Andi had gone over every system in *Nightrunner*, with Yarra in tow. She was still an old ship, and far from a luxury ride, but Durango and his shady team of engineers had done right by her. They'd charged her almost every credit she had, but they'd gotten the old ship ready to go, as promised.

"It was a big job for us, Andi. We usually fix ships that are banged up, or where some old system finally gave up the ghost. You guys had one hell of a fight out there. We barely managed to get her back in shape for you."

Andi didn't elaborate on the battle. What had happened in the Osiron system was between her and her crew.

"There's one other thing…"

Andi turned toward the engineer. "What is it?" She wasn't sure if Durango was going to try to pull something, some kind of last-minute scam. She tensed up.

"I've got a pretty good ear to the ground, Andi…I think you know that."

"I do." She was confused. *Where is this going?*

"Well, you don't have to tell me what went on out there—in fact, I'd actually prefer you didn't—but there have been some folks asking around about a ship. A ship called *Nightrunner*."

Andi stared back at him, her eyes like lasers. "Some folks?" She knew he could do better than that.

He looked around, in both directions, and then he leaned toward her. "Sector Nine." For the first time since she'd met him, Andi could hear fear in his voice.

"Sector Nine is looking for us?"

Durango looked around again, in both directions, an uncomfortable look on his face. "Well, all I've heard is the ship's name. I can't speak for what else they know…but it might not be the healthiest thing to fly back to Dannith and broadcast your arrival."

Andi shook her head. *Great, just great.* She needed to get back out here, and the Spacer's District was the first step to that. *What the hell am I going to do now?*

"I might be able to help." His voice dropped down to a whisper, and he looked around again before he continued. "I've got a line on a beacon, Andi...the whole setup. And, it's been wiped."

Andi looked back, as understanding began to flow through her mind. All ships were required to carry beacons that transmitted their identification. They were usually hardwired, impossible to reprogram.

"You mean you can..."

"It's illegal as hell, of course, but my contact can give us the beacon, and set up a file in the registry for a new ship. Complete with background, location of construction, and everything."

"You mean, disguise *Nightrunner* as..."

"As some other ship. One with enough cover out there to satisfy all but the most diligent search."

"And you can install it?"

"I can. I'll do it for nothing, fair enough considering what I already charged you. But my contact with the beacon's going to want platinum for the hardware."

Andi held back a sigh. "How much?"

Durango looked both ways again, and then he leaned forward and whispered to her.

It was a lot, especially in the current situation. But she could come up with it, barely.

So much for filling the fuel tanks and the food locker...

"Let's do it. And as quickly as possible." They really *had* to get back out there, even more than before. She had never felt so poor, not even when she was combing through the garbage for food.

"We can get it done in two days, three tops." A pause. "There's just one thing...we'll need a new name."

Andi hadn't even thought about that. She'd never named anything in her life, and she had no idea what to tell him. She stood where she was, her eyes dropping to the deck, moving to the sack she'd dropped to the deck about a meter away. It was her stuff, her meager collection of clothes and other possessions.

Her eyes fixed on one small spot on the bag, a rectangular shape, pushing out against the fabric. She knew what it was immediately. The old book, the Marine's book, the one she'd taken with her when she'd left Parsephon.

And, suddenly she knew the new name for the ship, without a slightest doubt.

"Let's name her *Pegasus.*"

The Andromeda Chronicles Will Continue With

Wings of Pegasus

For Those Who Haven't Read Blood on the Stars,
it Begins with

Duel in the Dark

64311149R00182

Made in the USA
Middletown, DE
29 August 2019

From SHOWING OFF to
SHOWING UP

An Impostor's Journey
from Perfect to Present

NANCY REGAN

NIMBUS
PUBLISHING
— NIMBUS.CA —

Nimbus Publishing Limited
3660 Strawberry Hill Street, Halifax, NS, B3K 5A9
(902) 455-4286 nimbus.ca

Printed and bound in Canada

Editor: Whitney Moran
Design: John van der Woude
Cover photography: Timothy Richard
NB1577

Library and Archives Canada Cataloguing in Publication

Title: From showing off to showing up : an imposter's journey from perfect to present / Nancy Regan.
Names: Regan, Nancy (Television news anchor), author.
Identifiers: Canadiana (print) 20210379065 | Canadiana (ebook) 20210379162 | ISBN 9781774710319 (softcover) | ISBN 9781774710647 (EPUB)
Subjects: LCSH: Regan, Nancy (Television news anchor) | LCSH: Women television news anchors—Canada—Biography. | LCSH: Television news anchors—Canada—Biography. | LCSH: Women television personalities—Canada—Biography. | LCSH: Television personalities—Canada—Biography. | LCSH: Public speaking. | LCSH: Self-confidence. | LCGFT: Autobiographies.
Classification: LCC PN4913.R44 A3 2022 | DDC 070.92—dc23

Nimbus Publishing acknowledges the financial support for its publishing activities from the Government of Canada, the Canada Council for the Arts, and from the Province of Nova Scotia. We are pleased to work in partnership with the Province of Nova Scotia to develop and promote our creative industries for the benefit of all Nova Scotians.